# The Iron Army

## BOOK 3 OF MOTIONLESS

## DARYL WALKER

# Contents

# CHAPTER ONE

# In the Dark

"How long are you gonna keep me down here, Marion?" Matt shouted, his voice echoing off the bare stone of the dungeon. He gave an unamused laugh. "You can't hold me forever, bitch!"

He wasn't sure how much time had passed since the witches' iron soldier had captured him, but it had to have been several months by now. He wondered how the rest of the group was faring with the Wizard. It seemed telling that there'd been no rescue attempts, at least none that he knew about.

He leaned his head back against the wall and sighed. Looking up, he rattled the shackles that were bound tight around his wrists and chained to the wall. The spikes on the inside of the shackles were embedded deep under his skin, blocking his shadow-stepping ability and severely weakening him.

He'd gotten used to the pain, telling himself he no longer really felt it. He'd also become used to not being able to move from the current position he was in and not being able to see anything because of the pitch-black darkness.

The darkness had once been his ally but now, here he was, tied and bound with no way out and nowhere to go. He'd had no one but himself and the unfriendly darkness as his only companions for what he assumed was months and he was starting to get sick of it, sick of the sound of his own voice.

"MARION!" he shouted again, his voice once more echoing off the walls. He swore to himself when there was still no answer. He knew she could hear him.

He moved back slightly, leaning his back against the cold wall as he sat there, carelessly rattling the chains, trying to get the feeling back into his arms. He looked up at the shackles, trying to once again figure out if there was some way he could free himself.

Since his capture, he had tried everything he could to get out. His first attempt, obviously, had been to shadow-step his way out. When he'd found he was unable to, it had completely set him back.

He wouldn't forget the amusement on Marion's face when she'd found out for sure that he couldn't get himself out.

After that, he'd been determined to prove her wrong, trying everything he could to get the shackles to either break or unlock. But nothing had been successful.

He shook his head again, knowing that he had to keep trying to break himself out of these shackles. He didn't know exactly what the witches had done to them, but it seemed to be some type of ability-binding spell, and he certainly wasn't a fan of it.

Steadying his breathing to try and psych himself up, he shifted his position, feeling pain in multiple places as he managed to get to his knees.

The pain in his shoulder was getting worse, even though he tried to tell himself it wasn't. He was sure it was damaged a lot more than it originally had been from the banshee attack. Even though the nurses in the Oz infirmary had tended to the wounds, it hadn't been long after that that Marion had captured him and locked him down here.

Staying on his knees, he yanked his arms forwards, trying to ignore the pain as he did so. It was the only way he could think of to try to loosen or break the chains on the shackles.

"Come on," he muttered to himself, shutting his eyes against the pain as he pulled forwards again, keeping the tension on as the cold metal dug into his wrists.

He felt the spike in the top of his wrists shift, making him grimace. He'd somehow forgotten about that small factor of the shackles.

The chains stayed tense as he pulled against them continuously, not feeling any sort of relief from the pressure.

He cursed to himself. It was no use; he wasn't getting out anytime soon. Sighing, he shifted back to a sitting position. He moved back against the wall, leaned his head on it, and shut his eyes again.

"You can't keep me down here forever!" he shouted. "MARION!"

"God, he never shuts up," Heather complained as she listened to Matt yelling again from the dungeon. It was muffled but enough to annoy her. "Someone, please shut that man up!"

"No one's going down there," Marion said harshly. "He'll wear himself out soon enough. The more he struggles against those shackles, the more they seem to sap his energy. He won't be carrying on for much longer."

Heather glared at Marion who ignored it. She had better things to do than worry about Heather not liking Matt.

"What are you going to do with him? He's been down there for three months," Carmen input, turning the page of a spell book. "I thought you would've killed him by now."

"Not yet. He needs to suffer a bit more," Marion said as they heard Matt shout again. Marion knew he was calling for her, but she wasn't about to give him the satisfaction of her presence just yet. "He knows something I need to know, and he won't say anything. Once I have all I need, that's when I'll kill him. Or Hunter will. I haven't decided how I wish to go about it yet."

"Well, he's escaped Hunter before," Heather spoke up. "What makes you think he won't and can't do it again?"

"If you hadn't noticed, he's locked away in your dungeon," Marion said matter-of-factly.

Vivian entered the room and Carmen motioned for her to clean off one of the tables that was stacked high with books.

"He's been down there in the dark for three months," Marion continued. "I somehow doubt he'll be getting away from Hunter again if we keep him locked in those shackles."

Heather just gave a shrug, switching her gaze to Vivian who didn't return it as she carried books between the table and the bookcases. "What does *she* know about this?"

Carmen and Marion both looked at Vivian, who continued what she was doing. Vivian didn't say a word, not letting onto the fact that she was listening into their conversation.

"Know about what?" Carmen asked, looking back at Heather who continued to eye Vivian suspiciously.

"You know ... him," she said, hinting rather than saying it.

"She knows nothing, and it will remain that way," Marion said seriously. "Now we're not speaking of this again. He'll tire himself out soon enough and he'll shut up, simple as that. No one goes down there unless I say so."

"You can't let him starve," Carmen said.

Vivian finished wiping the table over and left the room, still having said nothing. Marion watched her leave before turning her attention back to Carmen.

"He hasn't been. I've had someone else on that task."

Carmen just rolled her eyes, not saying anything more.

"What about Chris? What are you doing with him?" Heather asked.

"He won't be an issue," Marion said. "That stuff you gave me worked like a charm and he should be fine for a while. Please make sure there's more of it so, if it starts wearing off, I can administer another dose."

Carmen nodded. "We can do that."

"I'm happy to hear that it worked," Heather said cheerfully as Matt called out again. "For the love of whatever, shut him up!"

"I already said no," Marion snapped, causing Heather to glare at her. "Let him shut himself up. He'll get sick of his own voice soon enough."

"Well, he needs to shut up before I shut him up myself," Heather hissed, pushing herself out of her chair.

"Don't," Marion warned.

Heather stared her down for a few seconds before looking away.

"I'm just going to go and have a word with him," she said, walking out.

Marion shook her head and looked at Carmen. "If I find she's done something to him, I'm going to personally kill her myself."

Matt looked up when he heard the dungeon door open. Someone walked down the steps, coming to a halt in front of his cell.

A slight smirk crossed his face. "Not who I was asking for, but I guess it'll do."

"You need to shut it," Heather warned, pointing at him.

Matt laughed before leaning his head against the wall again.

"Why?" he challenged, feeling the wave of tiredness run down his body. He knew it was from the shackles, and he hated being so worn down all the time. "What are you going to do? You going to kill me?"

"Don't tempt me."

Matt gave another tired laugh. He looked at her, only really able to see the basic features of her because of the lack of light.

"Then do it," he urged her. "Kill me. Put me out of my damn misery. Just do it."

Heather smiled at him. "I'd get into trouble if I did that."

"Well, guess I'll go back to shouting, then."

She shot him a glare, but Matt ignored it and shut his eyes, still leaning against the wall. In a way, he was hoping she'd just kill him, but he also knew there wasn't much chance of it. He was sick of being held in the dark and any way out right now was good enough for him.

"Marion needs you for a bit longer," Heather said. "But believe me, once she's done with you, I'll be first in line to end you."

"You're the one who brought me here in the first place," Matt laughed, opening his eyes and moving his head off the wall as he looked at her, the tired amusement clear on his face. "You had your chance to kill me, but you did nothing. So don't you dare get snappy with me."

"You'd better watch your mouth," Heather warned, pointing at him again.

Matt shook his head and smiled. He hadn't lost his sense of humor over the past three months; but he was so damn tired.

"You'll be dead before you know it," Heather hissed. "No one's coming to get you, Shade."

"You don't know that. You don't know anything."

"If someone was coming for you, they'd have been here by now. No one has approached this place. How does it feel to know that even your closest friends aren't coming to get you out of here?"

"Shut up," Matt growled, causing Heather to smile this time.

"No one's coming," she repeated. "Just remember that when you're sitting down here in the dark on your own."

Heather spun around and left.

Matt listened to her climbing the staircase and shutting and locking the door at the top once she was out.

He sighed and rested his head back again as he rattled the shackles and chains around his wrists, feeling the pain in his shoulder again.

Maybe Heather was right. Maybe no one *was* coming for him.

"Bullshit," Matt said out loud, refusing to believe it. "She doesn't know anything."

# CHAPTER TWO

# Regrets

"So, how are we going to make ourselves an Iron Army?" Abel asked, watching Zeke.

Zeke shook his head, tapping the pen on the table, deep concentration on his face as he stared at the blank piece of paper in front of him.

"I have absolutely no idea," he said, still thinking as he spoke. "We've got to get our hands on one of them to see how they work."

"How?" Nixx asked as Zeke kept tapping his pen, not looking away from the blank paper. "We can't get anywhere near them, let alone get our hands on one. How do you propose we get one?"

Zeke shook his head again, clearly coming up blank on ideas. "I honestly don't know. But it's our only way of matching them. We get our hands on one of those soldiers, we're set."

"Our problem is getting our hands on one, though," reminded Nixx.

"I know," Zeke sighed, leaning back in his chair and slowly shaking his head again. "There's got to be something we can do."

"Like what?" Abel asked. "Zeke, this is a dead-end. We have to think of something else."

"What? What can we do besides this?" Zeke snapped, finally tearing his gaze away from the paper to look at Abel. "We've got nothing that can match Marion and her army. Nothing. We're all as good as dead unless we get our hands on one of those soldiers."

"Even if we manage that, once they realize one's missing, they'll send the rest and that's when the full-on attack will start," Nixx spoke up. "We don't know when they're planning on attacking and we might not even have time to see how they work. We're literally grasping at straws here."

Zeke slammed the pen onto the table, making the other two jump. He shoved his chair back and stood up.

"Well, when you boys come up with a better idea, write it down and come find me."

"Word on the street is that you'll be down here for a while yet."

Gates was sitting, leaning uncomfortably against the back of the cell, the stone cold, even through his shirt. He looked over as Zeke stopped on the other side of the bars.

"Well, hey," Gates said, not moving. "Didn't think you still existed, but it's nice to know you do."

"Yeah, I know. I'm sorry," Zeke apologized, hands in pockets as he stayed where he was. "This is the first time Vincent's allowed anyone to come down and see you. You know how he is."

"Unfortunately, yeah, I do."

Zeke sighed, looking at Gates who still hadn't moved at all. "Look man, I'm trying to convince Vincent to let you out of here. You shouldn't be down here. We need you."

Gates gave a shrug, finally shifting a bit but not saying anything.

Zeke sighed again. "Come on, man. Don't be shunning me like that."

"Give me one good reason not to."

"Because we're friends. No, we're family," Zeke said sadly as Gates looked away. "Please, just let me talk to Vincent and we'll get you out of here."

Gates shook his head. "Vincent won't listen. He's not about to listen to you or anyone else, especially about my case. He's going to leave me here to rot in this cold, dark dungeon and you'll all be fucked. You all need me, and he knows it. He's setting you all up for failure."

"We're not going to fail and you're not going to be rotting away down here for much longer."

Gates sighed, not saying anything more on the matter. He switched his gaze back to Zeke who gave him a bit of an encouraging smile.

"So, what have I missed?" Gates asked, reluctantly pushing himself up off the dirty floor.

He brushed himself down before coming over to the front of the cell, stopping near Zeke. He gripped the bars and watched one of Vincent's guards go past.

"Not a lot," Zeke said in response. "Besides Chris being gone."

Gates switched his gaze to Zeke. "What?"

"Look, it was a misunderstanding and Vincent's fault," Zeke said with a shake of his head.

"See! What the fuck did I say? I said it, didn't I?" Gates said, pushing back off the bars and throwing his hands in the air. "This is unbelievable! That man knows absolutely nothing about how this type of stuff works, how Marion works. He's useless, a sorry excuse for a leader."

"Well, this sorry excuse for a leader has every right to leave you down here."

The two of them looked over to see Vincent standing behind Zeke, looking very unimpressed.

Zeke moved aside slightly as Vincent joined him.

Gates took up his position at the front of the cell again, once more holding the bars. "You're seriously unbelievable, Vincent. You just keep messing it up, over and over again."

Vincent gave an unamused laugh. "Like you'd know," he said, looking Gates up and down. "Anyway, I didn't come down here to argue or change opinions."

"Then, what *are* you here for?" Gates asked. "I've got all the time in the world down here."

"I don't know if Zeke's informed you yet," Vincent began, Gates glancing at Zeke before looking back to Vincent. "But we might need your help on a mission."

Gates shook his head. "No."

Gates pushed back off the cell bars, turned his back on Zeke and Vincent, and went back to his place at the back of the cell.

Vincent sighed, crossing his arms as he glared at Gates. "What *is* your problem? Really, Gates, why do you refuse everything I ask?"

"I have my reasons," Gates said as he sat down in the same place as before, his back against the wall. He closed his eyes. "Now, I'd appreciate it if you got lost. I don't want to talk to you."

Vincent shook his head, uncrossing his arms. "Your choice. The longer you refuse, the more time you spend down here."

"It's not like I have anything else to do!" Gates called after him as Vincent disappeared around the corner and was gone. "Prick. He's never going to let me out as long as I disagree with him."

"Then, maybe stop disagreeing," Zeke said, sitting down where he was and leaning against the bars.

"Not gonna happen, Zeke," Gates sighed, leaning his head back. "He's going to get everyone killed, you'll see."

Zeke grunted in response, staying where he was. Neither of them said anything for a good few minutes.

"What mission?" Gates suddenly asked, making Zeke look up. "What's he talking about?"

"I don't know," Zeke sighed, back to leaning his head against the bars. "Vincent wants to do a lot of things. I've lost track by now."

"How did Chris disappear?"

"Vincent sent him out alone," Zeke began, shifting his position a bit but still staying against the bars at the front of the cell. "Well, by alone, I mean without any of us. He was with that team we went out with when Heather grabbed Matt."

"Well, say no more. Those men were useless."

"Yeah, well, they're certainly useless now."

Gates frowned, seeing the look on Zeke's face. "What do you mean?"

"Marion turned them all to stone, all except Chris and one other."

That got Gates's interest.

"Stone?" he queried, Zeke nodding. "As in, *stone* stone?"

"As in the stuff you're currently leaning against," Zeke said.

Gates looked at the wall next to him before looking back at Zeke.

"Chris is apparently under her influence now," continued Zeke. "We've lost another one."

"You think he can break out of it?" Gates asked, a thoughtful tone to his voice. "I mean, if this stuff she's used on him wears off, he might be able to get Matt out of there."

"There doesn't seem to be much chance of that right now."

"Well, give it a bit of time. We don't how long it'll work for," Gates said. "That's what we never included as a factor. Matt's not going anywhere without inside help. It's the only way we're going to get him out of there."

"Well, we can't get word to Chris. Let's just hope he's smart enough to think of it when he's himself again."

Gates nodded. "Chris is smart. He'll think of something to get himself *and* Matt out of there. I just hope Marion hasn't done anything to either of them. Last thing we need is both of them dead or incapacitated."

"Marion needs Chris," Zeke said with a shake of his head. "She won't kill him."

"She doesn't need Matt, though," Gates said. "She's only got him so she can make him suffer before he meets the blade. She's probably killed him by now."

"If she has, she has. Nothing we can do about it now."

Gates nodded and fell silent for a minute or two.

"Either way, we're going to make sure we do the right thing by him. Dead or not, Matt is family," he said.

"Yeah," Zeke said, nodding in agreement. He paused before speaking again. "What are *you* going to do once this is all over?"

Gates frowned. "Why do you ask?"

Zeke shrugged, looking down at something on the dusty floor. "Just curious."

"Fair enough," Gate said, more to himself than Zeke. He sighed. "Honestly, Zeke, I really don't know. Part of me wants to go home, but the other part knows I can't. I can't just pick up where I left off, but it's about time I went home. What about you? What are you going to do?"

Zeke shrugged again, still looking at the floor.

"I don't know yet. Guess I just see what everyone else is doing," he said. Gates gave a nod of understanding. "But now that you've mentioned it, going home does sound good."

"Just a matter of explaining where we've been for eight years."

"I somehow doubt anyone would believe us if we told them the truth."

"What are we even meant to tell our families?" Gates asked seriously. "I mean, we can't tell them the truth. I can't tell Skye where I've been."

A small blue cat caught Zeke's attention. Gates noticed it as it slipped through the cell bars, and he just watched it as it came over to him.

"I don't know, Blaine," Zeke sighed. "Guess we play the amnesia card and tell them we don't know. It's been eight years. Who even knows what's happened in that time?"

"But how? How do we explain it all?" Gates asked again, the sadness clear in his tone as the cat rubbed up against his leg. He returned his gaze to Zeke. "How do we explain how we disappeared? Why we disappeared? We can't. We'll all be locked away if we say anything."

The cat meowed at Gates, but he didn't even glance at him. Gates paid Alex no mind; he didn't have the time or energy for him today.

"Well, if I go back home, I'm sticking to my story," Zeke said.

Gates frowned. "Which is?"

"That I don't know," Zeke explained. "I was out with you guys and the next thing I knew, I was somewhere I didn't recognize. You guys were there too, but we got separated not long afterwards. Everything after that's just a blur. By the looks and sounds of it, someone spiked our drinks and abducted us."

"You've certainly put some thought into this," Gates accused, as the cat tried to get his attention. "Just how long have you been planning on going home?"

Zeke shrugged again. "I don't know. Two years, maybe?"

Gates shook his head. "You've been working on your story for two years and you're still here?"

"What can I say? Gotta get it perfect."

Gates shook his head again. Alex still wouldn't give up on harassing him, continuing to rub against him.

"So, you're going to go back home after we've defeated Marion and these witches," Gates began, Zeke nodding along. "And you're going to tell them that you don't know where you've been for the past eight years because someone spiked your drink."

"Everything after that is a blur," Zeke shrugged.

"Jesus, Zeke," Gates said with a sigh. "You really think they're going to buy that story? For real? What are you even going to do? Go to your place in the hopes that your family still lives there?"

"Well, logically, I'll go to the cops."

"OK, hang on. So, you're going to go home, wander into the cop station, and tell them what? That you've been missing for eight years? Man, that's not going to happen."

"Well, what are you going to do if you go home?" Zeke asked seriously, crossing his arms as Alex continued to meow at Gates. "Enlighten me."

"I haven't had as much time to think about this as you have. I hadn't thought of going home in a long time before Matt brought it up a few days before he got grabbed."

"Matt brought it up?"

Gates nodded.

"Yeah, don't know why," he said, that sadness back as he finally looked at the cat. He reluctantly picked him up and placed him on his lap. The cat meowed happily. "Matt hasn't spoken of home ever since Viv, you know. Just really caught me off guard."

Zeke nodded slowly. "Yeah, that's very unlike Matt."

"That's what I thought. I don't know what happened in that other reality, but something must have triggered it in Matt's head. Something must have reminded him of home. He thinks it's too late for him now, has nothing to go back to. His family is still up there, but they probably think he's dead and never coming back. All our families probably think we're gone forever, always wondering where they went wrong and where we are. If we are…"

Zeke shrugged, a sad look on his face as the cat closed his eyes and dozed off.

"Really, though. What are you going to do when you go home?" Zeke asked, keeping his voice down as someone approached and glanced at them as they went past. It was another one of Vincent's men.

Gates shrugged, listening to the cat purr contentedly as he slept.

"Well, I'm not going to make a scene," he said, thinking on the spot. "I'm going to get back into the real world—home—and I'm going to start to wander the streets with this dazed look on my face. Someone will eventually stop me and ask if I'm OK and I'll pretend I have no idea where I am. From there, they'll probably take me to the cop station, and they'll sit me down and ask who I am and where I live. I'll tell them my name and that I live in Los Angeles. After that, they'll probably check the missing persons' records and find I'm there before they call someone to come get me. I'll play it up for a bit and then eventually get back into the everyday routine."

Zeke laughed, Gates looking at him with a slight smile.

"And you think I put thought into *my* story," Zeke laughed again. "If you play it right, that might actually work. You've totally thought that through."

Gates gave him another slight smile before looking down at the sleeping cat.

"Yeah, just depends who they call," he said quietly, the smile gone. "They'll probably call Mom or Dad, maybe Skye, if I'm unlucky. Just … she's probably moved on by now."

"You never know until it happens," Zeke said sadly. "She might have waited. Maybe she never moved on. Guess you've just got to wait it out until you can go home."

Gates shook his head. "If I was in her position, I wouldn't have waited eight years. Just really miss her."

Zeke looked at him sadly, not saying anything; the look on Gates' face was enough.

"Just wish … none of this shit ever happened," Gates said. A few tears ran down his face. "Wish we'd never come down here in the first place. We've been down here for eight years with nothing to show for it. Eight years of our lives, gone. We're never getting this time back and it was all because of a stupid, accidental find. Sometimes … sometimes, I wish we never went out that night and we'd just gone to Matt's instead, or yours, or mine. Eight years we can never replace."

# CHAPTER THREE

# Influence

"*W*hy would you do that? What's wrong with you?*"

Marion looked at Chris, a rather innocent look in her eyes. But he knew this woman was evil. There was no shred of innocence left within her.

"Why do anything, Chris?" she asked.

Chris never took his eyes off the woman in front of him. He watched as she switched her gaze to the unmoving stone; the people that she'd just turned into statues with a wave of her hand. "Well, what a shame. I left one alive."

Chris finally broke his gaze away from her and looked over at where she was looking. One of the people from the scouting group was standing there with a shocked look on his face. Chris was sure the man was shaking, and he didn't blame him. Seeing your entire team turned to stone was quite a traumatic experience.

Turning his attention back to Marion, Chris was suddenly blinded by some form of dark dust enveloping him.

*"What the...?"*

Chris awoke with a start, sitting up straight and breathing hard. A frown crossed his face as he looked around, temporarily blinded by the light streaming in through the window. A cool breeze wafted through, moving the thin white curtains inwards.

"The hell?" he muttered to himself, tearing his gaze away from the window. His eyes adjusted properly as he looked around the rest of the room, wondering where he was and how he'd got here.

The room was small. The biggest thing was the double bed he was currently sitting in. There was a wardrobe to his left, and the window on his right. There were a few stacks of books on the floor near the door, but that was pretty well the extent of the entire room.

The frown remained on his face as he cautiously pushed the sheets back. He moved so he was sitting on the edge of the bed. The stone floor was cold under his feet, sending a shiver up his spine as he sat there and tried to remember how he'd gotten to this unknown place.

He had been out somewhere and that was all he remembered. He couldn't even begin to pinpoint the reason he was here or even where here was.

Standing up, he walked over to the closed door. He stopped and pressed his ear against it, trying to hear something. When all he heard was silence, he moved back, opened the door, and looked out into the deserted corridor.

He left the door open as he cautiously stepped out of the room. He saw a staircase leading downwards, and he wondered if he was on the top floor of wherever he was. He headed down the winding staircase, hearing someone talking as he got closer to the end.

"How long is he going to be kept down there? All he's done for three months is shout and sit in the dark. Believe me when I say, he's better off dead."

Finally reaching the end of the staircase, Chris stepped out into a room and saw who was talking. Marion and Heather both looked over as he stopped where he was, still rather confused at what was going on.

"Chris," Marion said, a bit of a smile on her face. Why was she looking at him like that? "Good to see you're awake. I didn't think you were ever getting out of bed."

"What's going on?" Chris asked, still very foggy about this situation as Heather looked him over.

"You mean, you don't remember?" she asked.

A sad look crossed her face, but something in her tone didn't sound right to Chris.

"If I knew what was going on, I wouldn't have asked," he said with a frown.

Marion sighed and stood up, straightening out her dress. She looked at him and linked her fingers together.

"You took a pretty hard hit, so it makes sense why you don't really remember it all," she began. The frown remained on Chris's face as she spoke. Marion sighed again. "Vincent sent some people after the four of us. They thought we were going to attack them and now they've started a serious war. We've had to prepare to make sure we're safe."

"Riiiight..." Chris said slowly.

The sad look remained on Marion's face.

"Don't you remember? Vincent's trying to kick us off our land," she continued, making Chris nod slowly. It seemed to make sense. "But we won't let him win. He has no right to be invading this area when it's rightfully ours."

Chris just gave another slow nod, Marion smiling at him now as she spoke again.

"I have someone downstairs that you might like to have a bit of a chat with," she said.

The frown returned to Chris's face as he listened to her. He was still a bit out of it but felt he was slowly getting there.

"He tried to break in," continued Marion. "So, we had to lock him down in the dungeon. He works for Vincent and used to be a friend of yours."

She indicated for him to follow her as she headed out of the room without saying another word. Chris glanced at Heather who gave him a bit of a suggestive smile before he followed Marion out. Heather followed, not far behind.

Marion unlocked a door near the back of the castle. Chris had more-or-less figured out that's where he was. He didn't know where this castle was, but he knew he was in one.

He followed Marion through the door and down the staircase. Behind them, he heard Heather shut the door once she was in as well, clearly not wanting anyone else to follow them.

The first thing Chris heard was a frustrated shout, followed by the sound of rattling chains. Marion stopped in front of a cell, and Chris and Heather stopped next to her.

The cell was small, but it took up the whole room. The bars were all that separated the prisoners from the jailers.

A bit of a laugh came from whoever was in the cell just a few feet away from where they were standing. Chris could see a figure on the left, sitting in the dark. That was clearly who was laughing, although Chris didn't know why.

As his eyes adjusted to the gloom, Chris could see that this person was chained to the wall.

"Well, finally gone to the dark side, have we, Chris?"

Chris didn't say anything, causing the man to laugh again. *Matt*, he thought. *His name is Matt.*

"And Marion, you've finally come down to see me again. Thought you were finally dead."

Marion's lip curled as she considered the man. She clearly didn't like him. "You can't kill me that easily, Shade."

Matt laughed again and leaned his head back against the wall. He sounded very tired, but that wasn't stopping him from being amused at the slightest of things. Matt turned his head to the side to look at the three of them, his head still leaning against the wall.

"So, what do you want?" he asked. "Come to finally torture me into telling you shit you don't even want to know?"

"Not just yet," Marion said with a bit of a smirk. She looked at Chris before returning her gaze back to Matt. "Just thought I'd stop in with Chris. Let you know he's here."

Matt gave another laugh, turning his head back to face the front so he wasn't looking at them anymore.

"Fuck you," he said quietly.

A scowl appeared on Marion's face. "Excuse me?"

"I said, fuck you," Matt growled, back to looking in their general direction. "Fuck you, fuck her, and fuck him."

"You'd better watch your language," Marion warned, causing Matt to laugh again.

"Why?" he challenged. "Seriously, what are you going to do, hmm? You've left me to rot down here for months, Marion. You won't do anything."

Chris saw Matt switch his gaze over to him. Even in the darkness, he knew that's where he was looking now.

"I hope you burn in hell, fucking traitor."

Matt fell silent, back to looking at the empty space in front of him.

Chris didn't like the way he'd just been spoken to. "Traitor? Really, Matt?"

Matt stayed silent, not even acknowledging that Chris had said anything.

"You look at me when I'm talking to you," Chris continued.

Matt laughed. He'd been in the dark for so long that anything was amusing to him at the moment.

"What? You going to *make* me look at you? Force me to?" he dared, still not looking at him.

Chris looked at Marion who returned his gaze for a couple of seconds. Clearly seeing what he wanted to do, she unlocked the cell door.

Chris strode over to where Matt was shackled to the wall. Matt kept his eyes closed as Chris crouched next to him, his back to Marion and Heather.

"Chris, you need to get out of here," Matt said, his voice incredibly low so the others couldn't hear him. A frown crossed Chris's face. "You're not meant to be here. I know she's done something to you."

"Why?" Chris asked, his voice down as well.

Matt turned his head to the side again, eyes open, and looked at him tiredly. He was worn out and, by the looks of it, he was ready to give up.

"Please," was all he said.

Chris looked at him sadly, wondering if what he'd just said was true. He still wasn't in the right frame of mind, but now he didn't know what was truth and what wasn't.

"I see you need a bit of time. I'll leave the keys in the door, and you return them to me once you're done," Marion spoke up.

Chris looked over to her and nodded, receiving one in return.

Marion and Heather headed back up the stairs, and Chris waited until he heard the door close at the top. He turned his attention back to Matt who once again had his eyes shut.

"You've got to get me out of here, man," Matt said, still not opening his eyes. "I've been down here for months, I think. I don't even know what day it is."

"I can't help you," Chris said, as Matt opened his eyes and looked at him again. "I'm sorry, Matt. I don't even know why you're down here."

"And you think I do?" Matt asked. There was a desperate look in his eyes. "Please, Chris. You've got to help me. It's only a matter of time before she decides to do something. I'm not going to be of use much longer. There's only so long I can hold out from telling her what she wants to know."

"Which is?"

"The journals, the fucking journals!" Matt said, desperately trying to get his point across. "She wants to know where the four journals are."

"Why does she want to know?"

"She needs whatever's in them. She doesn't know who has them and for some reason she thinks I know."

"Well ... do you?"

Matt looked at him, that desperation gone, replaced by a dangerous look. "Why should I tell you? You're basically her bitch now, Chris. You're nothing to me."

Chris sighed as Matt looked away. "If you tell her, she might let you out."

Matt scoffed. "Yeah, 'cause she's going to let me live."

"So, you do know where they are?" Chris asked, continuing to push for an answer. But Matt wasn't about to budge. "If you tell me, I can let you out. She left the keys in the door."

"You could just let me out anyway. Either that or just fucking kill me."

"I'm not going to kill you, Matt."

Matt looked at him briefly before going back to looking across the cell, not saying a word.

Chris felt sorry for Matt, though he really didn't even know right now if he could be trusted or not. He still wasn't quite with it, but hopefully within the next few hours he would start to remember the reason he was here.

"What happened to you?" Matt suddenly asked, his tone sad and voice down as he looked at Chris. "What's she done to make you like this?"

"I have no idea what you're talking about," Chris said truthfully.

"This," Matt said, indicating to Chris with his head since his wrists were shackled to the wall. "If you were really you, I wouldn't still be locked up in these damn chains."

He rattled the chains around his wrist, bringing Chris's attention to them.

"Just get out, Chris. You're no help. Fuck off and leave me alone. I'd rather talk to myself than to you. Fucking traitor."

Chris just looked at him sadly again before standing up, seeing he was no longer wanted. Without another word he left the cell, grabbing the keys and relocking it as Matt put his head down.

With one last look, Chris turned and headed back up the stairs, leaving Matt alone again in the dungeon.

# CHAPTER FOUR

# Silent Messages

"He said he knows where they are," Chris said.

"Did he tell you where?"

Chris shook his head, and a disappointed look appeared on Marion's face. She sighed and turned to Heather.

"I need you to get my doctor here," she said. "If anyone can force Shade to tell, it'll be him. I need him here as soon as possible. Until then, Hunter will be in charge of getting the information I need."

Heather got up and headed out of the room.

"How exactly are you going to get him to tell you?" Chris asked, not liking where this was going.

Chris hadn't seen any sign of Hunter yet, but he was sure he'd be skulking around the castle grounds somewhere.

"It doesn't matter how. We need him to tell us where those journals are," Marion said. "They hold vital information that we need to overthrow Vincent and get him to back off once and for all."

Chris was unconvinced. He didn't trust either side here just yet, but he didn't want Matt to die over this. "What happens once Matt talks? Are you going to kill him?"

"It depends on what happens," Marion said, irritated that Chris was shooting all these questions at her. "What happens, happens. It's not something that can be avoided. If he dies, he dies. It's that simple."

Chris stayed silent, deciding that it was his best option right now. He was going to play this out however he could until he knew for real whose side he truly was on.

"You OK?" Zeke asked as Gates suddenly frowned.

Gates put his head on the side like he was listening to something.

The small blue cat looked up at him from his lap and meowed. Gates signaled for Zeke and Alex to be quiet.

The three of them stayed silent for a minute or two before Gates quickly stood up, knocking the cat off him, and coming over to the front of the cell. Zeke was on his feet now too and the cat joined him on the other side of the bars.

"I need a piece of paper and a pen," Gates rushed, a frown on Zeke's face now.

"Huh?"

"Just do it!" Gates said, gesturing urgently at him. "Paper and pen, quick, before I forget."

Before Zeke could move or say anything, the cat rushed out of sight. Zeke and Gates both watched him go.

"What's going on?" Zeke asked as Gates impatiently waited for the cat to come back, hopefully with paper and a pen.

"Don't talk. I can't risk forgetting."

Zeke didn't say anything more and it wasn't long before Alex reappeared, no longer the cat.

Gates grabbed the paper and pen from him and quickly scribbled something on it. Once he was done, he stopped and looked at what he'd just written down. He looked up at Zeke.

"You need to get me out of here," he stated.

"I can't," Zeke said, taken aback by Gates's determination to get out now. Earlier on he hadn't cared, but something had clearly changed. "What did you write down?"

"It's an address," Gates said, looking back down at the paper.

"Whose address?" Alex asked, looking intrigued.

"I, ah, I think it's Matt's," Gates said, looking back up at the two, only to be met by confused looks. He sighed. "I think, I don't know, but I think it's his address topside."

Gates suddenly held his hand up to signal silence again, staring off and looking like he was once again hearing something.

Zeke and Alex watched as Gates quickly scribbled something else on the paper, frowning as he looked at it once it was written down.

"Another one?" Zeke asked, getting a nod from Gates.

"Yeah, but this one isn't back home. This is one from down here in the City," he said, trying to figure out what was going on. He looked up. "Zeke, I seriously need you to break me out of here."

"How?" Zeke asked quietly as a guard walked past and looked at them suspiciously. Once the guard was gone, Zeke spoke again, his voice even quieter now. "I don't have any keys, Blaine. How am I meant to break you out? I can't pick locks."

They watched as Gates tried to think of a possible way to get out. He folded the piece of paper up and put it in his back pocket with the pen.

"You've got to weaken the bars," he said.

Zeke sighed and crossed his arms. "I can't do that. I won't do that, not after last time."

"Then bring Ash down here and she can break them for me with her ice powers," Gates snapped, unimpressed, throwing his hands up. "Just do it, Zeke. I need to follow this up."

"Why did you write them down?" Alex asked, interest on his face.

Gates looked at him as Zeke tried to decide what he wanted to do.

Gates shook his head. "I don't know. I swear someone told me to."

Alex frowned as Zeke sighed in defeat and pushed up the sleeves of his jacket. Gates gave him a nod of thanks.

"Like, told you in your head?" Alex asked.

Gates nodded as Zeke looked around to make sure no one was close before he turned his focus onto the bars. He grabbed them and Gates stepped back.

"I can't explain it, but, yeah," Gates said, watching the metal of the bars begin to glow orange where Zeke was gripping them firmly. "I need to follow this up before it's too late."

Zeke yanked his hands back, shaking them out as the metal bars slowly cooled down.

"Don't touch it yet, it's still hot," he said, looking uncomfortable as he shook his hands out again. Alex was sure he saw smoke coming off them.

"What did you do?" Alex asked, watching Zeke kneel down and grab the bars closer to the ground.

"Burned through them," Zeke said as the orange glow came back, making him wince. "It's hot, too. That's why I don't do this very often."

"I didn't know you could do that," Alex said, watching in awe as the bars continued to heat up until Zeke quickly pulled his hands back again, feeling the heat.

"You'd be surprised what I can do. We both know a few more tricks than what you've seen," Zeke said, standing up and looking at Gates. "Alright, the top two should be OK to touch now. Push them out and the lower half will do the rest itself."

Gates gave a grateful nod, and pushed hard against the bars Zeke had heated up. They broke off suddenly, hitting the ground hard, the sound echoing around the dungeon.

Gates looked at Zeke guiltily. "Sorry, didn't realize it would be that loud."

"Let's go before someone comes to check," Zeke said, already heading off. "I hope you know you're going to have to lay low for a while."

"I will, don't worry."

Zeke shook his head as Gates and Alex followed him up the stairs. The door at the top was already open from when Alex had returned earlier. Zeke checked before they left, making sure no one was around.

"Where are we going?" he asked as Gates and Alex joined him in the corridor.

Gates pulled the paper out of his back pocket and unfolded it, looking at what he'd written down.

"Merchant Square, number eight," he said, the other two looking over his shoulder. "That's where we're going."

"Why Matt's address though?" Zeke asked as they began walking.

They remained quiet and tried to appear normal as they passed a few people who didn't seem to know that Gates wasn't meant to be out and about right now.

Gates shook his head. "I don't know. It clearly means something though, otherwise I wouldn't have written it down."

They headed out of the castle and out on to the busy street. Gates took up the lead as they walked, heading towards the arena. He was sure Merchant Square wasn't far from it.

Zeke and Alex trailed along as Gates made his way down a few different streets until the arena came into view.

"I think it's around here somewhere," Gates said, stopping outside the arena and looking at the street signs.

"It's over the back, I think," Zeke said, Gates nodding.

"Hey guys, what are you doing?" they heard, making them all look around to see Abel coming out of the arena. He frowned as he saw Gates. "Are you meant to be out?"

"Don't tell, I'll explain later," Gates said with a wave of his hand. "Do you know where Merchant Square is?"

Abel looked between the three of them before nodding.

"Yeah, it's about three streets over from here," he said, pointing to his right. "Come on, I'll show you. I need a break anyway."

He headed off, indicating for them to follow.

# CHAPTER FIVE

# Merchant Square

"This is it, Merchant Square," Abel said. "Why'd you want to come here?"

Gates didn't bother answering. He held tightly to his piece of paper and headed down the street and into the square.

It was a small community. The houses were close together and an open circular area in the middle separated the houses on each side. A few people were strolling along the paths, nodding to each other as they passed.

"This is the one," Gates said, stopping outside number eight. "Number eight, that's what it said."

"Who lives here?" Abel asked as they joined Gates.

Gates shrugged and knocked firmly on the door. A minute later, the door opened to reveal Don, the sixteen-year-old mind-reader. When he saw who was standing on his doorstep, his face lit up with relief while Gates just looked confused.

"Thank God, you got my message," Don said. "I didn't know if you'd get it."

Gates shoved the piece of paper in his face, forcing Don to step back. "Why did you give me this?"

A man going into the house next door looked at them suspiciously. He didn't say anything but quickly stepped inside and closed his door behind himself.

Don indicated for them all to come in, looking both ways to make sure no one else was watching. He moved aside, ushering the four of them in quickly, making sure the door was shut and locked once they were inside. He moved past them, and they followed him down a passageway into the dining room.

Don sat down at the table, offering them all a seat. Gates sat down opposite him, while Zeke sat next to Gates. Abel and Alex moved around and sat on the opposite side with Don.

"Why are we here?" Gates asked, smoothing the paper out on the table in front of him. "Were you the one who told me this?"

He indicated to the paper, getting a nod from Don.

"It's only a very recent discovery, but I can contact people," he explained. "I can talk to them but, at the moment, they can't respond to me. I need to try and get that communication line going."

"Jacob would be able to help you out. He seems to enjoy training you," Abel suggested. "Just talk to him about it."

Gates cleared his throat, getting Don's attention again. He indicated to the paper again.

"Why did you tell me about Matt's address? How do you even know it?" he asked, wanting to get to the bottom of this mystery.

"Oh, I didn't actually know whose place it was," Don said, sighing when the look of confusion crossed Gates's face again. "Look, not long before Matt disappeared, he caught up with me. He told me the address, but I don't know why."

Zeke looked at Gates. "Why would he tell him that?"

Gates shook his head, his gaze focused on the address on the paper as he thought.

"He'd have to have a very good reason to tell someone his address," Gates said after a few minutes. "He doesn't just tell people things for no reason, especially personal things. Why *his* address though? I've no idea."

"Maybe it's just in case something happens to him," Alex suggested. "Being prepared?"

Gates shook his head. "No, Matt wouldn't tell just anyone his address. It's not his Wonderland one. This is his real home one. His topside address."

Realization appeared on Alex's face as Abel frowned.

"I didn't think he'd been home in years," Abel said.

"He hasn't, none of us have, except you," Zeke said, thinking. "You go upstairs a lot, right? You could check it out for us. See if you can figure out why he gave us the address."

Abel didn't say anything, and Gates shook his head, seeing a flaw in Zeke's plan.

"We can't afford to leave right now. Whatever this is, it has to wait," he said. "Matt's the one with the keys to his place. He still has them, and we can't get into the Underground Wonderland to get the spares."

"There should still be a spare in the backyard," Zeke said, the two of them in their own conversation now. "He always kept one near the back door."

Gates sighed. "How do we even know the house hasn't been sold yet?"

"We don't, but Matt clearly knows," Abel spoke up, the two of them looking to him. "Tell me where the spare keys are, and I'll do it."

Gates looked at Zeke. "You want to do this?"

Zeke nodded, and Gates looked at Abel and nodded too.

"I think it'd be wise to take someone with you, though," Alex said.

"You want to come?" Abel asked. A grin lit up Alex's face as he nodded eagerly. "Well, then, it's settled. Where does Matt live?"

"California. I've got the address for you," Gates said. He looked at Don. "You got a pen?"

Don nodded, getting up from the table and going over to the bench. He grabbed a pen and threw it to Gates who caught it easily.

Gates drew a quick map on the back of the paper before sliding it over to Abel who took it and studied it.

"The spare key is usually around the back door somewhere. He moved it every time he used it," Zeke said, getting a nod from Abel. "Once you're in, just have a look around and see if you can figure out why he'd point us there."

Abel nodded again and looked at Alex. "Let's get going then."

Alex grinned, getting up as Abel did.

"Thanks for this, Abel," Gates said gratefully. "We really appreciate it."

"Anything to help and find what we need. We'll get him back," Abel said. Gates nodded but didn't look very convinced. "We'll see you in a couple of days probably. We have to get back to the Room of Doors before we can get out."

Gates nodded and Alex and Abel headed out.

Once they were gone, Gates looked at Don, who gave him a smile. "I kind of need to lay low for a bit. Think I could crash here for a couple of days?"

"Sure," Don said, a bit of excitement in his voice. He seemed to like Gates for some reason. "We'll have to clear it with my mom, but it should be OK once we explain it to her. Why do you need to lay low?"

"It's complicated. Believe me when I say, you don't need to know and you're better off not knowing."

Don nodded, not pushing the matter any further. He looked at Zeke who just returned the look without saying a word.

"What about you?" he asked, the look on Zeke's face showing that he hadn't even thought about what he was going to do. "Do you need to lay low, too? If so, I'm sure it'll be OK for you stay here as well.""

Zeke looked at Gates as he thought.

"You did break me out," Gates said with a shrug.

"Yeah, I should probably hang around," Zeke said, sighing and looking back at Don. "God knows what Vincent will do if I go back, and he knows what's happened."

"He's probably already figured out that I'm gone, and you were the last one to be seen down there with me," Gates said. "Alex wasn't there when Vincent showed up, but you were. I think it'd be best if we both stayed off the streets for a bit, just to be safe."

Zeke gave a nod of agreement, knowing that Gates was probably right. The last thing they wanted right now was to get locked up. Gates wasn't going back there any time soon and Zeke certainly didn't care to join anyone down there either.

"What did you do?" Don asked, looking between them and making the two men look at him. "Was it something serious?"

Gates shook his head. "It's nothing serious but it's better if we're not seen for a while. You don't want to get yourself caught up in this shit, kid, believe me when I say that."

# CHAPTER SIX

# Doctor's Orders

"Chris."

Chris looked over upon hearing someone call his name. Marion smiled at him from where she stood in the doorway. Hunter and his dog loitered in the room behind her.

Chris glanced at Hunter who scowled at him before turning his back and walking away. His dog growled at Chris before turning and following his master. Chris still didn't like that dog.

Marion walked over and sat in the chair next to him. The smile remained on her face as he heard a door slam somewhere deeper in the castle.

"I was wondering if you'd be able to keep an eye on Hunter for an hour or so," she said, making Chris frown. Wasn't Hunter capable of looking after himself? "My doctor will be down in the dungeon with him, but I don't think I'd like to leave either of them alone with Shade. The doctor and Hunter don't always get along with each other. Best that someone else be there to keep an eye on them."

"You want *me* to keep an eye on them?"

Marion nodded, before speaking again.

"Like I said, I don't really want to leave them down there with each other and our friend," she said, Chris giving a slow nod. "I've got to go out and take care of a few things, so I can't keep an eye on them. It'll only be for an hour at the most."

Chris sighed, knowing he didn't really have much choice. He gave a reluctant nod, making Marion smile. He didn't know what he would do if Hunter and this doctor didn't get along and something happened. What was he meant to do?

He watched Marion stand up, and he got to his feet too.

"They're probably both already down there now," she said. "Just make sure they don't hurt each other and make sure they don't kill my prisoner."

Marion looked Chris over briefly before leaving the room.

Once she was out of sight, he headed down to the dungeon. As he walked, he noticed the silence in the rest of the castle. It looked like Heather and Carmen were out as well.

He made sure the door that led down to the dungeons was shut before he descended the stairs.

As he neared the bottom, he heard Hunter say something. He presumed he was talking to the doctor.

Both of them looked over as they saw Chris reach the end of the stairs. They were both still outside Matt's cell and the door was still closed.

The dog growled at him, making Chris glance at it before he looked at Hunter.

"I was told to come down and keep an eye on things," he said, looking at the doctor as well before returning his gaze back to Hunter. "Marion's orders."

Hunter glared at him but stayed silent before looking back at the doctor.

"As long as you stay back and don't do anything, we won't have any problems," the doctor said, unlocking the door and entering the cell.

Chris didn't say anything, just watched the doctor walk over to where Matt was sitting, still in the dark and not saying a word. The doctor crouched down in front of him and slapped him hard across the face. Matt growled but otherwise stayed quiet.

"I'm going to ask this nicely, just once," the doctor said. "Where are they?"

Matt turned his head back to the front to face him. "Where are what?" he said, his voice down but sounding rather dangerous, even in the state he was currently in.

The doctor stood up and walked back to the front of the cell. Hunter and Chris watched him exit the cell and head off to his left, disappearing into the dark.

"What are you doing?" Matt suddenly asked, a hint of worry in his voice.

Chris didn't like hearing that; it was a bit unnerving.

The doctor reappeared, pushing a metal surgical trolley with vicious looking tools on it. The sight of it was enough to make Chris feel sick.

"The fuck are you doing with that?" Matt tried again, desperation evident in his voice as the doctor wheeled the trolley into the cell. Matt pushed himself back against the wall as far as he could. "You stay the fuck away from me."

The doctor ignored him and placed the trolley off to the side of Matt who looked over to the front of the cell, catching Chris's gaze before looking back at the doctor who was deciding what implement he wanted to use first. Chris watched the doctor pick up a very sharp knife, Matt shifting his position again as he also watched.

"This is how it's going to work," the doctor said crouching down in front of Matt again, inspecting the knife as Matt watched him very carefully. "You tell me what I want to know, and I won't hurt you. You mess me around, and you're going to regret it. I'm not here to play games and I don't appreciate it when people don't tell me what I want to know. You talk and you don't get hurt, get it?"

Matt looked at him, pushing his head back against the wall. "You kill me, and you've got Marion to answer to."

The doctor laughed. "By the time I'm done here, you'll wish I had killed you."

A smirk appeared on Matt's face this time, a bit of a laugh escaping him. "You'd be doing me a favor."

The doctor shook his head and roughly grabbed the back of Matt's head. He violently pulled him forwards and the chains around Matt's wrists lost all slack. The doctor pushed the tip of the knife under Matt's chin, Matt wincing a bit from the violent jerking movement. It looked like his shoulder was hurting.

"I'm not about to do you any favors," the doctor growled as Matt tried to pull out of his grip. "You're going to tell me what I want to know and then Marion will deal with you how she sees fit."

"Get your hands off me," Matt growled, pulling against him.

The doctor tightened his grip. "Who's got them?"

Matt pulled against him again, only to be forced back into the position he'd been in, the knife still touching his skin.

"There are four and I know you have the locations of them and who put them there. Where are they?"

Matt stayed quiet, directing a glare at the doctor. The doctor stared Matt down, neither of them saying anything. Matt wasn't one to back down and, by the looks of it, he'd be in a world of pain before the end of the day.

"Nothing to say?" the doctor asked. Matt just glared and stayed silent. "Well, I've given you the only chance you're getting. Speak up now or else this is going to hurt."

Matt pulled back again, but the doctor increased his grip and pulled him forward again. The tip of the knife dug deeper into Matt's skin.

The doctor suddenly pulled the knife away and forcefully stabbed it into Matt's already-injured shoulder, making Matt cry out in pain.

"Where are they?"

Matt looked at him, that glare still on his face as the doctor kept the knife in his shoulder and twisted it.

"Fuck you," Matt said, sounding strained. He was so tired and worn out. "Find them yourself."

The doctor pushed the knife further into Matt's shoulder, Matt managing to hold back a cry of pain.

"Want to rethink that answer?"

With the glare still on his face, Matt spat in the doctor's face. The doctor growled and wiped his face before looking back at Matt. He twisted the knife deeper, and Matt couldn't help but cry out this time.

The doctor looked over to where Chris and Hunter were standing, indicating for Hunter to come over and help him.

Hunter did as asked, entering the cell with his dog prowling behind him. Chris moved, loitering in the cell doorway now. The doctor left the knife in Matt's shoulder and gestured for Hunter to get another one of the metal tools from the table.

Hunter looked the tools over, his dog sitting down near him, its gaze on Matt who now had his head down. He handed one of the tools to the doctor, a thinner, harsher looking knife with a serrated edge. Without hesitation, the doctor stabbed the smaller knife straight down into Matt's thigh. Matt once again held back a cry.

"This is only going to get a lot worse the longer you refuse to tell me where they are."

"Get fucked," Matt snapped, trying to ignore the pain. He switched his gaze to Chris, looking a bit more confident despite what was going on. "You too, Chris. You're dead to me."

# CHAPTER SEVEN

## Against the Law

"I want you to explain something to me," Jacob said. He stood in front of Zeke and Gates, disapproval clear on his face. "Why the hell did you break him out and why the hell are you two here?"

The two men looked anywhere but at Jacob as Jacob kept looking between them both. They knew they were in a lot of trouble.

"Well? One of you care to answer me?" he asked, crossing his arms.

Don stood just behind him, looking extremely uncomfortable with the situation. He'd ended up bringing Jacob back with him after he'd been to the arena to train. It hadn't felt right not to tell Jacob what was going on.

Gates sighed, finally meeting Jacob's gaze. "We needed to talk to Don. Zeke broke me out because I needed him to. He didn't want to, but I convinced him to do it."

Jacob looked at Zeke briefly before returning his gaze to Gates.

"Why did you need to talk to Don?" he asked, glancing at Don.

"I asked him to," Don spoke up. Jacob turned his attention to him fully now. "I contacted him to come and see me urgently. It was important."

Jacob sighed, understanding what was going on now. "Don, you said you wouldn't do that."

Don looked down shamefully.

"It was important," Gates spoke up, bringing the focus of the conversation back to him. "And it turned out to be crucial. This could help us get Matt back and we weren't about to deny that chance."

A frown crossed Jacob's face. "How?"

"Matt told me an address before he disappeared. He told me to keep it quiet until it was necessary," Don said. "I had to tell them. They're his friends and they needed to know."

"Alright, well, I hope you know I still have to tell Vincent where you are and why you're here," Jacob said with a sigh. He looked tired and sad as he just stared at Gates.

Zeke looked disappointed as he shook his head, while slight alarm crossed Gates's face.

"You can't," Gates pleaded as he leaned back on the sofa he and Zeke were sitting on. "Please, Jacob. He'll lock me up again. Maybe he'll kill me because he knows I can get out. You don't know what he'll do, and you can't tell him!"

"He'll know you're gone by now," Jacob said. "You've been gone for nearly twelve hours. I think he'll know by now."

"So, you're just going to tell him where we are, and let him lock us both up?" Gates asked seriously. "He needs us to help him take down Marion and the witches, but he doesn't fully realize it yet. If he locks us up, then we're all screwed, and he won't realize until it's way too late."

"It's my job. I can't just let you roam around here when you've done something against the law," Jacob argued. "What do you think is going to happen if people find out about this? If word gets out that you two have messed around with the law and gotten off scot-free, what do you think will happen? Others will think they can get away with it as well. I have to turn you both in."

Don looked at him. "It's my fault they're here, that they broke the law."

Jacob ran his hand through his hair as he looked at Don. He wasn't overly impressed with Don at the moment for harboring fugitives.

"Technically, Alex and Abel are involved too," Gates spoke up. He was about to drag as many people into this as he had to in order to get Jacob off this case. "If you arrest me and Zeke, you have to arrest Don, Abel, and Alex, as well. That's five people Vincent won't have for his mission, and all of us know how to use our abilities more than anyone in the rest of the Emerald City and surrounds. Think about it."

Jacob looked at Gates, thinking and realizing he was caught in the middle of this situation now. Gates had a very valid point. It didn't leave Vincent with many skilled people who had control of their abilities.

Jacob shook his head. He knew his back was against the wall on this one.

"Fine," he said, throwing his hands in the air. "But you can't stay here. If I'm caught helping you lot, I could lose my job. From now on, you do exactly what I say and don't argue back, got it? One fuck up and I'm sending you both straight to Vincent, understood?"

Gates and Zeke nodded, and Jacob signaled for them to follow him as he headed out of the room. He was still incredibly unimpressed with the two of them right now.

Gates and Zeke followed Jacob to the front door and outside. For some reason, Don also followed along behind.

"If either of you get caught out, it's your own fault," Jacob said as he headed down a side street. "Vincent probably has people out looking for you, so don't be surprised if we see guards or officers."

Gates nodded as they passed a few people. He wondered where they were going.

"Where are Abel and Alex?" Jacob asked, looking over his shoulder at them briefly.

"Um, around," Zeke said.

Jacob stopped suddenly. He wasn't about to take any stalling answers today. "We don't move until you tell me. We stay right here until you tell me where they are. It's your choice how long we're here for."

Zeke and Gates exchanged looks before looking back at Jacob.

"They went back upstairs..." Zeke said, trailing off as he saw the look on Jacob's face.

With a shake of his head and no words, Jacob started walking again, sidestepping a few people who were walking the opposite way.

Gates, Zeke, and Don followed closely, none of them saying anything as they walked the streets. Gates kept looking around, worried about the guards and officers that may have been looking for them.

After a little while, they turned down another street. Gates and Zeke didn't recognize the area. Jacob halted outside one of the houses at the end of the street, turning and looking at the three that were still with him.

"You're staying here until we figure this out," he said. There were no protests. Jacob looked between Gates and Zeke. "You are not to leave this house, got it?"

They both nodded.

Jacob turned to face the door and checked to see if it was unlocked. Finding it wasn't, he glanced over his shoulder and unlocked it before opening it.

He held the door for them, motioning for them to head inside. Gates and Zeke did as asked and Jacob indicated for Don to go inside as well.

Jacob followed them in, shutting and locking the door after he was inside.

Gates, Zeke, and Don all looked around the front room they were in, intrigued.

"Is this your place?" Gates asked as Jacob walked past him.

"You break anything, you pay for it," was all Jacob said as he disappeared into the next room.

Gates looked at Zeke as Don followed Jacob. "I'll take that as a yes, then?"

Zeke shrugged before following Don. Gates rolled his eyes and did the same.

The next room was the kitchen. Don was sitting on a stool at the bench, while Jacob searched for something in the fridge.

"You do not say a word about this to anyone," Jacob said, taking something out and shutting the fridge. "You don't tell anyone why you're here. You don't say a word. Is that clear?"

Gates and Zeke nodded as Jacob placed a jar and some butter on the bench before going to get something out of one of the cupboards.

"As I've already stated, I could get into a load of trouble because of this. I could lose my job and, believe me, I can't afford to lose that. I somehow doubt my wife would be overly pleased with me if I got fired, or locked away for that matter."

"How long have you been married?" Gates asked, trying to get the subject onto something else.

"It'll be twenty years this year," was Jacob's answer as he placed a loaf of bread on the bench, He went back to the fridge. "She won't be too impressed that you're here so expect some disapproval at first, but she'll get used to it."

"So, what are we doing about this predicament?" Zeke asked, watching Jacob as he went about making a sandwich for himself, clearly not in the mood to offer anyone else anything.

Zeke didn't blame him; he'd been dragged into the middle of a problem he shouldn't have been.

"We'll figure something out," Jacob said, taking a bite. "But until then, neither of you are allowed out of this house. I'll see what Vincent wants done before I say anything. Just assume you'll be here for a while."

## Chapter Eight

# Upstairs and Unlucky

Alex looked around nervously as Abel unlocked one of doors within the Room of Doors. It was a worn, white door that looked like it hadn't been opened or used in a very long time.

"You sure this is the right door?" Alex asked as the door clicked open.

"Yep."

"Doesn't look like it's been used in a while," Alex continued, the nervousness coming through in his tone.

Abel put the key away and looked at him, his hand on the door handle. He sighed. "You didn't have to come along, you know. I know my way."

Alex finally met his gaze, the worry still etched across his face. He shook his head, wanting to go through with it and help Abel with their task. He didn't want him to go alone.

Abel gave Alex one last look before he pushed the door fully open.

All they could see on the other side was darkness. It certainly didn't make Alex feel any better about the situation.

Abel went through the door without hesitation, having done this many times before. Alex warily stepped through behind him, just able to see Abel not far ahead of him.

"Close the door. We don't want any unwanted guests."

Alex shut the door and heard it lock as it clicked shut. He now couldn't see Abel at all.

"Is this the only door that leads to where we're going?" Alex asked, trying to see where he was going as he cautiously followed Abel. He held out his hands, hoping Abel was still up ahead and hadn't taken some unknown and unseeable turn without alerting him. "Where *are* we going?"

"California," Alex heard Abel say from a few paces in front. He felt better knowing Abel was still with him. "We're going right up top. This door is the one that exits Wonderland, but it has a few different places to choose from when we get to the end of the tunnel."

Alex nodded. "Have you ever been to this ... California before?"

"I live there," Abel said in reply, Alex nodding once again. That was kind of cool. "Not the same city as Matt though."

"Where do you live?" Alex asked, trailing along behind in the dark, still unable to see Abel. "And what about Matt?"

"I live down in L.A., Los Angeles," Abel said. "Near Hollywood. It looks like Matt's in San Diego, which is a couple of hours drive from where I live."

"I've never been Upstairs," Alex said, starting to get excited about going somewhere new.

"Well, today's your lucky day, Alex."

⟢⟢❖⟣⟣

"Alright, this is it."

There was a solid white wall in front of the two travelers, disappearing into the dirt walls on either side of them. They'd entered a cavern, and Alex was glad to see a few lights set up around the small area. The white wall had four doors to choose from: a red one, a blue one, a black one, and a dark green one.

"Which one do we need?" Alex asked as Abel went over to the red door to inspect it. "I mean, you've been here before and apparently come this way all the time, you know?"

His tone came off as rather unsure as he stood back and watched what Abel was doing.

"Luckily this area wasn't affected by the tragedies back in Wonderland," Abel began.

Alex moved into the cavern a bit more, not liking the eerie darkness in the tunnel behind him. He thought he heard scratching within the dirt near where they were standing and it was starting to freak him out.

"Guess it's far enough out that it can't spread this far," Abel continued. He looked away from the red door and met Alex's gaze.

"So, which door is it?" Alex repeated.

Abel looked at the red door again.

"I only know where the blue one goes," Abel admitted, and Alex felt his heart sink. "The blue one leads to downtown L.A. That's the one I use whenever I go home. We've also got the problem that we need to get back down to Wonderland once we're done."

"Well, how do we do that?" Alex asked. He was starting to wonder if Abel knew what he was doing. "Because it would be kind of useless to get this far and then not be able to get back."

Abel nodded, moving over to the black door and inspecting it, clearly looking for some kind of indication of where it might lead.

"We've got four ways out and I don't know how many ways back in," he said, running his hand over the black door as Alex watched. "I know the way in from Pennsylvania and L.A., but they're the only ones. Pennsylvania's where Chris is from, where I got down here last time. I don't know where Matt would have found one if he was home in San Diego. I really don't know." He paused, thinking. "Unless he was in L.A. at the time; that's always a possibility."

"So, what do we do?"

"Well, we have two options. Either we take a complete guess and go through one of these doors and end up God knows where, or we go through the blue one to L.A., which means we have a lot of distance to cover to get to this address."

He turned away from the black door and looked at Alex to see what he wanted to do. Alex nervously fidgeted, trying to decide what the best course of action was.

"Can we come back through the door if we end up somewhere else?" Alex asked, his brain going a million miles an hour as he tried to decide what to do.

Abel shook his head. "It locks once we're through. Once we choose a door, we have to fully commit to it."

"What are the chances we aren't anywhere near Matt's place?"

"Well," Abel said, a bit of thought on his face as he went over to the green door to see if it had any clues that might tell where it would lead to. "I know the blue one leads to L.A.; that's at least the same state. My guess would be that the others would lead to completely different states, and we don't how far away we'd end up."

He kept his focus on the green door, Alex still fidgeting as he tried to make up his mind. Knowing they had to make their decision, Alex walked over to Abel who looked at him.

"Let's take the green door," Alex said, committing to the door.

Abel nodded. "Let's take the green door."

Alex nodded in return as Abel grabbed the handle of the green door, the one they were already standing in front of. The door opened and a bright light shone through, making them both shield their eyes from the sudden light change.

Abel kept hold of the door and went through, and Alex reluctantly followed. The sound of people talking interrupted what had been silence. It was the first thing that both Abel and Alex noticed as their eyes adjusted to the light.

A warm breeze was present as they looked around. They were in the middle of a beach, near some food outlets.

The green door behind them clicked shut and locked.

"Dammit," Abel sighed, running his hand through his hair as he looked around. "We're in goddamn Miami."

Alex watched groups of people stroll past. There were a lot of people here in one area and they all seemed very busy, compared to what he was used to back in Wonderland.

"Is this a bad thing?" he asked.

Abel looked at him, already feeling the heat due to his clothing choice of all black. He was used to it, but it didn't make him feel any better about their current problem of positioning.

"Yeah, it's a bit of a problem," he said. He indicated for Alex to follow as he started walking, wanting to get away from the bustle of the crowds. "We've got a very long way to go. We should have just gone straight to L.A. It wouldn't have been as far. We're on the complete opposite side of the country."

"So, what do we do?" Alex asked as he followed Abel onto the sand. More groups of people pushed past as Abel made his way to the edge of the beach to get back onto more solid ground.

"Well, I've got to figure that out," Abel said, just managing to miss someone coming the opposite way at a decent speed. A group of kids laughed at him as they passed by. "We've got to get this done as soon as we can, which means we're going to have to make our way over to L.A. Once we get there, we can figure the rest out."

"How are we going to get to L.A.?"

Abel shook his head and sighed, walking up the steps that led to the sidewalk. Alex made sure he stayed close. He didn't wish to get lost up here with no idea of where he was, where he was going, or even how things worked.

"I need to think about this," Abel said, coming to a stop on the sidewalk. He thought for a few minutes, then pulled his phone from his pocket. "Alright, just give me a second to make a call and I'll see what I can do."

He checked the signal then dialed. Alex looked around as Abel waited for someone to answer his phone call.

"Mom, hey," Abel began, when someone finally answered. "I've got a bit of a problem and would seriously appreciate a bit of help."

Alex continued to look around, having never seen anything like the buildings and structures that were around this area. He liked it almost as much as he liked the heat.

"Yeah, I'm sorry to be calling you like this," Abel continued, glancing at Alex. "A friend and I are kind of stuck in Miami. My card's disappeared so I can't get any money out or anything and I need to get back home. Do you think you could help us out and get us some plane tickets to get back? I'll pay you back when I get home."

Alex finally looked back at Abel who was looking a bit unhappy. He assumed it was because they'd chosen the wrong door.

"Awesome, thank you so much. You're a life saver. Alright, thanks. I'll let you know when we get back. I owe you one and I'll pay you back within the next few days. Thanks Mom, love you. Bye."

He hung up and put his phone back in his pocket. He looked relieved now that he had a plan and everything was beginning to work out.

Abel looked at Alex. "We have a way to L.A."

# CHAPTER NINE

## Vivian

"He won't say anything," the doctor informed Marion who had a rather unimpressed look on her face the entire time he was speaking. "He's not budging, no matter what we do to him."

Marion sighed irritably. She was losing and she knew it. She switched her gaze to Chris who, in turn, just returned the look.

"He wouldn't talk to you either, I'll take it?" she said. Chris shook his head. "Wonderful. Alright, just leave him down there for now. Hopefully he'll come to his senses and say something. Leave him to his misery."

The doctor headed out of the room. Hunter shot a glare Chris's way for some reason before he also left. Chris shook his head as Marion returned her gaze to him.

"He'll tell us eventually," she said. "But for now, he's a lost cause. The longer he refuses to talk, the longer he stays locked up in that cell."

"Why are you after these journals, anyway? What do they have in them?" Chris asked, crossing his arms.

"It's complicated," Marion said, dismissively waving a hand at him. "Anyway, Chris, it's been a long day so I'm going to get some sleep. You should do the same. There's something I need to show you tomorrow."

Marion walked out, leaving him in the room by himself. Sighing, he decided to head back to his bedroom.

He hoped that Matt would just give up the locations of the journals to end his suffering. But it didn't look like that was going to happen anytime soon.

It was very quiet as he walked up the stone steps that led to his room, but as he neared the top, he heard someone talking.

The door to his room was open and, by the sounds of it, whoever was talking was in there.

Chris stood in the doorway and saw that it was the young woman who worked for Carmen and Heather. She was making the bed, while a young boy sat on the chair at the desk, watching what she was doing.

The boy couldn't have been much older than about five.

"And as I've already told you, Riley, you're not allowed to go out unless I'm with you," the young woman said. "You know the rules."

Chris felt bad, as he was sure she didn't know he was there.

"But you're always busy, Mommy," the boy complained, crossing his arms as he watched her.

"Uh, hey, sorry," Chris suddenly said. The woman jumped and looked at him. The boy also looked over, but not as startled as his mother. "Sorry, didn't mean to startle you."

The woman gave him a bit of a smile before fixing up a small crease in the blanket on the bed.

"It's OK. I'm sorry," she apologized. "I'm almost finished."

Chris smiled at her before glancing at the boy who was staring at him with a happy grin on his face.

Chris looked back at the woman. "I didn't get your name. I've seen you around a few times today."

The woman subconsciously plucked at her shirt to straighten it. "Vivian."

Chris frowned. Where had he heard that name before?

It was like he knew her from somewhere but couldn't quite place where. Chris looked at the boy who was still smiling as he swung his legs back and forth, unable to reach the floor from where he was on the chair.

"You helping her out here?" Chris asked the boy with a bit of a smile.

"I'm here to make sure she does her job right!" the boy said happily, making Chris laugh.

"Well, she's done a good job and it's been done right," Chris said. He looked back at Vivian. "Thanks, you seem to do a lot around here."

Vivian shrugged, glancing at her son. "You should be in bed, it's getting late," she said, causing a disappointed look to appear on the boy's face. "I'll be down in a few minutes once I'm finished here, OK?"

The disappointment stayed on the boy's face as he got off the chair and headed to the door. He stopped next to Chris in the doorway.

"I can finish up whatever you need to do if you've got to get him to bed," Chris offered.

An unsure look crossed Vivian's face. "It's fine, it's my job to make sure everything's done."

"Well, at least let me make sure your son gets to his room," Chris tried, the uncertainty still on Vivian's face as she tried to decide what was the best thing to do.

After a bit of hesitation, she nodded reluctantly. "Thank you."

"Any time," Chris said.

Vivian smiled at him before turning her attention back to tidying the room.

Chris looked down at the boy who looked happier having someone to escort him to his room. The boy took Chris's hand and pulled him towards the stairs.

"I'm Riley," the boy said, giving Chris a grin as he let go of his hand and began heading down the stone steps. "What's your name?"

"Chris."

Riley looked over his shoulder and gave him another smile as Chris followed him down the steps.

"Do you live here, too?" Riley asked as they reached the end and headed down another corridor that Chris hadn't noticed before.

The hallway was rather dark, with nothing lighting it.

"I do at the moment," Chris said. "Have you always lived here?"

Riley nodded and stopped outside a room, pushing the door open. There were a few candles lit in the small room. It had no window and was furnished with only two single beds, a small cupboard, and a small desk with a chair.

"Yeah," Riley said as he went over to the bed that was against the wall. "Mommy doesn't like it here. She cries a lot when she thinks I'm asleep. I know she misses Daddy."

Chris stood in the doorway as Riley sat on the edge of the bed, his feet once again unable to reach the floor. He looked at Chris with a bit of a sad look on his face and pointed to the other bed, asking Chris to sit on it.

Chris did as asked. "Did you know your dad?"

Riley began to swing his legs back and forth as he watched Chris. He shook his head and looked down at his legs. "Mommy said he died before I was born. I want Mommy to be happy."

Chris looked at him sadly, not really knowing what to say. Before he could say anything, Riley spoke again.

"I should do as Mommy said and go to sleep," he said. "Thank you for walking down here with me, Chris. Mommy would appreciate it."

Riley grabbed the blankets from the end of his bed, pulling them over himself as he lay down.

"Any time, kid," Chris said, getting up. "I'll let your mom know you're in bed."

Riley nodded and smiled at Chris before closing his eyes. Chris gave a smile in return before heading out of the room, shutting the door quietly behind himself.

It was very quiet in the castle, and it was making Chris feel uneasy. The silence just didn't feel right.

Trying to push the feeling of dread away, he headed back to the steps, ascending them quickly back up to the top where his room was. The door was still open, and he stopped in the doorway again.

Vivian was straightening a few things on the desk. She looked over when she saw him.

"He's in bed," Chris said.

"Thank you," she said. She looked around the room before looking back at him. "Everything should be where it's meant to be. The bed has been remade, and I've cleaned up a few things."

"I appreciate it."

Vivian nodded. "Just let me know if you need anything. I'm around twenty-four seven."

Chris moved aside and she left the room. He watched her walk to the steps.

"Do they really make you work all night, too?" he asked, making her stop and look over to him. "They shouldn't be overworking you like that. It's not fair on you or your son."

Vivian looked down briefly before looking back up. "Riley's used to it," she said with a sigh. "He shouldn't be, but he is. I am, too. But I'm the only one who does anything around here, so I don't really have any other choice. They've never gotten anyone else, so it's just me here to do everything they don't want to do themselves."

"If there's anything that I can do for you, don't hesitate to ask, OK?" Chris said seriously, noting that Vivian looked uncomfortable with his offer.

"You shouldn't have to do anything for me," she said in return. "I appreciate it, but I don't want you to get yourself into trouble with any of them, especially Marion. Just don't get on her bad side, OK?"

Chris gave a nod of understanding. "I know, but if there's anything you need, tell me. Please."

Vivian gave a reluctant nod. "Thank you. Goodnight."

She headed down the steps and Chris watched her go. Something about her was still niggling at him. He was sure he knew her from somewhere. Whether it was someone having mentioned her name, or whether he'd met her before, he just didn't remember.

For some reason he couldn't place where he knew her from.

# CHAPTER TEN

## Sold Out

"I think I've figured it out," Zeke said, pulling Gates's attention away from what he was looking at on the wall.

"Figured out what?"

"How we can get our own Iron Army to counter Marion's," Zeke said, standing up from the kitchen bench.

Don was next to him, and Jacob was currently somewhere else in the house.

Gates crossed his arms, looking at Zeke.

"Alright, how?" he asked, glancing at Don who looked rather interested in what Zeke was about to say. "How are we going to get our own Iron Army to counter Marion's?"

"Well, we first need to get our hands on one of her soldiers so we can find out how they work," Zeke began. "I pitched the idea to Nixx and Abel earlier, but we didn't know how to get one. I think I've figured out how."

Gates and Don exchanged looks before they both looked back to Zeke as Jacob came back into the room.

"How?" Gates asked. "You've seen first-hand what they're like. How are we going to get one when we can't get near them?"

"Heather was controlling them, telling them what to do," Zeke said. "If we can either get her to send them out without her, or we grab her before she tells them to do anything, we can get one of them. I'm going to need you with us, because you can stop them with the barrier."

Gates sighed, messing his hair up a bit as he took in what Zeke was saying.

"Let's say this works," he began. "How are we meant to go about it without telling Vincent? We have to say something to him about it because we'll have to find somewhere to store this soldier while we dissect it and find out how it works so we can replicate it. We can't talk to Vincent about it while we're in this predicament, Zeke. It's not possible."

"We have to try," Zeke said, a bit of disappointment in his voice. "We have no other choice. We have to go see Vincent about this."

Gates gave an unamused laugh, shifting his position.

"We can't," he emphasized. "Zeke, I don't know if you realize, but we're not exactly Vincent's favorite people right now. I'm certainly not someone he likes. He'll lock us both up this time, not just me. We can't go to him with this because we're technically fugitives. It's a great idea, but I somehow doubt he's going to be up for the idea if you and I are the ones going to him about it."

Zeke looked at Jacob who returned the gaze without a word. When he realized why he was looking at him, he shook his head.

"Uh-uh, no way," Jacob said, making Zeke sigh. "I'm not telling him anything on my own. You're the one who wants to create your own army, so you go tell him. He'll know something's up if I say anything, since you're the one who originally came up with the idea. Take some initiative and tell him yourself, don't drag me into this any further."

Zeke looked at him with a bit of disappointment as the front door opened and they heard people talking.

"We have to do it," Zeke said, his gaze back on Gates. "We have to try. This might be the only way to get Matt back, Blaine. We have no other choice but to go to Vincent with this."

Gates didn't say anything as a woman appeared in the entranceway to the kitchen, getting everyone's attention.

"Hey," Jacob greeted her. He looked at the others in the room. "Everyone, this is my wife, Kim. Kim, this is Zeke, Gates, and you already know Don."

Kim looked at Jacob with an unamused look on her face. "What are they doing here?" she asked with a sigh. "There are people looking for those two all over the City!"

Jacob glanced at Gates before looking back at his wife. "I'll explain later."

Kim shook her head and walked past Zeke to the bench.

"Are the kids with you?" Jacob asked.

"They're probably in the living room, like always," she said. "Now, everyone out, stop crowding the kitchen."

Jacob indicated for everyone to leave the kitchen. They all headed for the living room, to find three boys there, as Kim had said.

"Hey, guys," Jacob said, as Zeke, Gates, and Don hung back a bit.

"Hey, Dad," one of them said. He appeared to be the oldest. "Who are they?"

"Just a couple of people from work," Jacob said. "I'll explain later once your mom knows."

The boy looked at Gates and Zeke, sizing them up. "You're the guys from the markets, aren't you?"

Zeke and Gates exchanged looks before looking back at him.

"Yeah," Gates said in response, the boy nodding in understanding. "Not our finest moment, but, yes, that's who you're looking at."

Zeke looked at Gates. "We really have to go see Vincent."

Gates sighed, knowing Zeke wasn't about to give up on this. It was a good idea, but he wasn't sure if he was ready to face Vincent and his wrath just yet.

"Yeah, OK," he said in defeat. "But if this gets us into a fuck load of trouble, I'm putting the full blame on you, got it?"

Zeke nodded and Gates looked incredibly unhappy about what he'd just agreed to do.

"You want me to come with you?" Jacob asked. "Just a bit of extra back up, just in case something happens."

They both nodded.

"Alright, let's get going."

"Vincent, there's someone here to see you."

Vincent looked up from what he was working on. Nixx and Ash were with him. The door opened and three people came in, causing Vincent's mood to instantly drop.

"Where the hell have you two been?" he snapped.

Gates and Zeke both looked uncomfortable, while Jacob stood off to the side.

"I've had people out looking for you all damn night and now you just show up out of nowhere? What the hell do you think you're doing?"

"We have an idea on how to get one of the soldiers from the Iron Army," Zeke said straight out.

Vincent's expression changed to surprise, showing he was caught off guard. He looked between them before settling his gaze on Zeke.

Ash gave Gates a disapproving look to which he just returned one of his own. There was still tension between the two of them and, most days, they tried to stay clear of each other to avoid making it awkward for everyone.

"Well, what's your idea?" Vincent asked, crossing his arms as he stared at Zeke. He pretended Gates wasn't even there.

"We lure Heather out with a few of them," Zeke said. Vincent's expression didn't change. "We get her away from the soldiers and then Gates can help get one using his barrier. We get one, bring it back here, and Nixx can figure out how it works since he's more of a scientist than any of us."

Vincent glanced at Nixx before returning his gaze to Zeke.

"This doesn't excuse either of you from what you've done, got it?" he said. "Count yourselves lucky I haven't just thrown both of you back down into those dungeons; lucky you're not shackled to the wall! How do you plan on getting Heather out of the way?"

"Ash can do it," Gates nominated. Ash pointed to herself before scowling at him. "You've got a grip on your ice ability; you can freeze her to the spot while we do the rest. It's all you'll have to do and then we can all come back here."

Ash looked at Vincent, the expression on her face saying that she didn't want to do this.

"I'm not going out there, not with him and not with anyone," she stated.

"Why don't you just fucking help for once?" Gates snapped, getting her attention. "You're so damn self-centered, even after everything that's happened. If we don't take Marion down, you're going to die, too. You really think she's going to let you, out of everyone, live? I know for a fact that you're the last person she'd want alive, Ash. Just step up and do this for the sake of everyone."

"I never said we were going to do it," Vincent said, finally looking at Gates. An annoyed look appeared on Gates's face. "What you men are saying is beyond a risk. What happens if none of you come back? Who are you planning on taking with you, because I need people here. Since Abel's disappeared, I only really have Jacob, Ash, and you two. Nixx has been helping with other things, so we don't have many left here."

"We want to take Jacob, Ash, me, Gates, and maybe some of our recruits we were training with," Zeke said confidently, not about to let Vincent shoot down his only idea. "We'll take Doug and Ruby. I know Ben will be more than happy to help you out here, Vincent. This is the only plan we have that could remotely work so we need to do this, please."

Vincent looked at him, clearly thinking over what his options were.

"If I let you do this, you'd better come back with something we can use," he said seriously, pointing accusingly at Zeke. "If you come back with nothing, or you don't come back at all, I'm not going to be pleased. You come back empty-handed, someone is going straight into shackles, got it?"

Both Zeke and Gates nodded to indicate that they understood what he was saying. Vincent waved them out of the room.

"Now get out. You've got forty-eight hours before I change my mind and pull the whole damn operation."

# CHAPTER ELEVEN

## Personal

"Chris, there you are. Come over here. I have something I want to show you."

Chris saw the subtle smile on Marion's face as she watched him walk over to her. Out of the corner of his eye, he saw Vivian going about her daily tasks, making sure everything was clean and still in its right place.

Marion headed out through the castle, and Chris followed along without a word. As he walked, he realized how quiet it was. He couldn't hear anything from Matt down in the dungeon, and that worried him. Normally, there was some sort of noise from down there, but today it was dead silent.

He followed Marion outside, and the sudden light change caught him off guard, temporarily blinding him.

"Where are we going?" Chris asked, his eyes slowly readjusting as he trailed behind her.

"You'll see," said Marion. "It's just up ahead."

They walked across the barren wasteland, until Chris saw what looked like a dilapidated castle up ahead that he hadn't known was there.

Marion didn't say anything else as she went down the small slope that led to the ruined castle.

"There's something I've been meaning to ask you," Chris said as they reached the ruins.

He saw figures standing in the shade of the old castle walls that were still upright.

"Ask me after I've shown you what we have here," Marion said as she came to a halt in front of one of the figures. "Whatever it is, I'm sure it can wait."

Chris frowned as he stopped next to her, looking at what was in front of him. There were a lot of them, all made of metal and none of them moving.

"What are these?" he asked, caution in his voice as he kept a bit of distance between him and these metallic ... soldiers.

"This is my army," Marion said, a triumphant smile on her face as her gaze never left the metal figure in front of her. "This, Chris, is the Iron Army."

She turned to look at him. "What do you think?"

Chris looked at the army, not sure what he was meant to say, before switching his gaze to Marion.

"Well," he began. "They're certainly ... impressive."

Marion nodded, satisfied with his answer.

"They definitely are," she said, turning back to the one in front of her. "They're going to help us win this war against Vincent and all who stand in our way. No one will stand a chance against this army. We'll be the ones left standing."

She turned to face Chris, but her gaze looked over his shoulder, an annoyed look appearing on her face. Chris turned to see Heather walking up to them with purpose, a non-caring look on her face like every other time Chris had seen her.

"I'm taking a couple of them," Heather stated with some irritation in her tone. "Vincent has sent some people out to do God knows what, and I won't stand for it. They're in *my* territory."

Marion seemed very displeased, narrowing her eyes as she watched Heather walk past. "Well, make sure you bring one of his people back. I don't care who."

Heather ignored her, clicked her fingers, and was gone, four of the soldiers disappearing with her.

Marion shook her head before looking back at Chris. "As I was saying, this is what's going to win us this war. Don't worry about Heather. She's a bit off the rails some days."

Chris nodded and Marion turned her attention to the soldier in front of her. It hadn't moved in the slightest.

"Marion," Chris said, making her look at him with a questioning look. "I want you to hire someone else so Vivian can work for me."

An interested and surprised look crossed Marion's face upon hearing his request.

An interested and surprised look crossed Marion's face upon hearing his request. She crossed her arms as she stared at him. "Why in the world would you want *her* working for you? Who else am I supposed to get to work here? It's not like anyone will come willingly."

"You're saying Vivian did?" Chris countered, a scowl appearing on Marion's face.

"You watch your mouth, Chris. Don't you dare speak to me like that," she said. Chris stood his ground and refused to look away. "Why do you want her to work for you?"

"Because you overwork her and she has a damn kid to look after," Chris said. "She's working nearly twenty-four seven. You'll work her to death."

Marion raised her eyebrows. "You say she has a kid?"

Chris nodded, concerned at the sly smile that crossed Marion's face.

"Well, that's certainly news to me," she said. "I'll find someone to replace her, and you can have full control over what she does from now on. She'll still be expected to work, though. There'll be no freeloading here."

A suspicious look crossed Chris's face. "I'm surprised you agreed so easily."

Marion shrugged as she walked past him, starting to head back to the castle. "What can I say, Chris? I'm just a kind person."

It was still quiet when Chris went down to the dungeon. He planned on checking to make sure Matt was still there and still alive. There hadn't been any sound whatsoever all day and Chris was worried that Matt was actually dead.

He walked down the stone steps, the candles on the wall flickering as he went past. Reaching the bottom, Chris was glad to see that Matt was still in the same place as when he'd left yesterday.

Matt didn't bother to look up as Chris stood on the other side of the bars.

"You come to finish the job, Chris?" Matt said. He sounded exhausted. "Or are you just going stand there like you did yesterday and watch me suffer?"

Chris looked at him sadly, and Matt finally looked up to meet his gaze. There was enough shadow that Chris was glad he couldn't see any detail on Matt's face.

"Well?" Matt asked, his tone bitter. "You going to just stand there? You going to do something? What are you going to do?"

"I wanted to make sure you were still alive," Chris said as Matt went back to his original position with his head down. "I'm not here to hurt you, Matt."

"You've already hurt me, Chris," Matt growled, not looking up. "By standing back and watching and not doing anything. By not getting me out of here, you've already hurt me. You're just as bad as the rest of them. I'm surprised Marion hasn't told you to kill me yet."

"She's not going to kill you until you tell her what she wants to know."

That made Matt laugh. He lifted his head, once more looking at Chris.

"She'll run out of patience soon enough. The bitch isn't going to ever know where they are," Matt said with another laugh, this one sounding a lot more tired. "She can guess all she wants. She can torture me all she wants. She will *never* find out where they are. I have nothing left, Chris. Nothing left to lose but my life. So why the fuck should I tell her, hmm? Why? Explain to me why I should tell her when she's going to kill me either way!"

Chris stayed quiet, not knowing what to say.

"That's what I thought," Matt said, shaking his head with another bitter laugh. He rested his head back against the cold stone wall, no longer looking at Chris. "Either way I'm dead, whether I tell her or not. I can't get out. I can't leave. I can't do anything but sit here and rot away. You can torture me all you like, but I will *never* tell anyone where they are. Not in here, not out there. Never."

Chris sighed. He felt bad for Matt and wished he could do something to help. There were a few reasons why he couldn't let him out. The main ones being that Marion would figure out he did it, and that he didn't have any keys to get in to let him out.

"I'm never getting out of here, Chris," Matt sighed, sounding defeated. "Just kill me."

"I'm not going to kill you, Matt."

"Then, fuck off. I don't want to talk to you anymore. Either kill me or get lost. I don't really care which one it is. I don't want to see you down here again unless it's to get me out. Tell Marion she can get fucked and that she won't ever know the location—or locations—of the journals. Is it one location, or multiple? She won't ever know, will she?"

He fell silent, head still leaning back against the wall. Chris shook his head to himself and headed back upstairs, making sure the dungeon door was shut behind him. Even though Matt couldn't get out, he still had to make sure no one, mainly Riley, was going to wander down there.

Walking into the main area of the castle, Chris saw Vivian still going about her usual duties. Riley sat on one of the chairs watching her.

"Hey," Chris said.

Riley gave him a bit of a wave, Chris giving a slight wave back before looking at Vivian. She looked up and gave him a bit of a smile before continuing on with what she was doing.

"What are you doing?" Chris asked.

Vivian frowned but didn't look up. "My job. What I always do."

"Did Marion not tell you you're under my instruction now?"

Vivian looked shocked at the news. Apparently, she hadn't been told. She looked at him and crossed her arms. "Why?"

Chris glanced at Riley, who was looking at one of the books on the table next to the chair he was in. He looked back at Vivian.

"I just ... I don't know, thought it would be easier on you," he said, the frown remaining on Vivian's face. "I mean, you've got your son to look after, and they overwork you. It's not fair on you two and under my instruction I can give you set hours or time off and everything. I'm just trying to help you out a bit..."

"I really appreciate it, Chris," Vivian sighed, finally looking rather relieved at the thought. "I mean, thank you, really. I seriously appreciate you doing this for us. You didn't have to."

Chris smiled at her and received one in return.

"It's fine. Marion said she'll get someone else to do some of the stuff you used to do," he said. Vivian nodded but looked a bit unsure about the new change of routine. "I want you to take the day off tomorrow. I'm sure Riley wants to hang out with his mom for a day or so."

Riley's face lit up with a smile as he looked at his mother. "Can we?"

"Of course we can," Vivian said, the grin never leaving her son's face. She looked back at Chris. "Seriously, Chris, thank you. I really mean it."

"It's fine, really," said Chris. "Just let me know if you need anything, OK?

## CHAPTER TWELVE

# Manipulation

"What do you think you're doing?"

Gates looked over his shoulder from where he was sitting on a rather large rock by the lake. Heather crossed her arms as she glared at him. Her four soldiers stood motionless behind her.

"This isn't your area," Heather continued, sounding extremely unimpressed. She looked around as Gates got up from where he was sitting. "Also, I'm pretty sure there's more than just one of you."

Gates shrugged as he put his hands in his pockets, staying where he was as he looked around too.

"Just me," he said, turning his attention back to Heather who glared at him suspiciously now. "I wanted to talk to you about something. I didn't know how else to get your attention other than by coming here."

The suspicious look remained on Heather's face as she looked Gates over, but he could see she was also curious as to why he was out here. "Alright handsome, you have my attention."

Gates gave her a slight smile as he walked around the large rock to the side she was on.

"Well, alright, then," he said. "I was thinking the other day, and I realized that you and I have something in common."

"What in the world would *we* have in common?" Heather asked, the interest still clear on her face. "We have nothing in common, whatsoever."

"Well, now, let's not go jumping to conclusions," Gates said with a bit of a laugh. "You'd be surprised. We have more in common than you'd think. I know for a fact, and this is what I came out here to talk to you about, that you don't particularly like Vincent."

Heather looked him over again, thinking. She returned her gaze to his face, but his expression was still the same.

"You work under him. Why do you have any reason to not like the almighty Vincent?"

Heather was surprised when Gates's expression changed to one of genuine displeasure.

"You'd be surprised," he said. He moved, walking closer to her and coming to a halt in front of her. "I don't know about you, Heather, but I don't particularly like being locked away in a dungeon just because I state my opinion."

An amused smile appeared on her face as she looked him over again.

"Oh no, has Vincent taken a disliking to you?" she asked, looking back to his face again. "You're not his favorite, I'll take it?"

"How did you guess?"

Heather smiled at him, but it was more of a sly smile than amusement.

"So, what do you plan on doing about it? Is this the reason you wanted to seek me out? To find a way of getting back at him?" she asked, taking a step closer, closing the distance between the two of them. "If that's the case, I don't know if I can believe what you're saying. You have a very good friend back at the Emerald City. What makes me believe you'd turn against him and the rest of your little gang and suddenly turn your back on them all?"

"Besides the fact that he didn't stand up for me and allowed me to be locked down in the dungeon?" Gates asked. He scoffed. "Please, I can give you multiple reasons why I should have left that group a long time ago."

The sly smile stayed on Heather's face as she crossed her arms. "Well, go ahead and tell me then. Prove to me you're not lying."

"If you insist," Gates said. "Where do I even begin? As I said, Zeke's done nothing for me. He left me down in those fucking dungeons for at least a week. Didn't visit once. I had to con one of the guards to come closer so I could grab the keys and get out. Not my proudest moment, I must admit, but I managed, nonetheless. Tell you what, the people Vincent employs aren't exactly the smartest."

"I've noticed," Heather commented dryly. "Seeing as they were all too stupid to realize they shouldn't get close to our territory. And now they've all been turned to stone, thanks to Marion."

"Anyway, besides Zeke being an unreliable asset, we have Ash," Gates continued. He could see he had Heather's interest now. "There are so many things wrong with that girl, where do I even start? She's manipulative and doesn't like it when she doesn't get her own way. She's good for nothing and only uses people to get what she wants. I can't even tell you how she's helped the group at all. I can't think of one single thing she's done that wasn't all about her."

"I don't know why she's still around to be honest," Heather said. Gates shrugged, "Good for nothing is a good description of her. Alright, I guess you've explained yourself enough. I don't particularly wish to be here all day. Correct me if I'm wrong, but are you saying that you want to ditch your little group of heroes, and join up with us? Is that what I'm hearing?"

Gates shrugged again. "If that's what you think you're hearing, then, yeah, that's what's happening."

Heather shifted her position, arms still crossed as she looked at him, no longer in the mood to play around. "Why should I believe what you're saying? How do I know if any of this is the truth? Why in the world should I believe you? Last time I checked, you were all on the same page. Has Vincent really screwed up that much in the past three months?"

"You know him better than I do, so you tell me."

Heather narrowed her eyes, summing him up as she tried to decide what to do. "I still don't know if I can believe you. Vincent might be a screw-up, but I just don't think you're capable of turning your back on him and your friends, even if they've all wronged you once upon a time. I just don't think you're capable of it."

"Well, Heather, you got me," Gates said with a bit of laugh, holding his hands up in his defense causing Heather to narrow her eyes at him. The smile disappeared from his face. "But, you see, the problem is, I've also got you."

Before Heather could move or say anything, Gates grabbed her, a blade already at her throat.

"You tell any of your damn soldiers to move or do anything, and I mean anything, I will slit your throat," Gates growled, holding Heather's arms against her sides with one arm, while his other hand kept the blade against her throat. "I'm not here to play games. You've had your fun, but this isn't going any further."

"What do you want?" Heather asked bitterly, seeing Zeke and a woman heading towards them. "Why did you lure me out here, truly? You going to kill me? Is that it?"

"I've no reason to kill you unless you do something stupid," Gates said. Heather gave a bit of a laugh, and he pushed the blade into her throat a bit more. "Shut it."

Zeke stopped next to him, giving him a nod before looking at the trees spread out for miles along the sides of the small lake. He gestured and Heather saw another three people emerge and head over to them.

Zeke switched his gaze to Heather who glared at him. He indicated to the soldiers, none of them having moved from where they'd originally appeared with Heather.

"How do they work?" he asked.

She laughed. "That's what this is about? You want to know how my army works? Please, like you're going to be able to defeat them. There are four of them and your little group couldn't even take on one. You're all pathetic."

"We never said we wanted to defeat them," Zeke said, a frown returning to Heather's face. "I'm not going to ask you again. How do they work?"

Heather stayed quiet, forcing Gates to push the blade a bit more against her throat, drawing a line of blood and making her wince.

"You're going to have to kill me," she sneered. "I'm not telling you anything. You're going to have to kill me, just like Marion killed your little friend Shade."

"We know he's not dead," Ash spoke up. Heather turned her glare on her. "We know for a fact that he's still alive."

"How would you know that? How can you be so damn sure that she hasn't killed him yet? All he did was complain constantly because he was unable to leave the damn dungeon. He wasn't of any use to any of us. He's dead."

"We know he's not," Gates said, Heather looking irritated now. "Because if he was, one of you would have left him on our doorstep to prove a point. We haven't seen any sign of him for months, so we know he's not dead. You're not as smart as you think you are, Heather."

"He's as good as dead if he doesn't speak up soon," she growled. "Marion won't wait forever, especially if she knows that you all know that he's only just breathing. He should have died months ago, right when Marion got her hands on him. She's too stubborn to let him die until he tells her what she wants to know. He's suffering and none of you can do a damn thing about it."

Gates looked at the metallic soldiers. "You ready to tell us how they work yet? None of us are going anywhere until you speak up."

"You ready to let me go yet? Same damn question!" Heather snapped. She gave a laugh. "If no one's going anywhere until I speak, then we're going to be here for a very long time."

## Chapter Thirteen

# Travelling L.A.

Alex looked around in amazement as Abel unlocked the front door, pushing it open and going inside.

Abel sighed, holding the door and clearing his throat to get Alex's attention. "You know we don't have a lot of time to waste, right?"

Alex looked at him with sudden realization on his face and he quickly stepped inside. Abel shut the door once he was in.

Alex looked around the front room they were in, fascinated by what he was seeing. It was a very nice house, and he found himself wishing he lived up here in a place like this.

"You live here?" Alex asked, following Abel through the house, looking at everything he could on the way past. He made a mental note to come back and properly look at the nice art on the walls.

"Yes."

Alex nodded, stopping in the doorway to the bedroom Abel had gone into. Abel opened the curtains, letting the light in.

"I like it here," Alex said. "Maybe I should move up here. It's a lot nicer than the draughty old castle back in Wonderland."

Abel didn't say anything as he went over to the closet, clearly after something.

Hearing a noise, Alex frowned and looked behind himself. Alex's eyes widened in surprise when he saw a small, black and white cat wind through his legs, heading into the bedroom.

"You have a cat?" he asked, the excitement bubbling over. "Cats are awesome!"

Abel gave him an unamused look as he threw a few clothing items on the bed. The cat jumped up onto the bed and Alex went over to it.

"Jamie and I have two cats," Abel said. "I have someone to look after them when I'm not around."

Alex nodded and crouched down at the end of the bed, beginning to pat the cat who didn't seem to mind.

Abel sighed, making Alex look up, still patting the cat.

"What?"

Abel shook his head. "Nothing, just thinking is all."

Alex frowned and stood up, which made the cat meow at him.

"About what?" Alex asked, watching Abel start to shove the clothes into a suitcase. He wondered why he was doing it.

"I don't know. A couple of things," Abel said, sounding distracted. "Like, maybe it'd be better to just come home and stay home. All this shit with Marion and everything is doing my head in. I mean, I don't want to leave you guys down there to fight without me, seeing as I pretty well started this whole thing, but just the fact of everything that's going on with Jamie, I was just thinking ... maybe it'd be better if we stayed up here for good, you know? I don't want anything happening to Jamie and now because of the whole baby and everything..."

"If you think it would be better for her to stay up here, then do it," Alex said. Abel looked at him sadly. "You don't have to fight, Abel, you know that. You can show me the way back after we do this, and I'll go back down to Oz and Wonderland and everything and you can stay up here. I can help Jamie find the way out, now that I've done it with you.""

Abel shook his head and sighed. "As much as I wish I could, I just can't."

"Maybe just bring Jamie up here then."

"But then what happens if I don't come back home again?" Abel asked sadly. "Seriously, Alex, what if I bring Jamie home and then go back to help you guys out with taking down Marion, and something happens to me? Who's going to tell Jamie when I don't come back home?"

Alex's expression fell at the thought, and he looked at Abel sadly. Abel shook his head and went back to packing the suitcase.

"Why are you packing stuff?" Alex asked, trying to change the subject as the second of Abel's cats wandered in and jumped on the bed with the first. It was also black and white.

"Because you never know how long we're going to be there and it's also going to look odd if we rock up to the airport and have nothing on us again," Abel said. "Better to be safe than sorry, you know."

"I guess," said Alex.

Abel finished putting things into the suitcase. He stood up straight and looked around the room, trying to figure out if he'd missed anything.

"How *are* we going about getting back to the ... airport?" Alex asked, making sure he was using the correct word. This place had some very different things than he was used to back home.

"Well, depends on what we think is the best way," Abel began. Alex went back to patting the cats as he listened. "Either I drive us to the airport, which I think might be the best option. The other option is that we get a taxi or something to take us over there."

Alex frowned. "Taxi?"

Abel sighed. He'd forgotten, somehow, that Alex didn't know how a lot of things worked up here. It was all so foreign to Alex and would take a lot to explain.

"Never mind, looks like I'm going to be driving us," Abel said. Alex looked at him blankly and Abel assumed he didn't quite get what he was saying once again. He paused. "Actually, why am I wasting money on planes when it's only a couple of hours drive to Matt's place? I'll drive. What am I even thinking?"

Alex gave a slow nod as Abel closed the curtains and grabbed the suitcase, indicating for Alex to leave the room ahead of him. Alex did as asked, and Abel followed behind.

"What are we going to do when we get to this place where Matt lived?" Alex asked as they headed for the front door.

Alex went outside. Abel was not far behind, and he shut and locked the door once he was out.

"We figure out why we've been sent there," Abel said, heading over to the garage with Alex in tow. "Once we know why we're there, we can go back down to Wonderland, get back to Oz, and see how far along the path everyone is. I'm just hoping we're nearly at the end of this damn war."

"It hasn't really started yet," Alex noted. "I mean ... has it?"

Abel lifted the garage door and pressed the key to unlock the car, making Alex jump slightly at the sound. He put the suitcase on the back seat, having decided that he was taking it regardless, just in case, even though he'd decided to drive instead of flying this time.

Abel opened the driver's side door, motioning for Alex to do the same on the passenger side. Once they were both in and the doors were shut, Alex copied what Abel was doing and put his seatbelt on.

"Honestly, Alex, this war has been going on for a long time," Abel said, starting the car and making Alex jump at the sudden noise. Abel looked at his phone and entered Matt's address, so he knew where he needed to go. "It's been going on for years, even before I got down to Wonderland. Matt's probably the only one who's been through the whole thing from the very beginning."

Abel looked over his shoulder and backed the car out of the garage, making Alex quickly grab the side of the seat from the unexpected movement. He was a bit unsure about this.

Abel grabbed something from beside his seat and pressed a button. Alex watched the garage door close by itself.

"Do you think Matt's still OK?" Alex asked. "Think Chris is doing OK?"

"I'm sure Chris has everything under control," Abel said, making sure no one was coming before he fully backed out of the driveway and onto the road. "If he's not under Marion's influence, then he should be able to get Matt out."

"But what if he can't get Matt out because he *is* still under Marion's control?"

Abel shook his head.

"Honestly, Alex," he began, seeing what looked like a traffic jam up ahead. "Chris is smart. He'll figure out something's up, sooner or later. I'm sure Marion's influence has an end to it. Depends on what she used to bring him around to her side because there's no way he'd go willingly."

Abel sighed as he stopped the car and tried to see how long the traffic jam was. This was going to take more than a couple of hours, by the looks of it.

"Well, obviously," Alex said. "But think about it. If Chris gets back to himself, we have an inside man."

Abel gave a shrug. "True, but he's going to have to be very careful not to alert Marion to the fact that he's not under her control."

## Chapter Fourteen

# Technical

"In all honesty, I'm surprised it worked. And you managed to get four of them, not just one," Vincent said, a frown on his face as he kept his distance from the motionless soldier. He looked at Zeke. "What did you do with the witch?"

"She's secured down in the dungeon. Ash is keeping an eye on her at the moment," Zeke said, Vincent nodding in satisfaction. "Ash won't let her do anything to get out."

Another nod. "Good to hear. The last thing I want is a witch loose in my city."

Gates rolled his eyes but stayed quiet. Vincent chose to ignore him, instead cautiously stepping forwards a few paces, still not too keen on getting too close to the metallic soldier.

"So, what's the plan now?" Vincent asked, crossing his arms as he looked the soldier up and down, that unsure look on his face the entire time. "I assume it's deactivated?"

Zeke shrugged and Vincent stepped back in alarm.

"No idea," Zeke said. "As far as we're aware, it needs to be told what to do, otherwise it'll just stand there and not do anything. We're hoping Nixx will take a look at it and see what he can do in the way of either dismantling it or replicating it. If we find out how it works, then we can try to replicate one of our own to take on Marion's army."

Vincent gave a slow nod.

"Honestly I think they're more Heather's army than Marion's," Gates commented. "We've only ever seen Heather out with them, never Marion. Heather seems to pride herself in them more. Marion will probably only use them when she launches the full attack on us."

"Either way, we need to get Nixx down here to have a look at this," Vincent said. "If one of you would be so kind as to make that happen, I'm going to go and have a bit of a chat with the witch."

"How long are you planning on keeping me here?" Heather asked. She pushed against the front of the cell, making sure she was right up against the bars, but Ash ignored her. "Oh, come on. Don't be such a bitch. Answer me!"

Ash switched her gaze to her, arms still crossed as she leaned against the wall a little distance away. Heather gave her a bit of a suggestive look.

"You're in here until you fucking die," Ash sneered, making Heather chuckle. "Don't push me. Shut it and don't talk to me again."

"Or what?" Heather dared. "You can't keep me in here for too long, you know. Someone will realize I'm gone and then the war will really begin."

Ash rolled her eyes, not saying anything.

"I somehow doubt they'll start a war over you," Vincent said as he came to a halt between Ash and the cell. A scowl appeared on Heather's face. "Marion has more pressing reasons to launch the war against the City. You're not really someone she'll care about going missing."

The scowl remained on Heather's face. "So, what, you're going to leave me here to rot in the dungeon?"

Vincent shrugged. "Isn't that what you've done to Matt over the past three and a half, nearly four months?"

A smirk replaced the scowl. "He deserves it, all the torture and the solitude," she said, enjoying the glare that appeared on Ash's face. "Oh, come on, even I know you don't like that guy. The world is a better place without that freak running around in it. He's as good as dead, you know."

"Well, Heather," Vincent said, walking over to the front of the cell, making sure to keep his distance in case she tried to grab him. "I mean, we're willing to let you go back to your dark castle for a price."

"Marion won't make a trade," Heather spat, already knowing what he was implying. "He's still of use to her. As you said, I'm not someone she cares about."

"So, Carmen won't want you back either, then?"

That made Heather stop and think.

"You're all in for a bit of a shock once my sister realizes I'm gone," she warned. "You won't be prepared for her attack. You thought Marion was bad? She has nothing on Carmen."

"Any ideas about how it works?" Zeke asked.

Nixx shook his head, still standing on the chair as he played around with the metallic soldier. The front of it was wide open, revealing bits and pieces within. Zeke and Gates were standing back, not wanting to get in his way.

"I've managed to deactivate it for now," Nixx said, a bit of a frown on his face as he tried to figure it out. "It shouldn't be able to move while we're taking it apart. Honestly, I've never seen anything like this before."

"Have you got even the slightest idea about how it could function?" Gates asked, crossing his arms as Ash appeared next to him. "Like even a little bit?"

Nixx shrugged, glancing over his shoulder as he continued to tinker around with the insides of the soldier.

"Honestly, Gates, at this point in time, I have no idea," he said. Disappointment appeared on both Zeke's and Gates's faces. "I'll keep digging and see what I can find, but as of now I have literally no clue how this thing works. My best guess is it's controlled by magic infused with other elements. It might take me a few days, but I'll find something, don't worry."

Gates nodded and switched his gaze to Ash. "Heather still locked away?"

Ash nodded. "Yeah, Vincent's got the security tight down there at the moment. He said he'd call on one of us if things get out of hand or it gets really bad down there. So, anyway, are we any closer to figuring out how to get Chris and Matt back?"

"No, still at a standstill," Gates said, shaking his head. "We figure they've lasted this long, especially Matt, that they can last a bit longer and we won't need to worry as much. We're focusing on getting our defenses up at the moment so we can be ready for when Marion decides to attack."

Ash nodded. "How's that coming along? Like what are we doing about that?"

"Well, glad you asked, I was just about to head out and see what I can do. See how much progress we've made, if you'd care to join me," Gates said. He looked at Zeke. "You right to stay here and help Nixx with this?"

Nixx pulled something out of the soldier, carelessly throwing it to the floor with a loud clang.

Zeke gave Gates a thumbs up and Gates nodded in response, signaling for Ash to head out.

"By the way, any word from Abel or Alex?" Gates asked, stopping in his tracks as he remembered that they'd sent two people out recently.

"Nothing yet," Zeke said. "If we hear anything, we'll let you know."

Ash followed Gates as he exited the room, the door shutting once the two of them were gone.

"Care to tell?" Nixx asked, throwing another piece of metal which bounced on the floor, before coming to a rest.

"They're on their own separate mission at the moment, trying to find out something that Matt left us a clue about," Zeke said.

Zeke watched as another piece of metal joined the others on the floor.

"Grab the table and put those pieces on it, we'll take a closer look at them in a minute," Nixx said, still focused on what he was doing. "If we can figure out why they're pieced together how they are, we may have a chance at figuring out how to replicate it."

"Is that a guarantee?" Zeke asked, doing as he'd been told and grabbing the loose pieces of metal, putting them on the table.

"It's a guess," Nixx said with thought in his tone as he reached further into the soldier. "Tell you what, there seems to be a lot of unnecessary metal in here. No wonder you boys had a hard time taking them on."

"They're a lot harder to fight when they use their abilities."

Nixx stopped and stared at Zeke who wandered back over from the table. "Abilities, you say?"

Zeke nodded to confirm that was indeed what he'd said.

"Well, maybe we can find out how they do that," Nixx mused. "Maybe they have some sort of mechanism in them that gives them their abilities."

"Guess there's only one way to find out."

# CHAPTER FIFTEEN

## *Defenses*

"Vivian, hey," Chris said, stopping Vivian abruptly in the hallway.

"Oh, Chris, hello," Vivian said, looking flustered, caught off guard. "Sorry, I didn't see you there. Is there something I can do for you?"

Chris frowned. "Are you OK? You're looking a bit overwhelmed."

"I'm fine, Chris, thank you," she said, giving Chris an unconvincing nod. He could tell something was up. "Just been rushing around today is all. Riley was a bit sick this morning, so I'm kind of behind on everything I need to do today."

"Oh, sorry for holding you up, then," Chris said. "Hope he's doing OK."

Vivian gave him a bit of a smile. She was glad someone cared about her son other than just her. "Thank you. I'm sorry, Chris, I should really get back to what I need to do today."

Chris nodded. "Of course. Before you go, though, there's something I need to ask you, which is the reason I stopped you."

Vivian frowned. "Sure, what can I help you with?"

Chris looked around briefly, making sure no one else was nearby. He was worried that Marion would be lurking nearby and hear what he had to say.

"Before, when Marion was in charge of you," he said, leaning in and keeping his voice down. Vivian leaned in as well to hear him properly. "Was she using something against me? Because recently I've been wondering about it."

The frown remained on Vivian's face. "How so?"

Chris sighed. "Well, for one, I'm almost one hundred percent sure that I'm not meant to be here. I'm pretty sure I never have, or ever will, work for Marion willingly. This is all wrong and I'm only just starting to really remember things. Did she, like, put something in my food or something like that? I don't even know how I got here."

Chris moved back a bit, giving her some space back.

"Honestly, Chris, I don't know," Vivian said. "I just take food to whoever it's meant to go to. I'm sorry, I don't have any role in preparing it."

"I just needed to check anyway, just in case you knew," he said. "But from now on, can you keep a very close eye on it? Don't give me anything they have lined up for me."

Vivian nodded confidently. "I can do that for you."

Chris felt more relieved now that he knew he had someone he could count on here. He still wasn't in the right frame of mind though and was hoping he'd start remembering what was really going on within the next couple of days.

"Anyway, I have to get on with what I'm meant to be doing," Vivian said. "I'll check in with you in a little while."

"Thank you."

"Ben, how are we looking?"

Ben looked up to see Gates and Ash headed over. They were on the outside of the City walls, working on the defense system. Doug and Ruby were working further down the wall with a few other people that Gates didn't know by name.

"Hot, as usual, and defenses are looking decent as well," Ben responded. He was crouched down, working on a minor detail at the bottom of the wall.

Gates shook his head. "I didn't ask how *I* was looking, but thank you. How are the defenses coming along? Any issues?"

"Nothing's been reported," Ben said, standing up and beginning to walk behind Gates as he headed down the length of the wall, inspecting it as he went. "So far, so good, boss."

Gates gave a nod of satisfaction, stopping near the main gate into the City. Ash took the time to look closely at what was being done.

The gate had been entirely reinforced with metal in an attempt to make it harder to bash down when the Iron Army eventually arrived. That, though, was only the beginning of the fortifications and defense system.

Halfway up the section of the wall they were standing in front of was covered in the same fortified metal, the intent being to stop anything breaking through the wall. A guard station was located just above the gate, but it hadn't been fortified yet.

Gates looked at Ash, seeing her admiring the work the civilians had been putting in. Ash returned his look.

"Impressed yet?" he asked, a half-smile on his face. "Came up with the idea myself."

"How did you manage to get Vincent to agree to this?" Ash asked, watching a group of four workers move a piece of heavy metal further down the wall, ready to install it in place.

"I told Alex who suggested it to Vincent who then agreed before he realized I was technically the project manager," Gates said, crossing his arms as a cool breeze brushed past. "This way we've got a bit more of a chance against the army when they decide to show up. They won't be getting through that gate as easily as they'd like. Plus, we have a bit more to top it all off."

Ash frowned, not sure what he meant. Gates gave her a smile but didn't elaborate.

"What do you mean?" Ash asked, her curiosity piqued. "What tops it all off?"

"Well, I'll show you if you like," Gates said, that smile still on his face.

Ash nodded, wanting to see what he had in store.

"I was wondering how we could try and fortify this as well as we possibly can," Gates continued. "So, I started playing around with a couple of ideas. This was all before Vincent decided to lock me up, mind you. I was down in the arena by myself at one point and had this brilliant idea.

"I've worked on my abilities quite a lot over the years, which means I've managed to learn how to do a variety of different things. I've also managed to get more ... coverage, I guess you'd call it. I don't particularly want to be stationed on the ground because I'd have to be on the front line."

Ash nodded and Gates indicated for her to follow him as he began walking back to the main gate. Ben also followed along behind them as they went through the entryway. There was a door off to the side of the guard's station, where they checked people who were on their way in.

Gates went through the door, the guard on duty not even bothering to check who they were. He clearly already knew. Ash and Ben followed Gates up the steps to the guard post they'd seen from the ground. Ben shut the door once they were all at the top. They were high up on the City wall and they all looked out over the land in front of the gates.

"So, anyway, I figured that if I didn't want to be on the ground and the front line, I could get a better post," Gates said, picking up from where he'd left off. "From here, I can keep out of the firing range and still reach people and stop as much as I can. More defense from up here. I can help the people on the ground. Not to sound egotistical or anything, but if I get taken out too soon, they don't have much of a defense at all."

"No, no, you don't sound egotistical, you're right," Ash said, looking down at the people working below. "You're our best defense at the moment because of what you can do. If they take you down, we're screwed."

Gates nodded and continued to look out at the land beyond the City, not saying anything.

"So, how far can you reach?" Ash asked with a bit of an amused smile on her face now as Gates looked at her. "What's your range and are you any good?"

"Wouldn't you like to know?" Gates responded with amusement. "Guess I can show you. It's not like I can impress you any more than I already have."

Ash shook her head, the smile still there. She indicated for him to go ahead and show her.

Gates turned his attention to a hole in the wall. It looked like it had once housed a window but that was long gone. He put his hands out in front of him, and Ash saw that the barrier covered the whole area of the wall in front of them, right down to the ground.

"I can go further but that's just so you know I can do it," Gates said, lowering his hands, the barrier disappearing. "Just in case you doubted me. Don't want to overwork myself just yet. Save the grand spectacle for when the real threat emerges."

"Well, at least you weren't lying to me about it," Ash said with a smile. "Won't that take a toll on you, though?"

"If it keeps Marion out for even a few extra minutes, that's all that matters. We have to keep her out long enough to get everything into order for when she breaks through, because we know she will."

Ash just hoped that Marion wouldn't be able to get through as easily as she expected. With the defenses all in place, and Gates at full strength, surely it would take her and her Iron Army a lot longer than she'd originally thought.

# CHAPTER SIXTEEN

# Released

A knock on the door made Chris look up. It was Vivian. She smiled at him as she pushed the door open a bit further so she could enter the room.

"How's the memory going?" she asked, placing a tray of food on the desk.

"It's getting there," Chris said. He raised an eyebrow as he looked at the tray. From where he was sitting on the bed, he couldn't tell what sort of food it was.

"I did as you asked and made sure I was careful with the food," she said. "Let me know if there's anything else you need."

Chris nodded and Vivian headed back out of the room, closing the door after herself, leaving Chris alone.

Chris turned his attention back to what he'd been looking at before Vivian had come in. He was pretty sure it was one of the journals Marion was after. He'd found it in his room, which led him to believe that it had been with him when he'd ended up in this castle.

How Marion hadn't gotten her hands on it yet, or even how she didn't even know he had it, was beyond him.

He went back to the page he'd been reading, a frown on his face as he tried to make out the words. The handwriting was rather bad. It had to have been written by a doctor if it was this illegible.

*'TEST SUBJECT 003 seems to be responding well to the treatment. At this rate I'll be able to find out what makes abilities work within individuals. Need for more test subjects is absolutely necessary.'*

The frown remained on Chris's face as he read further down the page. One name, in particular, caught his eye.

*'Haven't had much luck with the madman, Nixx. He's been uncooperative and doesn't seem overly fazed by me wanting to test things on him. I haven't begun yet, but will be returning shortly to begin the process. He is a very good test subject, as he has a very solid grip on his abilities.'*

Nixx. Why did that name sound so familiar? Chris's frown deepened as he tried to remember how he knew that name. He must have known who it was, else it wouldn't sound so familiar.

Before he could stop it, something in his mind clicked, sending a rather vivid recollection of something that had happened in the past.

*"The name's Nixx," he introduced himself, keeping eye contact with Chris the whole time. He straightened up and readjusted his top hat. "And who am I talking to?"*

*"Chris."*

*Nixx gave him another half-smile and a tilt of the head. "Honored, I'm sure.*

Suddenly, another intense memory surfaced in Chris's mind.

*"Don't touch him this time," Nixx said, moving around the doctor and inspecting him. "I think that touching him triggered the movement again."*

*"What is actually going on?" Chris asked. His heart was still beating a million miles per minute as he pushed himself back against the wall. His hands hung by his sides as he stared at the emotionless, motionless face of the doctor.*

*"That's going to be very dangerous if used for the wrong purpose," Nixx muttered to himself, thinking out loud. He looked at Chris. "The Queen will want to use that. Don't let her get her hands on you. The less she knows about your ability the better."*

Chris snapped back to reality, shaking his head from the sudden, unexpected throwback into time. He had no idea why it had happened, but he didn't like it and now his mind felt foggy. Nixx had said something about Marion wanting to use his ability for something bad, which meant he wasn't on Marion's side.

This, clearly, was not where Chris was meant to be.

Closing the journal, Chris stood up and went over to the door. He made sure no one was around as he walked down the stone steps to the lower level. He needed to see Matt and he needed to see him now.

Once again, it was quiet as Chris walked briskly through the main living quarters of the castle. Marion didn't seem to be around a lot lately, and Chris wondered where she was all the time. Now that he knew a bit more about what was going on, he believed she was plotting something big and dangerous.

Marion obviously figured Matt wasn't going anywhere as Chris found the door down to the dungeon unlocked again. He ducked in through the door, shutting it quietly and carefully after himself before descending the steps.

As usual, Matt hadn't moved. He had his back to the wall, and his head down.

"Matt," Chris called, making sure to keep his voice down in case someone upstairs heard him.

Matt jerked and looked up at Chris. He'd probably been asleep, which wasn't a bad thing considering how worn out he was all the time now.

"Oh, it's just you," Matt said unenthusiastically. He rested his head back against the wall, still looking at Chris. "Ready to kill me yet?"

"No, and I won't ever be ready to kill you," Chris said, seeing Matt roll his eyes, even in the dark. "I may have wanted to kill you a few times on the way to the Emerald City, but you're a friend and I won't kill you."

A frown crossed Matt's face, his confusion clear. "I'm sorry?"

"I need to know how to get out of here," Chris said, holding up the doctor's journal. "I know what's going on."

"Where did you get that?" Matt asked. His confusion was gone but his expression dropped. "You need to keep that out of Marion's sight. Why do you have that?"

"I must have had it with me when she grabbed me," Chris tried to explain. "I don't know how any of this has happened, but I know that Marion's the one we're trying to take down. I need to get out of here and back to the City as soon as I can. I need to leave now."

An unamused look crossed Matt's face. "I needed to leave four months ago, yet I'm still here. You're not leaving without me, Chris. You're not leaving me locked away down here!"

"How do I get you out? How do *I* get out?"

"You need to get the keys from Marion, well, from her or one of the other two. I know Heather has keys," Matt explained, sounding exhausted. "You unlock this door, you unlock these damn shackles, and you get me the hell out of here. You can't leave me locked away here, man, please."

"I'm not going to leave you here, Matt. Where do they keep the keys?" Chris asked.

"Most times, they have them on their person, so good luck getting a set of the keys," Matt said, leaning his head back against the wall again. "Can I get your word that you won't leave me here? Even if you can get out the front door, you will not leave without coming back for me?"

"You've got my word, I promise."

Matt gave a satisfied nod. Chris didn't blame him for being so desperate to get out. He'd been locked up for about four months, not to mention tortured, which was enough for anyone to wish they were dead.

Chris gave Matt one last look before he went back up the stairs and out of the dungeon, making sure the door was shut.

"Chris, there you are."

Chris froze, hearing Marion call for him. He still had the journal with him, and he knew he couldn't let her know he had it or let her get her hands on it. He was going to have to make sure she didn't catch onto the fact that this was one of the journals she was after.

"Marion," Chris said, turning to face her as he kept a firm grip on the journal.

Marion narrowed her eyes as she stayed where she was.

"What were you doing down in the dungeon?" she asked suspiciously. "And what have you got there?"

She pointed to the journal, and Chris looked down at it.

"Just a bit of light reading," he said, looking back at her. "Nothing special. Just grabbed the first book I saw and hoped it was good. Haven't started it yet, was heading back to my room to start reading it while I had something to eat, actually. Hopefully, Vivian's left my meal there by now."

Chris hoped she'd buy the lie as she looked him up and down with suspicion. She glanced at the book, then looked back at his face.

"Well, it's always good to keep up to date on what's going on in the literary world," she said, deciding not to push the matter any further. "Anyway, I should let you be on your way. If you see Heather, let her know I'm looking for her. I need to talk to her about a thing or two. Enjoy your dinner."

Chris nodded as Marion walked past him without another word. He breathed deeply once she was out of sight. That had been way too close for his liking. Making sure she wasn't still lurking nearby, Chris continued on his way. He walked down to Vivian's room at a fast pace.

The door was shut so he knocked and waited, constantly looking around and hoping that Marion hadn't decided to come back.

A minute later, the door opened a bit and Vivian looked out. When she saw who it was, she frowned and opened the door wider.

"Chris, is everything OK?"

"Do you have keys to the dungeon cells?" Chris asked straight out.

"No, Marion ended up with my set," Vivian said. Chris felt a wave of disappointment wash over him. "I can get a set for you tomorrow, though, if you want. I can't do anything at this time of night, I'm afraid. Carmen and Heather both have a set as well, but they lock their doors overnight. Can it wait until morning?"

Chris shook his head. "I need a set now. It's urgent. I have to get out of here before Marion comes back and I need to get something from the dungeon before I leave."

"I'm sorry, Chris, but I really can't help you right now," Vivian said sadly. "I wish I could but there's nothing I can do."

Chris nodded in understanding. "It's OK, thank you anyway. Look, either way, I need to get out of here. Can you help me? Do you know how I can leave?"

"Your best shot is the back entrance," Vivian said. "No one should be around at this time since it's getting late. If you leave now, you should be able to get out."

"Do you know how far away the Emerald City is?"

"It's a bit of a walk, I'm afraid. You should leave now before anyone sees you, else they'll know something's going on. Good luck."

"You should come with me, you and Riley," Chris urged. "You can't stay here forever, Vivian. It's not right and it's no place to raise a child."

"I'd love to, Chris, but I just can't," Vivian sighed. "If I leave, they'll definitely know something's happening and they'll launch their attack on the City. I can't be responsible for that. I'm sorry but I need to stay here so everything stays in order."

Chris nodded, understanding but disappointed. "Just take care, OK? I promise I'll do whatever I can to get you two out of here."

Vivian gave him a sad smile. "Thank you, Chris. Be careful and stop Marion however you have to."

# CHAPTER SEVENTEEN

## Making it Back

"When did he leave?" Marion snapped, a scowl on her face.

"He's halfway to the City," Carmen said. "He must have left during the night. He's nearing one of Vincent's alerts so he's out of our reach now."

Marion stormed out of the room, heading to the dungeon. She'd seen Chris coming out of there last night, so she needed to make sure Shade was still there. If he was gone, there was going to be a very big problem. She flung the door open so hard that it hit and bounced off the wall, and she practically ran down the steps into the darkness.

She stopped and gripped the cell bars tightly as Matt looked at her, wondering why she was disturbing his peace and quiet. He went back to his original position of head down and eyes closed, dismissing her.

"Well, I'm surprised he left you down here," she spat. "Thought he would have taken you with him. He's already halfway to the City, apparently."

"Let's hope he dies on the way, hey?" Matt said bitterly, not raising his head.

An amused smile crossed Marion's face as she shifted to lean against the bars. "Did he promise to take you with him? Oh, did I hit a sensitive spot, Shade?"

Matt stayed silent. He knew not to buy into her mind games. Then, he couldn't help himself; he was sick of being locked down here in the dark.

"If you're gonna kill me, just do it," he growled. "This has gone too far, Marion. Just kill me and get it over with. Then you can go and do whatever you want without me in your way."

"I'm not going to kill you, just yet," she said. "You still haven't told me where my journals are."

Matt finally looked up at her. Marion couldn't quite see the look on his face because of the darkness.

"Well, my dear, you missed your chance to get one of the journals last night," he said with superiority in his voice. He laughed, clearly seeing the expression on her face. "You're an idiot. You mean to tell me that you didn't search Chris when you grabbed him? You stupid bitch."

Marion growled, grabbed the cell keys from her pocket, and unlocked the door. Matt laughed again as she stormed over to him and knelt in front of him. She grabbed him by the throat, shoving the back of his head hard against the stone wall.

"How dare you speak to me like that! How dare you call me that," she snapped, keeping a firm grip on Matt's throat. "If you're not careful about what you say, you will never be seeing your friends again. I actually considered letting you out after you told me where those journals are, but I might have to reconsider."

"You've lost, Marion," Matt sneered, looking her dead in the eye as she glared at him but didn't loosen her grip. "Once Chris gets back to the City, and once they figure out why I gave them that address before you grabbed me, you're as good as dead. You won't ever know where those journals are, but they already do. They just don't know it yet."

Ash had wanted to go over some more things with her ability, so she and Gates were in the arena with Jacob. They stopped what they were doing when they spotted Vincent walking at a fast pace towards them.

"An alert's gone off," Vincent said urgently, sightly out of breath. "I need you three to go and check it out. We're short on people to send out at the moment, and you three can get there fast with the proper defenses."

Gates nodded and Vincent headed back across the arena to take care of something else. He seemed to be very busy lately, although no one really knew what he did.

Jacob looked at Gates and Ash before taking his phone out and checking something. Ash raised her eyebrows with a silent question.

"Alerts show up on here, in case you're wondering," Jacob said. "Just checking the location so I know where we're going. By the looks of it there's only one person."

He put his phone away and looked between Ash and Gates.

"You think it's a big threat?" Ash asked.

Jacob shook his head. "Nah, should be fine if it's just one person. Sometimes it's just a lost traveler. Let's go see what's happening."

Before the other two could say anything in return, Jacob's bright white light appeared, temporarily blinding them. Next thing they knew, the light was fading, and they were standing beside the Yellow

Brick Road. Gates blinked a couple of times, trying to get his vision back.

"Oh my God, Chris?" Ash exclaimed, rushing over to where Chis had collapsed on the road.

"Holy shit," Gates said, joining Ash as Jacob came over as well. "Is he OK?"

"We have to get him back to the City. Vincent will be able to fix him up," Jacob said. "He doesn't look injured, but we need to make sure he's right mentally. We don't know what Marion's done to him."

Vincent came out of the room, closing the door carefully behind him. "He's stable for now. He should be able to move around within the next couple of hours if he's feeling up to it."

Ash gave a worried nod. She was wondering where Alex was; she felt like she needed him around at the moment.

"Whatever was in his system from Marion should clear out in a few hours," Vincent continued. "He's lucky he made it back this far without one of them catching him."

Ash gave another nod and Vincent left. She jumped in surprise as someone appeared next to her.

"How's he doing?" Gates asked.

"Vincent thinks he'll be OK," Ash replied. "He said that he should be up and around in a few hours once everything in his system's cleared."

She headed off, and Gates followed her down the hallway and into the kitchen. He sat down at the table as Ash went over to one of the cupboards, seeing they were a bit low on food. She made a mental note to either get some or ask Vincent about it.

"Well, it's good he made it back," Gates said, pulling out his phone. "Don't know how we'd have handled having to fight against him if Marion's hold on him hadn't slipped."

Ash sat down opposite him. Gates was looking at something on his phone which was interesting to her, since it was the first time she'd seen him with one.

Ash nodded, not saying anything as Gates put his phone on the table, crossing his arms as he leaned back in the chair, his gaze on Ash.

"Ash, I want to apologize." He sighed. "Ever since we had that … altercation … a few months back, I've been a bit of a jerk towards you, and I want to apologize for it. It's unacceptable and I know things between us have been kind of horrible because of it. I just want to say sorry and that I know I've been a bit out of line because of it."

"Don't worry about it," she said with a shrug, confused as to why he was apologizing to her four months after the fact. "You've every right to treat me like that because of what happened. Honestly, Gates, I deserve it."

Gates looked at her sadly. He started to say something but was distracted by the screen on his phone lighting up. Ash got a quick glance at the background before Gates picked the phone up, looking at the notification that had just come through.

"Sorry, just Zeke needing me down there," Gates said, putting his phone back into his pocket as he stood up. Ash gave a nod of understanding. "Keep an eye on Chris. I'll be back up here in a while. If anything happens, come find us."

Ash watched Gates leave. Once she was sure he was gone, she got up and headed back down the hallway to Chris's room. She planned on sitting in with him just in case something happened.

As she walked, she couldn't help but wonder who was in the picture with Gates on his phone's background. She didn't recognize the woman, but she also didn't really know much about Gates.

Maybe it was someone he knew back in Wonderland? Maybe Ash would eventually ask but, for now, she was more focused on making sure Chris was alright.

She quietly opened the bedroom door and looked in. Chris was still completely out and most likely would be for a few more hours if what Vincent had said was true.

Ash sighed, going over to the desk and grabbing the chair before placing it beside the bed. She sat down and let her mind wander.

Had Chris just gotten lucky and managed to get out of Marion's grip? Had Marion let him go on purpose? Had Chris seen Matt while he was there? Was Matt even still alive? If he was, would Marion kill Matt now that Chris was gone? Had Chris even tried to get Matt out of there if he was still alive?

There were just so many unanswered questions. Hopefully, when Chris was awake and able to function properly, he would be able to answer those questions.

Until then, Ash would just have to wait.

# CHAPTER EIGHTEEN

# Metallic

$Z$eke looked over as he heard the door shut. Gates wandered over to him, stopping in front of him as he stood next to the deactivated and partially-disassembled soldier.

Nixx was at the table, looking over the bits and pieces he'd salvaged from the soldier. He glanced up and nodded at Gates, before returning his attention to the metal bits on the table.

"You called?" Gates asked.

Zeke nodded and indicated to the soldier. "Need your help with deactivating the other three."

They'd brought back all four of the soldiers Heather had with her when they'd captured her. Only one of them had been deactivated for now, as Nixx had decided they weren't really much of a threat without Heather to tell them what to do.

Now, though, they wanted to be sure that nothing was going to happen, as Heather was still in the building, even if she was locked away in the dungeons. She was still rather unpredictable, and they had no idea how she controlled them.

"Why do you need my help?" Gates asked, looking unsure about it as he followed Zeke over to the first of the other three soldiers.

"You're just here in case I hit the wrong thing while trying to deactivate them," Zeke said. He gestured to the chair next to the deactivated soldier that Nixx had been tearing apart. "Grab me the chair? I can't reach from here."

"Yeah, well, they're not exactly short soldiers and you're not the tallest guy.," Gates said, making Zeke smile. "Makes it harder to access their inner workings if you can't reach."

Gates grabbed the chair, brought it over, and placed it next to Zeke.

"Just keep a close watch in case I manage to screw this up," Zeke said, positioning the chair so he could reach what he needed to reach. "Don't particularly wish to get myself killed while trying to deactivate one of these."

Gates stood close and watched Zeke start to pry open the front of the soldier's chest. "We any closer to finding out how they work?"

Zeke shrugged as he forced the front plate open. He leaned forward, trying to get at something deep within the soldier.

"That's what Nixx is currently working on," he said. "We've taken out a few parts and he's seeing if he can figure it out before we go pulling more and more out of them. We'll probably end up completely dismantling that one, so we know exactly how it works."

Gates gave a bit of a nod, not saying anything as he watched Zeke work.

"Be careful with that, Zeke," Nixx called. "There are a few pieces you probably don't want to touch in there. You might accidentally activate it if you're not careful."

"Note taken," Zeke said, still concentrating on what he was doing. "If I set something off, you'll know. That's why Blaine's here. He'll stop it before it gets too far and tries to kill any of us."

"Thanks for the vote of confidence," Gate said, rolling his eyes.

Zeke shrugged, stepped off the chair, and moved back from the soldier.

He looked at Gates. "One down, two to go."

"I think you have to get rid of him. He's not about to tell you anything," Carmen said, watching Marion pace back and forth. "If Vincent's people already know where those journals are, there's not really much chance of getting them before they do."

Marion stopped pacing and looked at her, as an idea suddenly came to her. She remembered something Chris had said. There was still a slight chance that she could get Shade to talk.

"Heather's been gone for a few days," she noted.

Carmen shrugged, not bothered, as Heather often disappeared for weeks with no word.

"Is she the only one the Iron Army will respond to?" Marion asked.

Carmen shook her head. "They also respond to me, but I'll fix them up to follow your orders as well, if that's what you're asking."

Marion nodded and Carmen abandoned what she was doing.

"I'll be down in the dungeon with our friend," Marion said. "Once you've done that, bring one in."

Carmen nodded and left the room.

Marion smiled to herself. This might be the only thing that would make Shade talk.

"Chris, it's good to see you're awake," Nixx said, looking up as Chris and Ash wandered into the room.

Chris frowned, trying to work out what Nixx, Zeke, and Gates were doing. By the looks of it, they were dismantling one of four metallic soldiers they had. Chris wasn't sure how they'd managed to get one of them, let alone four.

"Heather's locked in the dungeon," Nixx said, looking back to what he was doing as he answered Chris's unspoken question. "Don't worry, she won't be going anywhere for a while."

Ash stayed close to Chris as Zeke went back to pulling bits out of the first soldier. He'd managed to deactivate the others an hour or so ago with no problems.

"So, are you alright?" Gates asked, crossing his arms and looking at Chris.

Chris nodded. "Yeah, I'm fine, thanks."

"What about Matt?"

"Last time I saw him he was still alive," Chris said, feeling bad and noting that the expression on Gates's face didn't change. "I was going to get him out, but I couldn't. There was no way I could get him out of there."

"So, you left him there instead of trying to find a way to take him with you," Gates stated, not impressed. "He's probably dead by now."

"I did everything I could," Chris said in his own defense, his tone lace with annoyance. "It's not my fault if Marion's killed him. I did what I could and he's lucky he was still alive when I was there."

"Well, you were there, you could have done *something*," Gates snapped, very unhappy now.

Zeke listened in but he kept going with what he was working on, not wanting to be a part of it.

"So, yeah, Chris, it kind of is your fault if Matt's dead now," Gates continued. "I'm certainly going to be blaming you."

"It is not my fault," Chris reiterated.

"You're so selfish, you know that?" Gates said with a shake of his head. "You left without him! You only thought of yourself!"

"You have no idea what the hell happened!" Chris snapped back, finally sick of the way Gates was speaking to him. "You weren't there so you have no idea what happened. I needed to leave as soon as I could before Marion got me back under her spell. I tried to help Matt but there was no way I could get him out, so don't you dare go accusing me."

Gates shook his head. "If he's dead, I'm still going to be blaming you."

Chris went to say something but stopped, having seen something moving at the back of the room. Gates frowned as he saw the look on Chris's face, turning his attention to what had caught his eye.

One of the deactivated soldiers was twitching and, a few seconds later, its eyes it up a dark red.

Without hesitation, Gates put his hands out, and the barrier appeared in front of them, creating a block from wall to wall.

The soldier began to slowly make its way over to them, completely unaware of the barrier.

"What's happened?" Nixx asked, hearing the commotion and dropping what he was looking at back on the table. He moved over to stand with everyone else. "Did one of you touch it?"

"Not since we were deactivating them," Zeke said. "I was careful with what I was doing, but maybe I touched something I shouldn't have."

Ash stayed just behind Chris who hadn't moved, and everyone watched as the soldier continued its slow pace towards them. It was twitching a bit as it walked and was halfway across the room now.

"I told you to be extra careful!" Nixx exclaimed.

"I was!"

"Clearly, you weren't careful enough," Nixx said with a sigh. "There's nothing we can do now. You boys know to take them down?"

"We actually have no idea," Zeke said and the look on Nixx's face said it all. "When we first encountered them, we couldn't do anything. Heather called them off. We don't know if they have any weaknesses or anything."

"Well, we need to figure it out now," Gates stressed. The soldier was nearly at his barrier now, which was just in front of him. "Because we all saw what happened last time."

"Well, you two did," Ash said.

"Now's not really the time, Ash," he said, focusing completely on the soldier. "Hey, is it just me, or is that not the same color as the rest?"

Everyone looked at the soldier, trying to see what Gates was talking about. Besides the eyes being a glowing dark red, the outer color of the metal was, indeed, not the same. This one was a dark grey, where the other ones were gold with black armor. This one still had the same black armor but was definitely different.

The soldier was mere yards away from Gates who was making sure he had a solid stance to be able to defend the five of them for as long as he could.

"I could have sworn it wasn't like that before," Zeke said with a frown. "Blaine, be cautious with it. We don't know if it has different abilities or anything."

"Oh, because I wasn't going to be cautious to start with?"

Zeke didn't say anything, and Chris moved over to join him, while Ash stayed close behind.

"Why is it a different color?" Chris asked. "Does that mean it's more dangerous?"

Zeke shrugged. "No idea."

"Guys, get ready to help me out here," Gates said. "We're going to have to work hard to take it down. Nixx, is there anything you can tell us? Have you found anything we can use to take it down?"

Nixx shook his head. "No."

The soldier suddenly stopped and stood motionless in front of Gates.

"Why has it stopped?" Chris asked, looking around.

Before anyone could answer, there was a metallic sound, which brought everyone's attention back to the soldier. A long, sharp-looking sword had appeared where its right hand had been only moments before.

No one said a word for a minute or so as Gates stayed where he was with the barrier up. He wasn't about to let anyone know he was a bit worried now.

"This isn't good," Zeke said. "Blaine, we need to leave now."

"We can't let it out of this room," Gates said, glancing over his shoulder at Zeke. "If it gets out, we won't be able to stop it. It'll kill everyone it sees, and we'll lose half the City. We have to keep it contained and try to get it deactivated again."

"Zeke's right, we can't stay here with it," Chris said. "We get out, close the door, and figure out how to stop it."

"It'll get through the door," Gates snapped. "These things are dangerous, Chris. They'll break through anything, and they'll kill everyone. We can't let it out. We have to work as a team and figure out how to take it down. I need you guys to back me up because, right now, I don't know how long I'm going to be able to last with this. I can only do so much. I need you guys with me here."

"We're not going anywhere," Nixx said. "Everyone get ready to defend. Gates is right. The only way it leaves this room is if we're all dead."

Zeke gave a nod of agreement now, not about to leave his friend alone with this killing machine.

Chris and Ash also nodded, although Ash looked very worried.

Nixx looked at Gates. "Last as long as you can. We're all here to back you up."

## CHAPTER NINETEEN

# Matt's House

"This has got to be the right place," Abel said, double-checking the address they'd stopped at.

He and Alex had arrived in San Diego less than ten minutes ago, and now they were parked outside the house they'd been told was Matt's residence before he'd ended up in Wonderland.

"You think anyone will be home?" Alex asked as Abel opened the car door and got out. Alex scrambled to follow him.

"Doubt it."

They stopped outside the closed front gate, and Abel double-checked the address again before deciding to go in. He pushed open the gate and headed up the pathway with Alex close behind.

"Where did Gates say the key would be?" Alex asked as he looked around. It was a very nice place, he thought, and he was interested to see what it looked like on the inside.

The front garden was very well kept, making Alex wonder who looked after it. Obviously, someone did, otherwise it wouldn't have been so nice.

"Does any of this strike you as a bit odd?" Alex asked as he followed Abel around to the back of the house.

"What do you mean?" Abel asked.

The back of the house also looked like it was well looked after. There was a pool, which had a cover on it, and the concreted, shaded area was clean with no dirt or dust.

Abel began looking for the key, figuring it was more likely to be somewhere out the back rather than the front of the house. Matt seemed like the type of person to put keys out the back and there were more places here that it could be hidden.

"Everything here is just too clean," Alex said. "Matt hasn't been home in years. Who's looking after the place?"

Abel shrugged. That hadn't really occurred to him. "Honestly, Alex, I have literally no idea. Ask him next time you see him."

Alex nodded and wandered off.

Abel stood for a second and looked around, trying to work out where Matt might have hidden the key. He walked over to a wooden table under the shaded area and picked up an ashtray. He didn't think Matt smoked, so it was a bit odd that he had an ashtray.

Alex's attention was suddenly brought back to Abel who held up a key.

"Now, let's get in and see what we're here for."

Alex nodded eagerly, very curious to see how Matt had lived here.

Abel went over to a sliding glass door that led into the house. The curtains on the inside of it were closed. He unlocked the door, then went and put the key back in its place under the ashtray.

He slid the door open and stepped inside. Alex followed him in and shut the door after himself.

"Lock it, just in case," Abel said.

It took Alex a couple of seconds to work out how the lock worked but, once he did, he locked the door and made sure to pull the curtains back into place before he looked around. It was a bit dark in the house, but he saw they were in the kitchen. It wasn't a very big house, but it seemed nice.

"Do we know what we're looking for?" he asked, as Abel headed out of the kitchen.

"No idea. Just have a look around and see if you can find anything that Matt might have been implying is here."

Alex gave a nod as Abel disappeared further into the house. Once he was out of sight, Alex moved through the archway and into the living room, beginning to look around.

There didn't seem to be anything out of place, but he also didn't know what Matt's house was normally like. For all he knew, the table might have been in the wrong place.

Finding nothing of use, Alex went back into the kitchen, seeing some papers that had been left on the bench. He went over and picked up one of the pieces. It had a list of expenses on it.

"Abel," Alex called, heading down the hallway in the direction that Abel had headed. "Have a look at this."

Abel looked out of the doorway of one of the rooms, and Alex held the piece of paper out to him. Abel took it, looked at it, and frowned.

"Looks like someone's been getting a bit of help with the gardening," he said, reading what was on the paper. "Someone called 'Kathryn J' is paying for the house currently. Also getting some work done on the garden, as I just stated."

Alex frowned. "Well, whoever it is, they're keeping the house in good order, even though Matt's not around. At least we have a name now."

Abel handed the paper back to Alex, indicating for him to put it back where he'd found it.

"We don't want to arouse suspicion when someone comes back. Anything you touch, put it back where you found it."

Alex headed back to the kitchen and placed the paper back where he'd found it, pushing it around with his finger until he was sure it was in the exact same position. He decided to join Abel in searching the room down the hall.

"You find anything yet?" he asked, watching Abel open the closet and began looking through it.

"Nothing yet," Abel sighed. He paused, hands on hips, as he looked around the bedroom. "What are we even looking for?"

Alex shrugged and opened the last drawer of the bedside table. He saw a folded piece of paper, which he grabbed and unfolded, finding a hand-written note saying, *'Third shelf up; closet'*.

"Hey, I think I've found something," Alex said, standing up and going over to Abel.

"What did you find?" Abel asked, turning around and seeing the paper Alex was holding out and the open bottom drawer behind him.

"It says the third shelf up in the closet," Alex said.

They both looked at the closet, which Abel already had open.

Before either of them could say anything more, they heard the front door being unlocked and someone talking. Alex looked at Abel with panic, while Abel went over and shut the drawer Alex had left open.

"Find somewhere to hide, someone's outside," Abel said, his voice low as Alex looked around, panic still on his face.

Alex dashed into the closet, glad he was able to fit. Abel indicated for him to move over to give him some room. They heard the front door open as Abel squeezed into the closet as well, quickly shutting the doors and hoping they hadn't been heard.

"I don't know why you insist on keeping it," a male voice said. "Kath, it's been eight years. He's not coming home."

Abel and Alex exchanged looks as they heard the front door close.

"You don't know that," a female voice responded. "I'd rather keep the house in good shape, just in case. You never know, Gary. Also, if Stella ever decides to move back into town, she can use this house. It's a nice house and there's no point in selling it when someone in the family might be able to use it. You never know."

Abel looked to his left, about to say something to Alex, but he wasn't there. Abel frowned, looking down to see the small blue cat sitting on the ground. A surprised look crossed Abel's face. He hadn't known they were able to use their abilities up here in the real world, but now he knew better, and at least he had more room in the closet now.

"Look, I know you're still hoping Matt's alive, but it's been *eight years*," Gary said. "We haven't heard anything from or about him in that entire time, Kath. He's gone. You've been looking after his house this entire time, but I honestly don't think he's coming back. He'd be back by now if he was coming home. Or we would have heard something from him by now."

"You can't tell me you don't miss him, too," Kath replied. "Also, this wasn't just his house, this was their house. Vivian's missing too, you know. It might have been eight years, but I really believe they're all still out there somewhere. Blaine and Zeke included. I know Skye and Casey miss them, too. Something clearly happened and I'm not about to give up my hope that our son is still out there, and they won't be giving up either."

Abel looked down at Alex, listening as Gary and Kath went into the kitchen.

"At least we know who's looking after the place," he said, voice very quiet so as not to attract attention to the fact that they were hiding in the closet in the bedroom.

Alex meowed at him and Abel shook his head and fell silent as he heard someone walking down the hallway, in their direction. Abel signaled to Alex to keep quiet, and the little cat laid down as someone entered the room.

Abel could just see out of the closet through the slight gap in the doors. He watched Matt's mother open the curtains and the window, probably making sure that the house wasn't always closed up.

He heard her sigh as she sat on the edge of the bed with her back to the door. She leaned over and grabbed the framed photo from the bedside table, looking at it with a sad expression.

"Maybe one day..." Abel heard her say quietly before she put the picture back.

She suddenly got up, fixing the bed covers where she'd been sitting before leaving the room.

Abel looked at Alex as he heard the back door open. "Think they'll be here long?" he asked quietly.

Alex meowed in response, then the little cat gently pushed the closet door open a bit and slipped out.

Abel stayed silent, still worried about drawing attention to the two of them. He watched through the open door as the cat jumped up onto the bed, then onto the bedside table.

Alex grabbed the framed photo in his teeth, jumped off the bedside table, and ran back over to the closet. Once he was in, Abel shut the door again and took the picture from Alex, who went back to his original position of lying down while he waited.

Abel looked at the photo with the small amount of light available in the closet. It was a picture of Matt and a woman, whom he assumed was Vivian. He didn't know who Vivian was, but she was clearly someone important to Matt.

"We're going to have to wait until they leave before we can do anything," he mumbled to Alex.

"Alright, let's go," Abel said, hearing the front door lock.

The curtains and the window in the bedroom had been shut and Matt's parents had finally left. It had taken them a few hours and Abel's leg was cramping from being stuck in the closet for that long.

Abel opened the door, and the little cat dashed out, jumping up onto the bed. Abel walked out stiffly, trying to stretch his back and legs.

"Alright, let's see what we can find up there," he said. Alex meowed in agreement. "I'm going to put you up on the third shelf. Think you can have a look around for me?"

Alex meowed again and Abel picked him up carefully. He placed the little cat up onto the third shelf in the closet, then stood back at the end of the bed. Alex walked around on the shelf, disappearing briefly as he wandered deeper into the closet where Abel couldn't see him.

A minute or two later, he appeared again, pushing something with his head. Abel frowned as the cat pushed three leather-bound books off the edge of the shelf, the books hitting the floor hard.

"Oh shit," Abel said, recognizing the journals.

He grabbed Alex from the shelf and placed him on the bed, before he picked the books up off the ground.

Alex jumped off the bed and changed back into a person. "What are they?"

"They're trouble," Abel said, opening one of the books to make sure they were exactly what he thought they were. "I have no idea why there are three here. I had one, Chris had one, and Nixx had two, so I don't know how Matt got his hands on them. I know I put mine out of sight and I doubt Nixx would have given his up. Why has Matt got three of them and how did he get them?"

"Well, this is certainly the last place I would have looked for them," Alex said. "What are they exactly...?"

"Marion's doctor's journals," Abel said. "They have some dangerous things written in the four of them. If Marion gets her hands on them, she'll be able to do more than just use her army. She'll have a lot more power at her disposal."

"But there are only three here," Alex noted. "You said there were four."

"Shit," Abel swore. "Chris has the other one and he's with Marion."

Abel and Alex looked at each other and didn't say a word for a couple of minutes.

"Let's just hope Chris hasn't realized it, and that Marion doesn't have it," Abel said with a sigh.

# CHAPTER TWENTY

# Terror in the Castle

"I t hasn't moved, why hasn't it moved?"

"I don't know, Chris, but right now we don't really have time to panic," Nixx said. "We have to stay calm and take this soldier on any way we can."

Gates was still standing in his defensive position, staring the metallic soldier down. Suddenly the soldier moved, swinging its sword at Gates's barrier. It slashed the sword in a straight line right across it, causing the barrier to disappear as Gates collapsed to his hands and knees.

"What the fuck?" Gates swore, doubled over on the floor. "Guys, get the fuck out! Now!"

Gates stayed where he was, and they all saw the blood on his hand when he moved it away from his stomach.

"Shit," was all he said, still doubled over in pain.

The soldier's attention was still on Gates as it moved forward to stand over him. Gates looked up as it raised its sword, ready to bring it down onto him to finish him off.

But before it could do anything, Zeke moved and the area in front of them went up in flames.

"Get out!" Zeke shouted at the others. "We're right behind you!"

Ash moved first, with Gates and Nixx following, heading for the door.

Zeke went to Gates and grabbed him, hauling him to his feet and getting a cry of pain in response as he dragged him over to the door. The soldier swung the sword down and just missed the two of them as the flames died out.

Zeke dragged Gates through the door, letting him go as they made it through. Gates collapsed onto the bottom of the stairs, as Zeke slammed the door shut, locked it, and put his back to it in an attempt to stop the soldier getting through.

The other three were halfway up the stairs, but Gates stayed where he was, trying to stop the bleeding. It had soaked through a lot of his shirt already.

"We've got to stop it before it gets any further into the castle," Chris said. "Also, Gates can't go very far, he's seriously hurt."

"I'm fine," Gates growled, leaning his head against the wall. "I'm not about to lay down and die just yet."

There was a very hard shove against the door, which jolted Zeke off it. He put his back to it again, hoping they were going to be able to contain it for a bit longer while they figured out what to do.

"We need to get moving, get out of here, and find Vincent," Ash spoke up, everyone apart from Gates looking to her. "He'll be able to help us."

Chris nodded as Zeke was pushed off the door again with a harder hit this time.

Nixx moved down the staircase, stopping at the bottom in front of Gates. "We need to get you to the infirmary. Let me take a look?"

Gates stayed silent, having nothing to say. He knew Nixx wasn't about to take no for an answer. Nixx crouched in front of him, as Zeke was pushed off the door once more. Nixx moved Gates's hand and arm out of the way, not liking the amount of blood on his shirt.

Nixx carefully lifted Gates's shirt up to assess the damage. The expression on his face was enough to determine the severity of the situation. There was a very deep slash right across Gates's midsection, caused by the soldier when he'd swung the sword at the barrier. It had been very quick and had done a lot of damage within that short time.

One of the downsides to Gates's ability was the physical wounds he suffered when his barrier was attacked, and this was a dire situation.

"We need to get him out of here now," Nixx said.

Gates hunched over again as Zeke was forced off the door one final time, landing on his hands and knees on the floor.

Suddenly, the soldier's sword came through the door, right where Zeke had been standing just moments ago, just above where his head was now. They were lucky this door was made of metal, else the soldier would have broken through right away.

Nixx moved up a few stairs as the sword withdrew back into the other room. Zeke quickly scrambled to his feet and moved to the stairs. The sword stabbed through the door again, sliding down this time with a harsh metallic sound, causing all of them to wince.

"Let's get out of here, we'll shut the door on top and try to slow him down again," Nixx said, moving up the stairs.

Ash and Chris took the hint and followed, while Zeke looked at Gates. He crouched down in front of him. "Come on, we've got to get you out of here."

Gates shook his head as the sword came through again, trying to slice its way through the metal door.

"Zeke, I can't get up," Gates said seriously, leaning his head back against the wall. Zeke saw a few tears run down his face. "I'm losing feeling. I'm bleeding out too quickly! I literally can't get up, man."

"I'm not about to leave you here, Blaine. I'm not gonna let you lay down and die," Zeke said, trying not to show Gates just how upset he was. "I'm not letting you die down here. You're gonna pull through this and you're gonna go home to see Skye, OK? I'm not gonna let you miss that chance."

Gates stayed quiet, just watching Zeke. Zeke looked up at the other three as the soldier continued to cut through the door.

"Go and get Vincent, and lock that door," he instructed. "At least stop it before it gets out into the City. Don't let it out of this castle."

Chris and Ash had both stopped, looking shocked and unsure, a few steps ahead of Nixx. Nixx nodded to Zeke and motioned for Chris and Ash keep going and get out. They did as they were told and Nixx gave Zeke and Gates one final nod of respect before running up the remainder of the stairs and through the door.

As the door at the top of the stairs slammed shut, the soldier managed to cut through the other door, pieces of metal clanging on the stone floor.

Zeke and Gates heard the door at the top of the stairs lock, and they looked at each other.

Zeke smiled sadly at Gates who looked like he'd lost any will to live he had left. "We fall together or not at all."

Ash looked on in horror as Nixx slammed the door shut and locked it. Two people passing by looked over but kept moving as Nixx moved back from the door.

"We can't just leave them down there to die!" Ash yelled.

"That's their choice," said Nixx. "Zeke chose to stay down there with Gates. If it gives us a bit more time to try and stop this soldier getting out, we need it. They might be able to hold it off for a bit longer while we work out how to contain it, to stop it. We need to do this as a team. If they die, it shouldn't be for nothing."

"What do we need to do?" Chris asked, knowing what Nixx was saying was true. If they didn't work together everyone was going to die.

"We need to get Vincent and Jacob, and we need as many other people as we can get," Nixx said. "The more people we have, the better chance we have."

Chris went to say something, but they were interrupted.

"Guys!"

Abel and Alex came to a very quick halt.

"Chris?" Abel said, sounding confused.

Chris gave him a brief smile as a loud bang came from behind the door causing all of them to look at it.

Abel looked at the group in front of him. "What's going on?"

"We fucked up and we're all about to die," Ash spoke up, Alex standing with her now and holding her arm.

Abel looked at her with confusion, so Nixx spoke up as they heard more noises coming from behind the door.

"We don't have a lot of time, but in short we have an active soldier down there," he explained. "Gates and Zeke are down there at the moment. Gates is seriously hurt, and he couldn't get up the stairs. Both of them are most likely going to die, but they're buying us time."

A very sad look appeared on Alex's face. Abel on the other hand, was thinking.

"I might be able to help them," he said. "Just get the soldier out of there so I can get to them."

Before anyone could say anything else, Abel ran off, disappearing quickly around a corner.

Ash looked to Nixx. He seemed to be in charge here. "What do we do?"

Something slammed against the door behind them. The soldier had made it up the stairs, which meant Gates and Zeke were most likely dead.

"We do as Abel said, we let it out," Nixx said. "If Abel can somehow get to Gates and Zeke, they may have a chance if they're still alive. We need to make sure the soldier stays on us, so we all have to attack it with everything we've got, understood?"

"Where are we taking it?" Alex asked, jumping as the door behind them shook with another hard slam.

"The arena," Chris spoke up, everyone nodding in agreement. "That's our best option. We get it to the arena. There we have open space and more people who will be training."

Everyone nodded, all of them on board with the plan.

"Alright, let's see who's on the other side," Nixx said, moving back to the door.

Everyone got ready as Nixx unlocked the door and swung it wide open, stepping to the side as he did so. The soldier stormed out and Nixx shut the door so it couldn't go back down.

"How are we doing this exactly?" Alex asked, the worry in his tone as he saw what they were up against. "What are we doing?"

"Someone attack it, I don't care how, just do it!" Nixx yelled.

The air became bitterly cold as Ash concentrated until a sheet of ice appeared, snaking along the ground. A set of spikes made of ice smashed into the soldier, managing to push it back into the shut door.

The soldier swung its sword wildly, smashing the ice and causing everyone to step back.

"Everyone start moving. Keep it on the group at all times," Nixx instructed.

Ash went for the soldier with her ice shards this time. Alex had now changed, but he wasn't an adorable cat this time. He was a huge, vicious-looking bear, albeit a blue one.

"Get it down to the arena and get help there," called Nixx. "I'm going to stay here and help Abel when he gets back and in case something else happens. Now, get moving."

# CHAPTER TWENTY-ONE

## Saving Lives

"We clear?" Abel asked as he and Jamie rushed over to Nixx.

Nixx nodded, wondering what he was planning.

Abel looked at Jamie. "We don't know if they're still alive or not. Think you can help?"

"I'll do what I can," Jamie said with a nod.

Abel opened the door and immediately saw Gates and Zeke at the bottom of the stairs. He quickly headed down, with Jamie and Nixx close behind.

"Zeke?" Abel called cautiously.

Zeke looked up. He had his arms around Gates's shoulders. Gates leaned against him, not moving.

"Abel?" said Zeke as Abel crouched in front of him.

Jamie came down the stairs very carefully, making sure she didn't fall.

"How the hell did you guys get past the soldier?" Nixx asked, crouching next to Abel.

"Luck," Zeke said, keeping his hold on Gates who still hadn't moved. "I managed to shield us both in fire and the soldier couldn't get through the flames. I assume it was due to the heat. It gave up pretty quickly when it realized we were encased and it couldn't get to us."

"Is he still alive?" Nixx asked, nodding at Gates.

Zeke shrugged and a tear rolled down his cheek as he held Gates against his shoulder. Everyone stayed quiet as Nixx carefully took Gates's wrist, checking for a pulse.

"I can't tell," he ended up saying, carefully placing Gates's arm back down. "I can't feel his pulse but that doesn't mean he's gone. We might be lucky."

Abel looked at Jamie as Zeke refused to let Gates go. "Can you do something?"

"I can try," she nodded.

Abel and Nixx moved back to give Jamie some space as she turned her attention to Gates. She took his hand and held it, shutting her eyes and concentrating.

Nixx and Zeke looked to Abel for an explanation.

"We found out recently she can heal people," he began, interest crossing Nixx's face as Jamie continued to concentrate. "She can't heal herself, but she can heal others. If he's not already gone, there's a chance she can help him."

Jamie opened her eyes and, keeping hold of Gates's hand, looked at Zeke. Zeke looked at her sadly.

"He's still here," she said. "Barely, but he's still with us. He won't be for much longer but for now he's hanging on."

"Can you help him?" Zeke asked desperately. "Please."

"I can try," Jamie said. "That's all I can do. I can't guarantee he isn't already too far gone, though. If he's too close to the Reaper, I may not be able to help him."

"Just please, do everything you can."

"I will, I promise."

"Just a bit further!" Chris shouted.

There were a lot of frightened citizens scrambling to get out of the way, making sure they weren't about to get caught up in the fight.

Ash and Alex worked on getting the soldier to take the last few steps into the arena.

The soldier swung at Ash who managed to jump back out of the way. Alex attacked the soldier's arm, clamping his strong jaws around it and shaking it, leaving dents in the outer metallic layer as the soldier shook him off.

Alex growled and pushed the soldier from behind as Ash threw more ice shards at it from the side. The soldier turned to face her and took a step.

"Come on, just a few more steps!" Chris said, urging them to get it to move a few more steps. "Get it inside and we'll have it!"

Ash nodded and moved in front of the soldier. She was just inside the arena now. The soldier followed her movement, getting closer to her.

She indicated for Alex to push it again from behind. Alex rammed the soldier hard and it finally took a step into the arena.

Everyone who was training had stopped what they were doing the moment they'd heard the commotion.

Ash managed to get the soldier to follow her further in, while Alex kept it from leaving.

Jacob was standing not far from Chris with his hands on his hips. "I assume something went drastically wrong with the deactivation."

"You guess right," Chris said, moving closer to him. "We need everyone's help to take it down. The only problem is that Nixx and Zeke are the only ones who know how to deactivate it, and they can't do that without opening it up. We're going to have to stop this one for good."

Jacob gave a nod, as Don joined him. Ben, Doug, and Ruby also headed over as Ash managed to halt the soldier by coating it with ice. Alex stood guard, making sure to avoid the sword the soldier was swinging wildly.

"It won't stay stuck for long!" Ash called. "What are we going to do?"

"We've got to use everything we've got!" Chris called back. "Everyone needs to go full force and keep it from doing anything. Keep clear of it at all times and attack from a distance!"

Ash signaled for Alex to swap places with her. He prowled around to the front of the soldier as Ash took up position a few yards behind it.

Chris looked at Ben. "You guys ready for some advanced training?"

"You know it," Ben said, studying the soldier with intrigue. "You need help, we're here to help."

The soldier suddenly broke free of its icy prison, swinging at Alex. Alex growled and lunged forward. He grabbed hold of its right arm with his jaws again, doing everything he could to immobilize it. The soldier used its left arm to swat Alex off, knocking him backwards where he lay unmoving. When Chris looked over, he saw that Alex was unconscious and had changed back from a bear into a person.

The soldier turned its attention to Ash again, presumably because she'd done quite a lot of damage to it on the way to the arena.

"Ash, keep it there!" Chris shouted' "Do not let it out of this arena!"

Ash moved back a few paces as the soldier moved towards her. It swung its sword at her, causing her to move back again, tripping over herself in the process. She landed on her back, smacking her head hard on the ground, causing her to become dizzy as the soldier loomed over her.

Chris moved quickly, doing everything he could to stop the soldier from harming Ash. He swore to himself as he realized his ability wasn't working.

"Someone stop it!" Chris shouted, looking over and seeing that Alex still wasn't up yet.

Everyone did what they could, but nothing seemed to affect the soldier.

"We can't stop it," Ben called. "Nothing's working!"

Ash was still on the ground, trying to get her bearings.

"Ash, get out of there! Move!" Chris called. "Move now!"

Ash looked up at the soldier, pushing herself back a bit as she stayed on the ground, her head still spinning. The soldier raised its sword above its head, but all Ash could do was watch and wait, unable to get to her feet.

The soldier swung the sword down hard, and Ash shut her eyes, waiting to die. She knew there was no way she would survive a hit like that.

When she didn't feel anything, she dared to open her eyes. The confusion, mixed with the dizziness, hit her hard when she saw the clear barrier just above her head.

She looked to her left to see Gates on his knees next to her.

"Move," he said, pushing his hands up to try and force the soldier off his barrier so he could get to his feet.

There was blood running down his arms, the cuts on his hands clear from the hard impact of the sword on his barrier. Ash thought Gates was scarily resilient, but he'd met his match with this soldier.

"Move!" Gates shouted at her, making her flinch. "Get the fuck out of here!"

Ash managed to push herself away from Gates as he pushed hard against the soldier, forcing its sword off his barrier and making it take a step back.

Zeke grabbed Ash by the arm, pulling her out of the way and to her feet. Abel took her, seeing she was still unstable from the hit to the head she'd taken when she'd fallen.

"How are we going to take it down?" Ash asked, still dazed as she watched Gates push his barrier at the soldier before it could raise its sword again.

The soldier was forced several more steps back, which allowed Gates to get to his feet, although the barrier was gone now.

"We couldn't do anything. Nobody's ability worked against it," Ash said when nobody answered her.

Alex was now conscious again. He knelt beside Chris and the others who were just watching as neither Gates nor the soldier moved, facing off against each other, waiting for the other to make the first move.

"Everyone needs to stand back," Gates said harshly, not taking his eyes off the soldier. "This one's mine."

"We need to work together," Nixx called. "You can't take it down by yourself."

Gates didn't say anything, still in the staring competition with the soldier who also hadn't moved as its dark red eyes stared directly at him.

Zeke moved forward a step, getting ready to help if he was needed. He had faith in Gates and knew that he could figure out a way to stop this metallic beast.

Gates suddenly put the barrier back up, separating him and the soldier. Everyone else just watched the beginning of the showdown.

"This isn't good…" Ash said, keeping hold of Abel so she didn't fall over. "He's actually going to die this time."

The soldier suddenly moved, swinging the sword at the barrier, having figured out that it would hurt Gates if it hit correctly. The sword connected, slashing across it like it had done before, making Gates shout in both annoyance and pain. But he was ready for it this time and he wasn't taking it anymore.

He pushed back hard, catching the soldier off guard and knocking it to the ground. Once it was down, Gates didn't waste a second, switching his position. The barrier reappeared, pinning the soldier's arms, legs, and torso to the ground.

It was obvious to everyone watching that Gates was already getting strained and hurt from the hits he'd taken. Blood ran down from his hands and stomach, splashing on the dirt at his feet.

"You're dead!" Gates shouted at the soldier, keeping it on the ground as it began to struggle. It may have been metallic, but it seemed to have a life of its own. "You think you can try to kill me and get away with it? You're dead wrong."

Gates was mad. He wasn't in the mood to play anymore.

"You should be dead," the soldier spoke in a grating voice. "You are all going to die."

"Think again," Gates said.

With one swift movement, Gates pushed his hands forwards before bringing them back quickly. The arms and legs of the soldier that had been pinned down were now separated from its body, and its torso was cut in half. The soldier let out a loud, metallic scream.

"Not fun being hurt, is it?" Gates snapped, as the soldier continued to scream. "This is what you get. You think you can just come in here and try to kill people? No, it doesn't work like that. Fuck you."

The barrier appeared one last time, this time around the soldier's throat. Gates pushed his hands forward again and the soldier's head split from the remainder of its body. The eyes flickered, then the dark red lights faded, and it fell silent.

Gates stood there looking at it for a few seconds before he collapsed hard to the ground. Zeke and Abel rushed towards him.

Ash stayed next to Nixx, while Chris and Alex headed towards Gates, Alex a bit unsteady on his feet

"He's completely out," Zeke said. "He's hurt again. We've got to get him to the infirmary before we do anything else. We might need Jamie again."

Abel gave a nod.

"I'll get some help moving these pieces back to the castle," Nixx spoke up. "Alex and Chris and a couple of the others here can help me. I'll see what I can find as to why it activated like that, and why we couldn't use some abilities against it."

Abel and Zeke nodded as they lifted Gates between them and started to head back to the castle.

# CHAPTER TWENTY-TWO

## Breaking Out

"You keep that away from me! Don't you bring it any closer," Matt said, pushing himself back against the cold stone wall of the cell, unable to move anywhere else.

Marion pouted. "What's the matter, Shade? Afraid of a little soldier?"

"This is how you're going to kill me? With one of your pathetic army men?" he sneered. "You're going to have to because, no matter what you do to me, I won't give up any information. Like I said, I'll happily die before I spill any words about anything to you."

"Well, I tried," Marion sighed. "Have fun down here in the dark for another few months. Maybe when you've gone insane from not seeing the light you'll cooperate."

She clicked her fingers, and the metallic soldier followed her out of the cell. She closed the door and locked it, leaving Matt in the dark again as she and her soldier headed back up the stairs.

Matt sighed as he heard the door at the top close. She no longer bothered to lock it; she knew he wouldn't be getting out.

He was getting sick of sitting in the dark, but he couldn't tell her anything, even if it meant she'd finally end his life. He wasn't about to let her win.

"How's he doing?" Nixx asked, startling Zeke who'd been slowly falling asleep.

It was late and they were in the infirmary. Gates was still unconscious, and Zeke sat on the chair beside the bed, not planning on leaving any time soon.

"He's stable," Zeke said, rubbing his eyes tiredly. "They say he should be out of here tomorrow if he's awake and feeling up to it. They're going to be keeping a close eye on him, though, for the first week if they do let him go back to his room. Ash is very lucky he didn't die, or she'd be dead too."

"We all would be," Nixx said.

Zeke gave a nod, resting his head on his hand as he looked at Gates.

"I don't what I would've done if Jamie hadn't managed to get him back," he said quietly. "I've known him for years. We've been friends for a very long time."

"Well, he's very lucky Jamie was able to help," Nixx said. "You said you managed to shield both of you from the soldier. Can I ask how?"

Zeke stood up and moved away from the bed, making sure he had enough room to demonstrate to Nixx how he'd done it. Nixx watched closely as Zeke set a circle of fire around himself before waving his hand above his head, then in front of himself. The fire stayed lit around him, fully encasing him within flames.

He clicked his fingers, and the fire barrier went out, leaving a scorch mark on the floor around himself. He didn't say anything as he went back to his seat beside Gates and leaned his head on his hand again.

"That's impressive," Nixx noted.

"Thanks," was Zeke's unenthusiastic, tired response. "Taught myself."

Nixx nodded and moved towards the doorway. "Well, let me know how he is. You should get some sleep, too."

Zeke gave a miserable shrug, not saying anything more. Nixx looked at him sadly before he left, knowing it would be better if he left Zeke by himself in the infirmary. The last thing he needed was to be harassed, even if it was by well-intentioned people.

"Hello."

Matt jerked awake and looked up upon hearing the unexpected voice. He frowned, looking over in the darkness to see a small boy, no older than about five, looking at him from the front of the cell. He was sitting near the bars with his legs crossed and his hands in his lap, just watching him.

"Hey, kid," Matt said, wondering how long he'd been there. "You shouldn't be down here. This isn't a place for kids."

"What are *you* doing down here?" the boy asked, curiosity clear in his voice.

Matt gave a slight laugh and looked down. "Believe me, kid, if I knew I'd tell you."

"You don't know why you're locked away down here in the dark?"

Matt shook his head and leaned it back against the wall. He was getting very sick of the cold stone at his back and wished for something else to break the boredom.

Also, why was there a kid in this castle? He was sure Marion didn't have any children, and he highly doubted it was either Heather's or Carmen's. So, whose kid was this?

"She doesn't like you much, does she?" the boy asked sadly, making Matt look over to him again.

"Who?"

"Marion," the boy said. "I hear you shouting down here a lot. She's done bad things to you down here, hasn't she?"

Matt looked at him, feeling the tiredness wash through him. Those damn shackles were keeping him so worn down all the time.

"You shouldn't be down here," he repeated, looking away from the boy and back to the floor in front of him. "This isn't a place for children."

"Will she let you leave?" the boy asked.

"I don't think I'm going to be getting out of here for a very long time."

The boy fell silent and just stared at Matt. Matt didn't say anything more. After a few minutes of silence, the boy spoke again.

"My name's Riley," he said proudly. "What's your name?"

"That's a nice name, kid," Matt said, looking at him again. The kid nodded with a smile on his face. "That was a name my wife and I considered calling our kid if we ever had one."

"What happened to her?" Riley asked.

"She's long gone. She's not coming back."

"Why?"

Matt shook his head and looked away from the boy again. "It's complicated, very complicated."

"My daddy isn't around anymore, either," Riley said with a nod. "Mommy never told me what happened to him, but she said he's not coming back. Is that what happened to you, too?"

"Yeah," Matt said.

He fell silent again, not in the mood to talk to some kid. He may have been sick of his own voice, but a kid wasn't really the best company.

"So, what's your name?" Riley asked, leaning forward and grasping the bars of the cell. "You didn't tell me before."

"Matt."

"It's nice to meet you, Matt!"

"Yeah, likewise, kid," Matt said unenthusiastically, still not looking at him. "You shouldn't be down here."

"Yeah, I know," Riley sighed, looking down and putting his hands back in his lap. "Mommy will get really mad if she knows I'm down here."

"Well, you'd better get back up top if you don't want your mom to be mad at you."

Riley shrugged, not moving from where he was.

Matt stayed silent but frowned when he heard the door above open. Someone was headed down. It was probably just Marion again. Or maybe it was Hunter coming to torture him some more or maybe kill him this time. If only.

"Riley?" he heard a female voice call from the stairs. "Riley, are you down here?"

Matt's heart jumped in his chest. He knew that voice, but it had been a very long time since he'd heard it.

"No!" Riley called back.

The woman sighed as she descended the remainder of the stairs. "What have I told you about coming down here? You're not allowed down here, you know that."

"Sorry Mommy, I was just talking to Matt."

The woman looked over, but Matt wasn't game enough to look up. He was imagining it; he had to be. It couldn't be who he thought it was. Marion had killed her five years ago. She was dead.

"Oh my God," he heard her say. "Matt?"

Matt finally looked up, forcing himself to look through the darkness and see her properly.

Vivian looked back at him from where she stood at the front of the cell and Matt felt tears run down his face. This couldn't be happening. What a sick joke.

"Please tell me this isn't real, you're not real," he said, shaking his head and looking down at the floor.

He heard the sound of keys clinking and unlocking the cell door. The door swung open, and Vivian rushed over to him, kneeling in front of him.

"I promise you, Matt, I'm real," she said, putting her hands on either side of his face, forcing him to look at her.

Matt shook his head, the tears still running down his face as Riley loitered in the doorway.

"I saw her kill you, right in front of me," he said. "You've been dead for five years, Viv."

"I don't know what you saw but it wasn't me," she said as Matt shook his head again, still trying to get his head around everything that was happening.

Vivian reached into her pocket, holding something in the palm of her hand and making Matt look at it. "Marion gave me this before she shipped me off to this place. She gave me this and told me you were dead."

Matt looked at the wedding ring in Vivian's hand. It was his. He didn't know how Marion had gotten her hands on it, but he'd been missing that for five years. He'd looked everywhere but hadn't been able to find it.

Vivian put her hands back on either side of Matt's face. "What have they done to you?"

"I was so sure you were gone forever," Matt said, unwilling to look away from her now that she was alive and right here with him. "I didn't know what to do."

"Matt, it's OK," Vivian reassured him. "Let's get you out of here. How long has she had you down here? I knew she had someone down here, but I never dreamed it was you."

"I, um, I think it's been about four months," Matt said, watching as Vivian tried to find the right key to unlock the shackles. "I don't even know anymore. I don't know what day or week it is. Whether it's day or night. I've been down here for too long."

"We're going to get you out of here," Vivian said, finding the right key. "You're going to be OK, Matt, I promise."

"I have to get back to the Emerald City," Matt insisted as Vivian managed to get one of the shackles unlocked.

Matt painfully moved his arm down and the shackle fell off his wrist. The spike that had dug into his wrist slipped out with a trickle of blood.

"I have to get back," he repeated.

"Just take it easy, OK?" Vivian said, unlocking the other shackle. "We'll all get out of here."

Matt dropped his arm, feeling the pain as he freed himself from the final shackle.

He looked at her tiredly. Vivian motioned for Riley to come over as Matt shifted his position, trying to get to his knees. Riley stopped next to Vivian, who dropped to one knee and looked at him.

"Riley, honey," she said as Matt tried to ignore the pain and bone-weary tiredness. "Sweetie, this is your dad."

Riley and Matt looked at each other with surprise.

"What?" Matt said, looking up at Vivian.

Riley broke out into a big grin and threw his arms around Matt who winced in pain before carefully returning the gesture.

Vivian smiled. Matt removed one of his arms from Riley, putting it around Vivian's shoulders and pulling her against him, keeping a firm hold on the two of them.

"I'm getting us out of here, I promise."

# Chapter Twenty-Three

## Family

"Well, hey there, savior," Ash said with amusement as Gates painfully made his way over to the table, moving very slowly.

Gates scoffed as he reached the chair. "Please, far from it."

Ash put down the book she'd been reading and watched him pull the chair out from the table and carefully sit down, wincing as he did so. He certainly got beaten up more than anyone else she knew.

"How are you doing, really?" she asked.

"I can hardly move, for one," Gates said, shifting slightly and regretting it instantly. "I'm very sore, have some brutal bruises, and will have a wicked scar once it heals up."

Ash smiled and looked Gates over. Both of his wrists and hands were bandaged up just like the last time he'd gotten seriously hurt from the damage done to his barrier. He was wearing a shirt, so she couldn't see the full extent of his injuries.

Gates grimaced and leaned back in the chair, wincing again. "I'm in so much pain."

"Maybe you should go lie down for a while," Ash suggested, watching Gates try not to move much. "You probably shouldn't be moving around, anyway. You need to rest and heal up. We need you at full health when Marion launches her attack."

"Where's Zeke at?" Gates asked, completely avoiding her suggestion. He could be rather stubborn sometimes and didn't like being left out of the action, even when he could hardly move. "He around?"

"You should be in bed, not asking where Zeke is," Ash scolded.

Gates rolled his eyes. "I'm thirty-five. I think I can decide for myself whether I should be in bed or not."

Ash raised her eyebrows. "Thirty-five?"

Gates looked at her with no amusement. "Thirty-six come July. Why? What's the big deal?"

"Nothing," Ash said as Gates shook his head and winced in pain again, clearly having moved slightly too much. "Just ... thought you were a few years younger than that."

"Whatever."

"If it makes you feel any better, I'm thirty-two."

"Not really, but thanks for the thought."

"Well, either way, you still look pretty good for thirty-five," Ash said. "Anyway, I've been meaning to say thank you for once again saving my life. That's twice now."

"And once again, you don't have to thank me," Gates said, still trying not to move. "We're a team so I'm not about to let anything happen to anyone, regardless of how I feel about them. Also, I don't plan on making a constant habit of it."

"So, we're just a team?" Ash asked. "Come on, by now I've got to have earned the friend title."

"Why do you think you've earned that?"

"Well, even if we're a team, we don't have to step in and save people all the time. There are plenty of others on the team," Ash explained. "Friends and family get saved before the team. We've known each other long enough to at least be friends."

"That what you think?" Gates asked, raising his eyebrows. "You think we're friends?"

Ash gave a confident shrug before resting her chin in her hand, still looking at him.

"I think so," she said. "I mean, we've known each other a while now. You've saved me twice and you even apologized about the way you acted towards me. If that doesn't make us friends, then I don't know what does."

"Well, how about you keep on wondering about that and get back to me when you have a more solid answer on why we're apparently friends."

Ash rolled her eyes, causing Gates to laugh a bit. Ash saw him try not to show how much it actually hurt.

They fell into a comfortable silence, neither one having anything more to say.

After a while, Ash forced herself to speak again. "Can I ask you something?"

Gates just looked at her and offered no response.

"The other day, I saw the background on your phone," Ash continued. "Who's the woman with you?"

Gates's expression fell and Ash saw that she'd hit a nerve. When he said nothing, she tried again.

"Is she the reason you got so mad at me after what happened between us?" she asked sadly. "She clearly means something to you, Blaine."

Gates looked away and Ash sighed.

"Don't call me that, you've no right. You know it's Gates to you," Gates said, trying to sound annoyed but it just came off as tired and sad. "Just don't."

Ash looked at him sadly. He certainly kept a lot to himself, but it was his personal life.

"I'm sorry."

"You should be," Gates said with a sigh, though Ash could tell he didn't really mean it. He put his hands on the table, forcing himself to stand up. The pain he was feeling was very evident. "Where's Zeke? I need to talk to him about something."

"You should really go back to your room and get some rest," Ash insisted, worried that he'd make himself worse if he was up and about too soon. "It'll make you feel better if you're not moving around."

"Where's Zeke?" he said, again brushing off her concern, but keeping one hand on the table.

He could be so hard to talk to sometimes, she thought as she stood up too. "He's probably helping Nixx down in the workshop. I'm going with you to make sure you get there."

"Ash, I'm fine," Gates said, the annoyance showing this time. "I don't need someone to be with me twenty-four seven. I'm capable of looking after myself."

"I don't care," Ash said, her tone also annoyed now. "You're seriously hurt, Gates. You nearly died. You look like you could collapse at any damn second! I'd rather make sure you make it to your destination than find you collapsed in the hallway. You'll end up back in the infirmary if that happens and I know you don't want to be there. None of us want you back there."

"You mean you, you don't want me back there," Gates said. "Why? Why do you care so much about what happens to me? Honestly, Ashley, why the hell do you care so much?"

"Because I know I can trust you!" Ash snapped. "You put up this stupid tough façade all the time, even when you're severely hurt. You don't want people to know that you care, probably too much. You might only see me and everyone else as a damn teammate, but I see you all as family."

"You don't know me well enough to call me family," Gates said.

"Well, too bad," Ash said harshly. "We may have only been shoved together as a group a few months ago, but we're a damn family whether you like it or not. We have to look after one another."

Gates looked at her for a few more seconds before he spoke.

"I need to find Zeke," he said, finally removing his hand from the table and turning towards the door.

Ash shook her head and watched him slowly make his way out of the kitchen, before he disappeared around the corner. She sighed, not about to let him leave by himself. She really didn't want anything happening to him.

She really hated the fact that she'd, for some reason, become rather attached to him. But she felt safe with him around.

Ash left the room, picking up her pace as she saw Gates not far ahead. Gates glanced at her as she fell into step with him, walking at his slow pace.

"You're really going to make sure I get there, aren't you?" he asked, sighing as she nodded. He knew he didn't have much choice. "Alright, then. I hope you're not in a hurry."

They continued on at a very slow pace in silence, neither of them having any more to say. It took a while, but they finally reached the door that led down to the workshop. It was very badly dented from when the soldier had been bashing its arms against it.

Ash held the door open for him, and Gates gave her a nod as he began stepping down the stairs, making sure both feet were on each step before attempting the next one. Ash shut the door and followed.

"You OK?" she asked when he was halfway down.

"Fine," Gates said through his teeth, looking very uncomfortable and obviously in a lot of pain.

At the bottom of the stairs, the second door that led into the workshop hadn't been replaced yet. It was completely gone.

Gates and Ash went in and stopped just inside the room. Nixx was at the table, writing a few things down as he studied a piece of the dismembered grey soldier. Zeke, Abel, and Chris were working on one of the other soldiers, the original one that had been getting dismantled.

The little blue cat was sitting on the table with Nixx, and he looked over when he saw the two new people enter the room. He meowed at them, making everyone else look over too.

"Hey, man," Zeke said, leaving what he was doing to go over to Gates. "God, you look awful."

"I feel exactly how I look," Gates said as Ash grabbed the vacant chair, the one they'd used to reach the taller parts of the soldiers. "I'm in a lot of pain and I can hardly move."

"Sit down," Ash ordered, placing the chair behind Gates. "Before you collapse."

Gates reluctantly did as he was told, sitting and wincing as he did so.

Zeke looked at him with concern and the little blue cat jumped off Nixx's table and wandered over to Gates and Ash.

"You shouldn't be moving around, Blaine," Zeke said, going back over to the soldier that the other two were dismantling. "You should be in bed, sleeping it off."

"I need to talk to you about something," Gates said, as Alex jumped up onto his lap. Gates ignored him, as usual, and Alex curled up, shut his eyes, and dozed off.

"Sure, what's up?" Zeke asked, glancing over at him.

Chris took a piece of the soldier over to Nixx's table, listening in to their conversation.

"That soldier," Gates said. "It spoke."

Nixx looked up. "We're still working on why that happened. Everything about that soldier was just completely wrong."

"Have you found anything yet?" Ash asked.

Nixx shrugged. "Nothing of importance. They're just metal, really. No idea how they work yet. No idea how to replicate it or destroy it, either. We got lucky with that other one."

Ash nodded and Alex suddenly perked up, his little ears twitching as he looked over at the entranceway that led up the stairs.

"What?" Gates asked him.

Everyone else saw that Alex had heard something, or at least thought he'd heard something, and they also looked where he was looking.

"You hear something?" Ash asked.

The little blue cat was now very alert and, without any indication of what was going on, he jumped off Gates's lap and dashed out of the room. Ash quickly followed him as everyone else looked at each other, confusion on their faces.

"What's happening?" Abel asked as Gates pushed himself off the chair, pushing the pain aside.

"Alex knows something we don't," Chris said, abandoning what he was doing and heading for the door. "We should check it out; he usually knows things before we do. Cats are like that."

He left the room, Abel not far behind him. Nixx also stopped what he was doing to join them. Zeke helped Gates move to the door, helping him up the staircase, moving a bit quicker than Gates was comfortable with, but he was keen to see what was going on.

"I can take it from here," Gates insisted once they reached the top.

Zeke was not convinced but knew Gates preferred to do things independently.

They continued on their way, seeing everyone up ahead in the hallway that ran from the rooms, past the kitchen, and into the group room.

"What's going on?" Zeke called, moving ahead of Gates who didn't really care.

He stopped at the edge of the group, surprise crossing his face as he saw what was happening. He pushed past everyone as Gates finally made it to the group.

Nixx looked at Zeke from where he was crouched in front of Matt, Vivian, and Riley. Matt looked ready to pass out, while Vivian and Riley were just confused, not too sure what was going on.

"Oh my God," Gates said, finally having pushed his way past a few people. "Vivian?"

Vivian looked up at him, a surprised look crossing her face.

"Blaine?" She looked at Zeke who was helping Nixx get Matt to his feet. "Zeke?"

"We thought you were dead," Gates said. "What the hell happened?"

Ash helped Vivian to her feet. Riley saw Chris and went over to stand just behind him, as he was the only one he knew here.

"We don't have time for that right now," Nixx said as Abel and Zeke supported Matt who could hardly stand. "We'll have time for that later."

Before anyone could say anything else, Abel and Zeke were moving, led by Nixx, as they maneuvered Matt along the hallway and down towards the infirmary.

Vivian looked at Chris, Riley still with him. "Chris, can you please look after Riley? I really need to go with them."

Chris nodded and Vivian nodded back gratefully before looking at her son. "You stay with Chris and your Uncle Blaine, OK?"

Riley gave a nod, giving Gates a shy smile. Vivian quickly headed off after the others.

The blue cat meowed, going over to Riley and sitting down in front of him. Riley's face lit up with a smile when he saw him. He grinned and sat down while Alex started rubbing against his leg.

Ash looked at Gates. "Did she just call you that kid's uncle?"

Gates looked at Riley. He seemed like a very happy kid.

"She may have," Gates said defensively, crossing his arms and regretting it due to the pain.

"Why?" Ash pushed, a suspicious look on her face. She was determined to find out more about his life.

"I, uh, I may have, possibly, been engaged to her sister," Gates reluctantly said, Ash raising her eyebrows with interest. "Not that it's any of your damn business."

"You were engaged to her sister?" Chris asked with surprise as Gates watched Riley play with the little cat who was thoroughly enjoying the attention. "So, wait, that would mean you were going to be Matt's brother-in-law."

"Why's this such a big deal?" Gates asked seriously. "Yes, I was engaged to Viv's sister. Yes, when I married Skye that would have made me Matt's brother-in-law. Why is this so interesting to the two of you?"

"Talk about a close family," Ash commented, looking at Alex who was still enjoying the attention from Riley.

Gates shook his head, not saying anything more. Chris looked at Riley who was still mesmerized with the little cat.

"How about we go somewhere with a bit more space?" Chris suggested. "Come on, let's get out of this hallway. Alex, get moving."

Chris indicated for them to move into the group room just down the hallway. There was a lot more space in there and available furniture that Gates could sit on. Ash wasn't the only one to notice that he badly needed to sit down.

Alex got up from where he'd been lying on the floor, making his way to the group room. Riley looked sad as he watched Alex walking away.

"Where's he going?" he asked with disappointment, still sitting on the floor.

"We're going to move out of the hallway and into a better room," Chris said, picking Riley up off the floor, knowing he wasn't about to walk himself. "You can play with Alex more once we get down there, OK?"

Riley nodded eagerly, holding onto Chris as he started walking. Ash stayed back with Gates as they followed.

Riley kept his arms around Chris, looking back at Gates and Ash. He gave them a wave and a smile. Ash smiled and waved back as she made sure Gates was OK to keep moving.

"Is Daddy gonna be OK?" Riley asked Chris as they went into the group room.

Chris turned the lights on and saw Alex lying in the open space in the middle of the room.

"He's going to be fine," Chris reassured Riley, placing him down near Alex. Riley's face lit up again as the cat rubbed against him, making him giggle. "We've just got to wait a bit, but he'll be OK."

Riley nodded, already distracted by playing with Alex again.

Gates collapsed onto one of the sofas with a sigh, and Ash took a seat next to him.

Chris looked at the two of them. "How are you holding up?" he asked Gates.

"Surviving for now."

Chris turned his attention back to Riley who was happily occupied with Alex. Hopefully, Matt would be OK. The last thing this kid needed was to lose his father for good when he'd just found him.

# CHAPTER TWENTY-FOUR

# Study

"I'm so glad to see you're OK," Zeke said, pulling Vivian into a hug. She hugged him back. "Matt was so lost without you. We're so glad you're alright."

"You've no idea how relieved I am to see you guys again," Vivian sighed, staying in Zeke's embrace. "It's been so long since I've seen any of you. I'm so glad you're all OK and still here. I really thought Marion would have killed you all by now."

"Oh, she's tried," Zeke laughed. He moved backwards, out of the hug, and looked at her. "You should get some sleep. Matt won't be around for a while, I don't think. If anything happens, I'll let you know, OK?"

Vivian nodded. It was getting late, and she knew Zeke was right. There was nothing she could do for Matt right now and she was getting very tired. She needed to check in with Chris who was still looking after Riley.

"Vincent should have been told by now what's going on. He'll probably stop by to see how everything's going," Zeke said. "Someone can show you to the room Matt was staying in. Get some sleep, and we'll talk more in the morning."

"Thank you, Zeke," Vivian said gratefully. "You should sleep too. If anything happens, someone will let us know."

Zeke gave a small nod but didn't say anything and didn't move.

Vivian gave him a smile before she headed out the door and back the way she'd come earlier when they'd brought Matt to the infirmary. She needed to check in with Chris and get Riley to bed.

"Hey."

Chris looked up from where he was sitting on the floor opposite Riley. Riley was patting Alex, who'd tired himself out and was now dozing, curled up in a ball.

Vivian smiled at Chris from the doorway.

"Hey," Chris said. "How's Matt?"

As Vivian entered the room. Riley gave her a wave, getting a wave in return from his mother. She sat on the chair near Chris.

"He probably won't be awake for a while," she said as Riley continued to pat Alex without a care in the world. "They're going to be doing some tests to figure out what Marion's done to him."

Vivian looked over at the sofas. The lights in the room had been dimmed an hour or so ago, and Gates had fallen asleep not long after that. He was still out, lying with his head on Ash's shoulder. Ash had her arm around him and her head against his with her eyes closed, but she wasn't asleep. She wasn't game to move in case she accidentally woke him, but she wasn't complaining.

"Is he OK?" Vivian asked quietly, nodding at Gates.

Chris glanced over at Gates and Ash before looking back at her. "We had a bit of a run-in with some trouble yesterday. It's going to take him a bit, but he'll be back on his feet soon."

Vivian gave a nod and looked at Riley. "Alright, let's get you to bed. It's getting late."

"But I wanna play with Alex some more," Riley protested stubbornly, crossing his arms.

"You can play with him tomorrow, sweetie," Vivian said, getting up and picking him up off the floor, startling Alex awake. "It's getting late, and you should have been in bed hours ago."

Riley hung onto her as she looked at Chris. "Could you please show me where Matt's room is?"

Chris smiled at her and led the way down to Matt's room. He stopped in the doorway while Vivian went in and put Riley on the bed. "If you need anything, just let me know."

She turned and gave him a grateful smile. "Thank you, Chris. I really appreciate it and thank you for keeping an eye on Riley."

Chris gave her a nod and Riley waved at him. Chris waved back, then turned and headed back to the group room.

Ash and Gates hadn't moved by the time he got back. Alex had disappeared, though.

"I should probably get some sleep too," Ash sighed, still keeping hold of Gates who was still out and leaning on her. "It's been a long day, and we all need some rest."

"You going to wake him up?" Chris asked with a bit of amusement. "I mean, you can't really go anywhere with him like that."

Ash looked unsure about what she should do. "I don't want to disturb him; he needs the sleep."

"Well, whatever you do, I'll see you in the morning," Chris said, heading to the doorway. "Try and get some sleep. We're going to need everyone we can get working down in that workshop tomorrow."

Abel looked over as Chris and Ash joined him in the workshop. It was still early, and Abel was the only one down there at the moment.

"No Nixx yet?" Chris asked as Ash went over to the chair that was still in the same place it had been in yesterday when Gates had been with them.

"He's staying up in the infirmary to help them with Matt," Abel said, placing a piece of the soldier on the table and looking over what was already there. The table was becoming rather full. "So, we're left down here with his notes to try to figure this out for ourselves. I appreciate you two coming down to help."

"Well, we want to figure this out before anything happens. Now, with Matt gone, Marion may decide to launch the attack very soon," Chris said, going over to help Abel at the table as Ash sat and watched. "Tell you what, that's what scares me the most. Not knowing when she'll suddenly appear at our gates. She's probably been improving the Iron Army all this time while we're still trying to figure this one out."

"For now, all we can do is hope she hasn't and that she won't turn up outside those gates until we're ready," Abel said, reading over what Nixx had written down the previous day. It wasn't making a lot of sense to him.

"Any news on Matt?" Ash asked as she leaned back a bit on the chair. She wondered where Zeke was today. She thought he would have been down here with them, especially since this had been his plan from the start.

"Nothing yet. As far as I know, he's still in the infirmary until further notice," Abel said. "Give him some time and he'll be back to his usual self. Matt's tough, he'll pull through."

Chris watched Abel move a few things aside on the table as he looked for a specific part.

"What about Gates?" Chris asked Ash. "How's he doing this morning? How did that go for you last night?"

"He was still asleep before I came down here with you," Ash said, crossing her arms. "I don't think we'll be seeing much of him for a few days at the rate he's going. He could hardly move yesterday."

"I saw that," Chris nodded. "So, you guys seem to be kind of close."

A surprised look crossed Ash's face as she realized what Chris had said.

"Why in the world would you think that?" she asked seriously. "According to Gates, we're a team, nothing more."

"Well, you clearly think differently," Chris said matter-of-factly, looking over as Riley appeared in the doorway, trailed by the little blue cat. "I've seen the way you've been looking at him lately. You like him."

Ash looked at him with no amusement as Riley wandered over to the table where Chris and Abel were. Abel glanced at him before looking back at the pieces of soldier on the table.

"You're full of it, Chris. You know that?" Ash said as the cat jumped up into her lap and settled down, happily purring.

"Just calling it as I see it, Ash," Chris said before turning his attention to Riley who had reached up to see something on the table. "Hey, what are you doing down here? Where's your mom?"

Riley stopped what he was doing, looking at Chris as Abel pushed a few things out of the kid's reach.

"Alex wanted to come for a walk and find friends," Riley said. "So, we left Mommy with Zeke, and we came for a walk. Alex heard you down here because the door isn't closed, and we thought we'd see what you're up to. What are you doing?"

Riley stood on his tiptoes to try and see what was on the table.

"We're just looking over a couple of things," Chris said. "We're working at the moment."

"Can I help?"

"I don't think there's really anything you can do for us, I'm afraid," Chris said. "How about you take Alex and show Ash your room? She'll be more than happy to hang out with you for a while until I finish up here. We can hang out once I'm finished here, OK?"

"OK!" Riley said cheerfully, abandoning his post at the table.

He came around to Ash's side of the table, grinned, and waved at her. "I'm Riley!"

"I'm Ash," Ash said with a smile. "Alright, let's go find something to do, hey? Leave these two here to do this boring work. Chris will come and find us when he's finished."

Riley nodded eagerly, looking at the little cat. "Come on, Alex!"

Alex perked up upon hearing his name and jumped off Ash's lap. He ran out of the room with Riley chasing him. Ash sighed and got up, giving Chris a look.

"Better catch him before you lose him," Chris said, turning his attention back to what was in front of him.

"Alex won't let anything happen to him," Ash said as she left the room.

Abel glanced at Chris as he tried to figure out what he was meant to be doing.

"So, that's Matt's kid?" he asked, picking a piece up and frowning as he looked it over. He didn't even know what he was meant to be looking for. Nixx's notes and everything here were so confusing.

"Yeah," Chris said, reading over something Nixx had written. He held it up. "Does any of this make sense to you?"

Abel shook his head with a sigh, putting down the piece of metal he'd been holding. "Honestly, Chris, no. Nixx knows what he's looking for and maybe how to find it. We've got no idea, and I don't have the slightest clue what any of these notes mean."

"So, what do we do? Do we wait until Nixx comes back and let him do what he does?"

Abel looked at him. "I think that's all we can do right now. I need to go and check in with Jamie anyway, see how she's doing."

"Alright, well, I'll go catch up with Ash and Riley, in that case."

"I'll catch you a bit later," Abel said, following Chris to the door and heading up the stairs next to him. "I'm going down to the arena once I've checked on Jamie. If you hear any updates on Matt, let me know."

# Chapter Twenty-Five

# Votes

Chris wandered through the hallways, trying to figure out where Ash, Riley, and Alex had gone. They couldn't have gotten very far in such a short amount of time.

Riley had certainly taken a liking to Alex, and it was nice to see. Alex also seemed to enjoy the attention. Chris wondered if Ash was a bit jealous, seeing as Alex was her best friend.

Approaching the group room, Chris heard Ash say something and Riley laugh. Chris stopped in the doorway and watched Ash and Riley in the middle of the room tickling Alex who was enjoying the love and attention he was getting.

Ash seemed kind of happy for once, which was nice to see, Chris thought.

Ash finally looked over and saw Chris watching them. She gave him a smile and motioned for him to come in and join them. Riley barely even looked up as he was happily occupied with Alex.

Chris went over to them and sat on the floor next to Ash.

"Thought you'd be down there a while," Ash noted, looking at him. "I didn't think we'd see you until late this afternoon."

"Abel and I are going to meet down at the arena later on," Chris said. "We can't make heads nor tails of Nixx's notes. He's going to have to direct us when he finishes with whatever he's doing in the infirmary, when Matt's better."

Alex wandered over to Chris, sat in front of him, and meowed.

"Do we know how serious it is with Matt?" Ash asked quietly, looking up as Vincent appeared in the doorway.

Chris shook his head, and Alex went back to Riley as Vincent entered the room.

"We're getting everyone in here in about ten minutes," Vincent said. "We have a few things we need to discuss." He glanced at Riley before looking back at Ash and Chris. "Might be an idea to find someone to look after the boy while we're all in here."

Chris gave a nod of understanding, and Vincent headed back out, presumably to go and inform everyone else of what was going on.

Ash sighed and stood up. "I'll go check in with Gates and get him here for this meeting or whatever you want to call it. I need to check on him anyway to make sure he's still alive."

"I'm sure he's fine," Chris reassured her, still not completely sure why she cared so much about Gates. He still couldn't place it. "I'll go find Vivian. Riley can stay with her for a bit while we get this out of the way."

Ash left the room, leaving Chris with Riley and Alex. Alex would also need to be around for the meeting.

"Alright, kid, let's go find your mom," Chris said, standing up and getting a disappointed look from Riley.

"Can't I just stay here with Alex?" Riley asked sadly.

"I'm afraid not," Chris said. "We've got some adult stuff to talk over. How about once it's finished, I'll come and get you and we'll go for a walk down to the arena? You'll get to see some cool stuff down there."

Riley's face lit up with a smile. "Can Alex come too?"

"He sure can. He's always welcome to come along wherever we go, OK?"

Riley gave an enthusiastic nod and got to his feet. Alex stayed with him. He'd taken it on himself to protect Matt's son, and Chris was sure Matt would be very grateful for it. Chris also wondered how Matt had taken the news that this was his kid. Or did he even know?

Riley trailed after Chris as they left the room, while Alex dashed out and disappeared ahead.

"Where's Alex going?" Riley asked as he tried to keep up with Chris, unable to match his stride, which wasn't really surprising.

"He's going to meet us down there," Chris said, slowing down a bit. Riley nodded but looked unconvinced. "Don't worry, he's not about to leave you."

Riley stayed quiet as Chris slowed his pace even more so he could keep up. They walked in silence down to the infirmary. Chris was fairly sure that was where he'd find Vivian, as last time he'd checked Matt was still down there.

They walked into the infirmary, and Vivian looked over from where she was sitting. The little blue cat was sitting on an empty chair next to her, but Matt was nowhere to be seen.

Riley rushed over to his mom, and she gave him a tired smile.

"Hey," Chris said. "How are you holding up?"

"As good as I can," Vivian said, picking Riley up and sitting him on her knee. "Just waiting, you know? That's the worst part."

"It sure is. Any news on what's happening?"

"Vincent said he's going to inform everyone at a meeting soon," Vivian said. "So, I guess you'll find out today sometime."

"He said the meeting's in about ten minutes, which is actually the reason I've stopped in," Chris said. "I need to leave Riley with you while the meeting's on. I'll come back afterwards and take him off your hands again for a few hours so you can stay down here without any distractions."

"You don't have to Chris, really."

Chris shrugged. "I don't mind. He's a good kid and right now you need all the help you can get. I know it's not easy, especially with everything that's going on with Matt."

"You've got that right," Vivian sighed. "Look, I really appreciate you taking the time to keep an eye on Riley. I know there are a lot more pressing matters you have to attend to, with the whole Marion thing and everything else. Really, Chris, I can't thank you enough."

"It's no trouble," Chris reassured her.

Riley looked at her and she smiled at him.

"Chris said we can hang out later. He said we can go do some cool stuff. He said Alex can come along, too!"

Alex meowed upon hearing his name, and Riley waved at him.

"Alright, I'll come back down in a bit," Chris said, turning to leave. "Hopefully everything goes OK down here. If something happens, come find us in the group room."

Ash knocked quietly on the door, looking in without waiting for a response. Gates was lying on his front on the bed, and he turned his head to the side to look at her.

"Hey," Ash said, entering the room and leaving the door slightly open. "Vincent wants everyone down in the group room. Thought I'd come and check on you and let you know."

Ash sat on the edge of the double bed. The curtains weren't open, and it was a bit dark in the room, but Gates hadn't left the bed at all, so it didn't matter to him how dark it was.

"I appreciate it," Gates said, shutting his eyes again. "I'll be down there in a sec."

"How are you feeling?" she asked.

Gates just lay on the bed, and she figured he was too sore to move.

"I'm in pain and I don't think I can get out of bed due to the position I've ended up in," was the mumbled response she got, making her smile. "As comfortable as this is, I think I've messed up my chances of getting out of bed at all."

"Need a hand?"

Gates sighed, opening his eyes to look at her.

"Nah, I've got it. It might take me a minute or two, but I'll manage," he said, shutting his eyes again. "What does Vincent want to chat about?"

"No idea," Ash said, putting her legs up on the bed and leaning back against the headboard. "He just said he wanted everyone in the group room in ten minutes to talk about a couple of things."

Gates still didn't move, and didn't answer her for a couple of seconds. She wondered if he'd fallen asleep.

"Hmm, well, I guess we'd better go find out," he finally said, tiredly. He opened his eyes, looking at Ash from the same position. "Think you could grab my shirt for me?"

Ash smiled at him and got off the bed. She went around to the side Gates was on and picked his shirt up off the floor. She threw it onto his back, getting a sigh from Gates.

"Thanks."

"Anytime," Ash said with a bit of a laugh. "Let me know if you need help getting out of bed. Don't hurt yourself any more than you already have."

"I appreciate the concern."

Chris looked over as Ash came through the door, Gates not far behind. He didn't look particularly well, but that was to be expected. Alex was tapping his feet impatiently as he watched Ash help Gates sit on the closest chair.

"I may not be able to get back out of this chair," Gates said. "I'm possibly going to be sleeping here tonight."

"You'll be fine. You managed to get out of bed," Ash said, sitting on the chair next to him. "Even if you did require a bit of assistance."

"Well, that's apparently what I get for sleeping in comfortable positions."

Abel came in next, taking a seat next to Chris. Alex continued to tap his feet nervously, wanting to know what was going on.

Nixx and Zeke came in next. Zeke went straight over to sit with Gates, while Nixx sat next to Abel.

"Anyone know what we're here to talk about?" Abel asked, looking around at everyone.

Everyone shook their heads; no one knew what was going on. Hopefully, it wasn't going to be anything too drastic.

Jacob came in and sat down without a word. Chris and Abel exchanged looks. If Jacob was here, then there was something drastically wrong, as he wasn't usually called in.

When no one else came through the door, Abel spoke again.

"So..." he began, everyone looking to him as he tried to get a conversation going while they waited. "If anyone wants to come down to the arena after this, Chris and I are headed down there..."

Zeke nodded. "I'm in. Need to get out of that infirmary for a bit."

Abel nodded, satisfied there was another person willing to join them.

"I'd join you, but I need to get back down to the workshop," Nixx spoke up. "You boys get anything done down there today?"

Chris and Abel both shook their heads. Before they could say why they hadn't gotten anything done, Vincent appeared, strolling in like he owned the place. Well, technically he did.

He took a seat, looking around at everyone as he spoke. "Glad you all made it. So, we've got a few serious things we need to talk about. That's why you're all here right now."

He sighed, looking down before he continued.

"We've been having a few problems with Heather, who's still down in the dungeon, as you know," he said, everyone exchanging looks. "If those problems persist, we might have to get rid of her."

"As in kill her?" Alex spoke up, looking worried. "We can't kill her. She'll die, and then they'll launch the attack on us, and we'll all die!"

"Alex, calm down," Chris said, seeing the panic on Alex's face. "We'll handle this."

"What's the problem with her?" Nixx asked.

"She's been trying to get out by casting spells on the guards," Vincent said as an interested look appeared on Nixx's face. "We don't know how to silence her, or stop her, without doing real damage to her. If anyone here has an idea then, please, speak up."

"You don't want to actually hurt her?" Ash asked with confusion. "I'm sorry, but do you know the amount of shit that she and her friends have caused. Matt's a prime example of that. Heather needs to be killed, no doubt about it."

"We can't just kill her," Chris spoke up. "That's straight up murder, Ash. You'd really be OK with killing someone?"

"We're all going to have to kill soon enough," Ash said, that worry appearing on Alex's face again. "In case you hadn't noticed, Chris, we're going to have to fight Marion and probably kill her. It's the only way to stop some people."

"So, you're saying you'd happily kill Heather? It's cold-blooded murder."

"Oh, and torturing Matt is acceptable? He's lucky he's not dead!"

"It might be different if she'd killed him, but she didn't. If she did, then you'd have probable cause to kill her, but as far as I'm aware Heather hasn't really done anything."

"Quit it!" Gates suddenly shouted, slamming his palms on the table, causing everyone in the room to fall dead silent. "For God's sake, just shut up!"

No one said a word as Gates looked between Ash and Chris.

"You two are like damn children," he snapped. "We can deal with this if we all just shut the fuck up and listen! Don't argue and don't push your opinions onto everyone else. I get it, one of you wants her dead and the other doesn't. If we take care of this civilly, we'll get a lot closer to a solution."

"What do you propose we do?" Vincent asked him, Gates switching his gaze to him.

"We take a vote, majority rules," Gates said. "We vote: kill her or keep her. No other options. And if it's a tied vote, we find one more person to decide."

Vincent nodded. "Looks like we have our options: kill her or keep her. The vote comes down to all of you."

# CHAPTER TWENTY-SIX

# Helping Matt

"All those who vote for killing Heather, raise your hand."

Ash didn't hesitate and was the first to raise her hand. Alex looked at her with that worry still on his face. He was very against this.

Gates was the next to raise his hand, closely followed by Zeke.

Nixx shook his head but didn't say anything.

Vincent looked around at everyone. "Anyone else?"

Abel slowly raised his hand, and Chris and Alex both looked at him with shock on their faces.

"Are you serious?" Chris asked him. "You can't be serious, Abel. You really want to kill Heather? You gonna do it yourself?"

Abel left his hand up as Vincent counted. "Four votes for killing her."

Abel looked at Chris sadly as he lowered his hand but didn't say anything.

Vincent looked around again. "Anyone against it, raise your hand."

Chris, Alex, Nixx, and Jacob put their hands up. It was also four; the decision was tied.

Vincent sighed, indicating for everyone to lower their hands. "Well, looks like I get the final vote seeing as the numbers are even. I'll have to think about it before I make my final decision so, once that decision has been made, I'll call everyone in again. Anyway, that's not all we have to talk about. I want to give everyone an update on what's going on with Matt."

Vincent paused but no one said a word.

"By the looks of it, it's going to take him a while to get back on his feet properly. It's going to be a rather slow process for him," Vincent continued. "We're going to keep him in the infirmary for a while, just to make sure he's going to be able to get back on his feet. We're also going to be keeping him unconscious for a while because he's very sick."

"What exactly do you mean by 'sick'?" Gates asked.

Vincent looked at Nixx and raised his eyebrows, silently asking him to say something. Nixx had been helping them figure out what had happened to Matt, so he had a better idea of what was going on, more than Vincent anyway.

Nixx cleared his throat before he spoke. "Matt's been severely poisoned. We don't know exactly what's caused it, but whatever they did when he was locked in that castle has seriously damaged him. We're trying to figure out what they used, and how we can get it out of his system before it does any more damage."

"Does anyone know why he couldn't get out of the dungeon when he was there?" Abel asked, looking around at everyone. "I mean, they clearly had some way of keeping him there, because he wouldn't have been gone so long if he could get out."

"I don't think he was able to shadow-step out," Chris finally spoke up, everyone looking to him. He'd had first-hand experience inside the castle and had seen what they'd done to Matt. "Something in that cell was stopping him. I don't know exactly what, but whatever it was had enough power to block his ability and drain his energy."

"Hmm, that's certainly interesting," Nixx said, his tone thoughtful.

"We have someone who might know," Jacob spoke up. "She's down in our dungeon."

"You want to talk to Heather," Ash stated. Jacob nodded. "Why?"

"Because she's our best bet at finding out how we can help Matt," he said. "If anyone would know, it's her. She's got inside knowledge. Before we decide what to do with her, we need to speak to her and find out what they did to him. If we don't, then it doesn't sound like he has much chance."

Ash seemed displeased. She didn't like Matt much to begin with, but she didn't like Heather, either.

"Jacob's right," Zeke said, Gates giving a nod of agreement. "We need someone to talk to Heather and find out what they did, what's poisoning Matt."

Ash rolled her eyes and crossed her arms but didn't say anything.

"Who wants to talk to her?" Vincent asked, looking around at everyone again. "We need someone who can get through to her without hurting her too much. Any volunteers?"

"I'll do it, but only if I can bring Alice with me," Chris said.

Vincent frowned. "Why would you want to bring her in? Also, she won't talk to anyone who's not Matt. We had this issue when we tried last time, remember? She refuses to do anything for anyone who isn't him."

"Let me talk to her," Chris said. "I'd like to have her there because it might force Heather to talk. I know I'd talk if I was threatened with Alice."

Vincent looked a bit unsure but nodded, nonetheless. "Alright then. Chris, you go and talk to Alice, but I want her back in her cell once you've gotten what you need from Heather. Gates, if you're able to, go check in with the current defenses at the front of the City. Zeke, you go with him. Nixx, you either go back to the infirmary and help them there or go and work with the soldiers we've got down in the workshop. Abel, you and Alex head to the arena with Jacob and help people out with their training so they're ready for whatever happens. Ash, you do whatever it is you do."

Everyone nodded, although Ash was obviously not impressed.

Vincent stood up and left the room. Everyone else took that as their cue to stand and go about their assigned tasks.

"I'll come find you in the arena once I've spoken to Alice and Heather," Chris said to Abel and Alex as they left the room together.

Alice looked up when she saw the door open. Her eyes narrowed in suspicion when she saw it was Chris.

"What do you want?" she sneered, ripping another few pages out of the book she'd been given. She couldn't read and she hated these stupid paper things. "I don't have time for you, Chris. I have books to destroy."

"I can see that," Chris said, looking around the room as he closed the door.

There was paper everywhere. The books she'd been given had been ripped apart and thrown around like trash. Alice didn't care. She felt more at home now that she had things to destroy.

"Get out of my room," Alice growled, tearing a few more pages out and throwing them violently at Chris. He didn't move as they drifted harmlessly to the floor, nowhere near to hitting him. "I don't like it when people are in my room."

"I thought you'd like to know we found Matt," Chris said, putting his hands in his pockets and leaning back against the wall.

Alice's head snapped up upon hearing Matt's name. An interested look crossed her face.

"Well, now," she said, tossing the half empty book aside. Chris watched it hit the floor with a thump, causing a few pieces of paper to flutter around it. "If you found him, then where is he? I thought he'd have come to see me by now if he's back."

"He's in the infirmary," Chris said. A confused look crossed Alice's face as she tilted her head to the side. "They did something to him when he was locked in the castle with Marion. He's being poisoned by something they gave him while he was there, and we don't know what. We don't know how to counter it which, in turn, means he's probably gonna die."

Alice growled. She wasn't about to let someone like Marion take Matt from her.

"Why are you telling me this?" she asked, crossing her arms as she looked Chris over. He would never be able to replace Matt.

"Because I need your help," Chris said. "We have Heather in a cell upstairs. I need you to help me talk to her. She knows what's poisoning him and how to stop it before it kills him."

"So, you finally need my help," Alice mumbled to herself. "Hmm, yes, I can help. Don't want him dead now, do I? Chris won't ever be able to replace him ... no, can't have that. Not part of the plan..."

"So, you'll help?" Chris asked, choosing to ignore what she was mumbling to herself.

"Yes," Alice blatantly stated. "I *will* help. On one condition though, Chris."

Of course there was a condition.

"What's the condition?"

"You let me talk to Matt once he's not dead," Alice said bluntly.

Chris saw her mouth twitch and he was sure she was going even crazier down here away from people.

"When he's feeling up to it, he'll come down here to see you, that's a guarantee."

Alice gave a satisfied nod.

"Hmm, yes, good, good," she mumbled to herself again, looking down at her hands. "All going according to plan..."

"Now, come on, we need to go have that chat with Heather," Chris said, indicating for her to join him near the door. "We don't have all day, and you'll be back in here once we're done, OK? That's the deal."

Alice nodded again, this time not saying anything. Chris nodded back, satisfied.

He opened the door and went out. Alice jumped off her bed and dashed out after him. A couple of the guards watched warily as Chris and Alice went up the stairs, but they knew better than to say anything.

Chris walked in front of Alice but kept glancing over his shoulder. He was sure she wouldn't try anything, since she'd regret it if she did and she knew it. But he still didn't like having his back to her.

Chris looked at the guards stationed outside Heather's cell. They moved out of the way, knowing not to mess with him.

Heather looked over from where she was standing at the back of the cell. An interested look appeared on her face, and she pushed off the wall, wandering over to the front of the cell.

"Well, hello, Chris," she said.

Alice growled from where she'd stopped beside Chris.

Heather looked at her with disgust. "What, in the name of all that's holy, is that?"

"This is Alice," Chris said.

Alice hissed at Heather, who took a half-step back. Even though she was on the other side of the bars, Heather was intimidated and wasn't about to take any chances.

"She's here to help me ask you a few questions."

Heather's interest was piqued and overcame her disgust. She moved forwards again, until she was standing up against the bars.

Alice didn't like the way Heather looked Chris up and down, not at all.

"What kind of ... questions ... are we talking about?" Heather asked, returning her gaze to Chris's face. "Are you going to let me out if I tell you what you want to know?"

"Not a chance," Chris said in response. Heather pouted at him, but he wasn't in the mood to be messed around by her. Matt's life was pretty well in her hands; she just didn't know it yet. "We want to know what you did to Matt."

"I never touched him," Heather said, crossing her arms stubbornly. She looked at Chris suggestively. "Sometimes I wish I did, though, he's certainly a fine man."

That caused Alice to growl at her again, and Heather glanced at her with disgust again.

"Cut the crap, Heather. I'm being serious," Chris snapped, Heather looking back to him now. "What did you do to him? I know whatever's happened to make him so sick wasn't caused by Marion. How did you keep him from using his abilities?"

A surprised look crossed Heather's face. Chris had caught her off guard.

"I'm sorry? Why would you think I did that?" she asked. "But thank you for the credit."

"Because to hold Matt, you'd have had to have something in place already when you got him, so what did you use?" Chris demanded to know. He was done with her avoiding the questions. "If you don't give me the right answer, I'm sending Alice in. If you hadn't noticed, she's quite fond of Matt and isn't impressed that he's sick."

Heather looked at Alice briefly, a bit of worry on her face this time.

"So, Matt escaped, did he? Marion won't be happy," she said, looking back at Chris and trying to change the subject.

"Tell us what you did to him," Chris warned, as Alice took a half-step forward.

"Alright, fine, if you really want to know," Heather said with a sigh. "Carmen and I managed to develop something that could block people's abilities. Every four hours the chemicals would release from the shackles and go directly into the bloodstream. We infused it with a hint of magic to help keep it going and to add a bit more security, I guess you'd call it. If you didn't know, abilities are born in the bloodstream. That would be why Shade is so sick. You can't just take someone off those chemicals. It's like a drug. You have to turn the dose down slowly, not just remove it completely, which is clearly what's happened. Or you use other chemicals to clear the first lot out of his system."

"How do we get it out of his system?"

Heather shrugged. "No idea."

"If you know, stop holding back and tell me," he snapped.

An unsure look appeared on Heather's face as she looked between him and Alice.

"If you let me out of here, I'll do it myself," she tried, but Chris shook his head.

"Not a chance. Tell me how to get it out of his system or I send her in."

Alice moved forward a bit more, startling Heather and making her take a few steps back from the bars.

"You keep that creature away from me!" she exclaimed, pointing at Alice who hissed at her again. "Don't you let her anywhere near me!"

"Then talk," Chris said. "I'm not here to fuck around. Tell me what I need to know, and she'll back off. The longer you stall, the more agitated she's going to get. You tell me what I want to know, and she'll be out of your face in no time."

Looking unsure but knowing she had no choice, Heather sighed and spoke again. "You need to mix a few things together; rare plants only found in certain areas of Oz and Wonderland. Once you've done that, inject it straight into the bloodstream of said victim. It'll take a couple of days to clear out. They won't get any sicker and they'll be up and around in no time."

"What plants?"

"Geez, you ask a lot of questions," Heather sighed.

Chris gestured to Alice, who stepped forward again and gripped the bars, putting her face right up against them.

"Alright, alright," Heather said, taking another step back. "Keep that ... thing ... away from me and I'll tell you."

Chris signaled for Alice to back off and she did so reluctantly. Heather stared at her before looking back at Chris.

"Well, one of them is Peppermint, which is good for healing."

"I thought you said 'rare' plants. Peppermint isn't a rare plant," he said with a frown.

Heather looked at him with annoyance. "Around here, Chris, it's very rare. You have to know where to look for it. I know the places to get all these things too, just so you know."

"What else do we need? Keep talking."

"Got to mix that with some Adder's Tongue," Heather continued, not missing a beat and making Chris nod. "To top it all off you need Anemone and Belladonna."

"Now, wait a minute," Chris interrupted, Heather looking at him questioningly. "I know for a fact that Belladonna is toxic. You can't expect me to believe you on that one. I've spent enough time on Pagan magic websites to know that's not something you want to use."

"Believe what you want, Chris," Heather said with a shrug. "So, we need Peppermint, Adder's Tongue, Anemone, and Belladonna. There's more to it, though. Do you still wish to know?"

"What happens when we mix it all together?" Chris asked. "Won't the Belladonna cancel out everything else?"

"Not if you mix it right," Heather snapped. "Anyway, as I was saying. You need a few more things before it's a cure for what's happened. The last three things you need are Carnation, Goats Rue, and Snapdragon. Got all that down?"

"How do I know you're telling me the truth?" Chris asked. He was very concerned about the Belladonna. "You could be telling us stuff that will make him worse or even kill him."

"I'm locked in a cage, Chris. What have I got to lose?" Heather asked, stepping forward again, but staying away from Alice. "You're going to need help finding everything. I know someone who knows. She's right in front of you."

She pointed to herself, mouthing the word 'me' to him.

"I know who you mean," Chris said as Heather looked at him suggestively. "But thank you, I'll talk it over with Vincent and I'll be back to see you if I need anything else."

Heather's expression fell. "You're leaving me in here? Are you serious?"

"Yes, you're not getting out that easily," Chis said, glad that he had a good memory and was able to remember what Heather had said he'd need.

"This isn't fair!" Heather screamed, stamping her foot. "You can't leave me in here forever!"

"You left Matt in your dungeon, you can rot down here too," Chris said.

He looked at Alice, "Let's get you back to where you belong."

Alice followed Chris, glancing over her shoulder several times at Heather until they were out of sight.

# CHAPTER TWENTY-SEVEN

## In the Arena

Vincent looked up as Dorothy and Chris walked into the group room. He was there on his own, sitting at the dining table, working on a few things. There were multiple notebooks spread over the table in front of him.

"Chris is here to see you," Dorothy said.

Vincent nodded and signaled for her to leave the room.

She did as she was told, pulling open one of the doors and heading out, closing it behind her. She was Vincent's secretary, so Chris assumed she had a lot to work to do.

Vincent pointed at the seat opposite him. "How did it go? Did you get any useful information?"

"I'd like to think so," Chris replied, sitting down.

Vincent nodded distractedly as he wrote something in the notebook in front of him.

"She told me what we need to get Matt back to health."

Vincent stopped and looked at him, interested now. "Did she now? Well done. What did she say we need?"

"She named seven plants that need to be mixed together and injected directly into the bloodstream," Chris replied. "One of them I'm not sure about, though. It sounds a bit off to me."

"Well, what did she say we need?"

"Peppermint, Adder's Tongue, Goats Rue, Anemone, Carnation, Snapdragon, and Belladonna," Chris said, watching a frown cross Vincent's face. "The Belladonna one is the part I'm a bit iffy about."

"You've every right to be worried about it," Vincent said with a concerned nod. "Belladonna is very toxic. She's one-hundred percent sure this is what we need?"

Chris nodded. "Yeah, she said she knows where to get everything, *and* she knows how to mix it correctly. I hate to say it, but we might have to trust her on this. We don't really have much of a choice at the moment."

Vincent gave a nod as he thought.

"Apart from the Belladonna, everything else sounds like it might help," he mused to himself as Chris just listened. "They've all got healing properties. A few of those you mentioned also help with health and strength, protection too. I think you might be right. We're going to have to trust her enough to mix it all together. Finding the plants, though, we may not need her. Nixx knows a thing or two about medicinal plants. It might be worth talking to him about it."

Chris nodded. "I'll get onto that straight away. Do you want me to send him up here to have a chat with you about it?"

He could see Vincent thinking again.

"It might be worth seeing how much he knows before we delve into this too far," Chris continued. "If we need to use Heather to find them, then we'll just have to bite the bullet and go for it."

"As much as I don't think it would be wise, I do have to agree," Vincent said, his tone thoughtful. "Anyway, go and have a talk with Nixx. He's in the workshop. Then, send him up here and I'll talk to him about it, too. I'll get him to come and find you once we've come to an agreement on what's the best thing to do."

Chris nodded once more and got up. Vincent turned his attention back to what he'd been writing as Chris left the room. Chris wondered what exactly he was writing. It must have been important, or he wouldn't have had so many notebooks on the table.

Making his way down to the workshop, Chris let his mind wander. What if Heather wasn't telling the truth? What if they got everything together, and it ended up killing Matt? Chris knew there were a lot of people who would want to be first in line to kill Heather if that happened.

Hopefully, Nixx would be able to help them make the right decisions about whether or not those were good plants that could help Matt recover, even the toxic ones.

The door at the top of the stairs to the workshop was closed as usual, but Chris could hear some noises coming from down there. He opened the door and went in, shutting it behind himself and heading down the stairs. The door at the bottom was still non-existent. He wondered if Vincent would ever have it fixed.

"Nixx? You down here?" Chris called when he was about halfway down the stairs.

"Depends who's asking," was the response he got.

As Chris entered the open workshop, Nixx glanced up from where he was making a few notes at the table, several pieces of metal on the floor near his feet.

"Chris," Nixx said, his focus quickly back on what he was doing. He picked up one piece of metal from the half-dismantled soldier. "Down here to help?"

"Not exactly. I came to talk to you about something," Chris said.

That made Nixx look up and meet his gaze. "What do you need to talk about? Is it something to do with Matt?"

Chris nodded and Nixx put down the piece of metal, his focus fully on him now. He indicated for Chris to speak.

"So, I had a talk with Heather," Chris said. "She's given me a list of plants that are supposedly going to help Matt recover. Vincent wanted to have a word with you about it to see if you'd be able to help out because we can't really trust Heather completely."

Nixx gave an interested nod. "Well, Chris, you're in luck. I know a thing or two about medicinal plants. Vincent wants me up there now, I assume?"

"As soon as you can."

Nixx abandoned what he was doing and headed over to where Chris was standing in the doorway. He went out past him, and Chris followed him back up the stairs.

"What are these plants Heather mentioned?" Nixx asked, opening the door at the top of the stairs and stepping through.

"Peppermint, Adder's Tongue, Goats Rue, Anemone, Carnation, Snapdragon, and Belladonna," said Chris, closing the door behind himself. "But I'm not sure about the Belladonna. I thought that was deadly."

Nixx stood there for a minute, not saying anything as he thought about the plants Chris had listed.

He started walking again. "Everyone else is down in the arena, as far as I'm aware. There's not really a lot left to do in the way of fortifications and preparations for when Marion makes her grand appearance. Apparently, the barricades at the front of the City are looking very good and should keep the Iron Army back for a bit. Hopefully, Gates is up to the task when the time comes, as he's one of the main sources of keeping people out."

"Hopefully," Chris said, walking alongside Nixx. "I'll head over to the infirmary and get Riley. Give Vivian a bit of a break. I'll take him down to the arena, so that's where I'll be if you need me for anything. Come and let us know what's going on when you get the chance."

"Will do."

Chris headed off down a corridor to his right, while Nixx continued forwards, heading to the group room.

It was rather quiet in the part of the castle where Chris was. He didn't pass anyone, and he wondered how many people Vincent actually had working for him. He figured he would need a lot to maintain a castle this size, but he never really saw that many people around.

The door to the infirmary was closed, as usual. When Chris went in, he heard the rumble of the machines that he always heard whenever he was down here. He hated the sound. It reminded him of hospitals back home. But at least the Emerald City had a good supply of electricity. It wasn't as primitive as Wonderland.

"Chris!" Riley exclaimed, jumping off the chair he was on, startling the little blue cat out of his sleep.

Alex had come back down here as soon as the meeting was over.

Vivian was talking to one of the nurses, but she looked over as Riley ran over to Chris.

"Hey, buddy. You ready to get out of here for a bit? Leave your mom to what she has to do?" Chris asked as Riley stopped in front of him.

Riley nodded excitedly, looking at Vivian expectantly.

She nodded and smiled at Chris before looking back at her son. "You be good for Chris, OK?"

Riley nodded again and looked at Chris. "Alex is ready to go, too!" he said happily.

The cat meowed upon hearing his name.

"Well, alright, then. Let's get going and see what everyone else is up to," Chris said. He looked at Vivian. "I'll have him back in a while. Give you a bit of time to yourself down here."

"Thank you, Chris," Vivian said as Riley headed out of the infirmary with Alex trailing along behind.

Chris gave her a smile before leaving too, not wanting Riley to get too far ahead of him. Even though Alex was with him, he wasn't about to let the kid out of his sight.

Riley and Alex were waiting for him in the hallway, a happy look on Riley's face as usual.

"Do you think Uncle Blaine will be at the arena?" he asked as he started walking with Chris, Alex running to keep up.

"He might be," Chris said. They headed towards the front of the castle. "You been out of this castle yet?"

Riley shook his head. "Nope."

"Well, guess this is going to be a new experience for you, hey?"

Riley nodded excitedly as they arrived at the double doors. Chris opened one and let Alex dash out into the street. Riley followed him.

Chris went out, making sure the door was shut behind him. There were a lot of people around, even though it was starting to get late. The day had gone by very quickly.

It wasn't even Market Day and Chris wondered if there was some event happening later in the week and people were setting up for it.

Chris picked Riley up, not wanting him to get lost in the crowds.
Alex also kept his pace up, sticking close to them, as people moved out
of their way.

There still seemed to be a bit of a problem with some of the ones
who worked under Vincent, ever since the 'incident'. Chris hadn't
even been there when it happened, but people still knew to move out
of his way, knew he was connected in some way.

"How far away is the arena?" Riley asked, looking at Chris.

"Not far, we'll be there in no time."

Riley smiled at him, Chris smiling back as he continued walking.
It had been a while since he'd been out of the castle and down to the
arena. He didn't really count the incident with the soldier. That wasn't
a training session. That was a safety issue.

Maybe that was why people were avoiding him. They'd been
around when Chris, Ash, and Alex had led the soldier through the
streets. He thought he recognized a few people who had been around
that day.

"Is that it?" Riley asked, pointing to the large structure just up
ahead.

"That's it. You ready to see what happens in there?" Chris asked as
they got closer.

Riley gave an eager nod again, happiness still on his face. Chris was
curious to see how Matt would be once he was awake, and he got
to spend time with his son. He hoped it would make him a bit less
cold-hearted, but he knew Matt hadn't always been like that.

Alex dashed on ahead into the arena. When Chris and Riley
entered, everyone was up the back where they usually trained. Ash
looked down to see Alex sitting at her feet. She looked over, and saw
Chris and Riley headed their way.

"Hey," she called with a bit of a wave.

Everyone else looked over too, Zeke clicking his fingers and putting the current fire out.

Chris stopped near them and Riley waved at Ash, then looked around. He clearly hadn't noticed Gates standing with Ash, but it was only a matter of time, seeing how he'd asked about him earlier on.

"Any news?" Abel asked.

"Heather gave me a list of plants and Nixx is going to have a chat with Vincent about it. It's complicated, but once we have a solid answer, we should be able to help Matt," Chris said.

Riley finally noticed Gates and his face lit up. "Uncle Blaine!"

"Hey, kiddo. You causing trouble for Chris again?" Gates said. Riley shook his head, the smile still on his face. "Alright, well, how about we give Chris a bit of a break so he can work on a few things and you and me go hang out for a bit?"

"Can we stay here?" Riley asked, still holding onto Chris.

"We sure can. Best we watch from a distance, though," Gates said. "Don't want you getting hurt, do we?"

Riley shook his head and looked serious. "No."

"I doubt your mom would be very happy if something happened while we were down here." Gates moved over to Chris. "I'll take him for a bit, so you're able to do some stuff."

Chris handed Riley over to him. Riley was excited and he made sure he had a good hold on Gates.

"You sure you're OK to take him?" Chris asked, noticing how Gates winced as he took the kid.

Gates nodded. "Yeah, I'll be fine. The things you do for kids, right?"

Chris smiled as Riley changed his position, deciding to hug Gates instead of just hanging on.

Gates just shook his head. "Alright, kiddo. Let's get out of their way."

Riley waved to Chris as Gates headed over to the edge of the arena where the barricade was. There were seats on the other side of it. The barricade was to make sure people didn't get hit or get into the arena when there was a fight going on.

"He seems to be doing a bit better," Chris said, watching Gates walk away. "Also, he seems to be good around kids."

"Lightens him up a bit," Ash remarked, Chris looking to her as Abel and Zeke went back to what they were doing. "He's pretending he's OK but he's not. He'll heal up eventually, though. You, though, are scarily good with kids. You don't look like someone who likes children much."

"Kids have never done anything wrong by me," he said, watching Gates keeping Riley occupied. "I don't know, sometimes you've got to learn how to deal with them. Kids deserve to have someone looking out for them when they're going through shit with family."

"You speaking from experience?" Ash asked, a bit of sadness in her voice.

"Would it matter if I was?" he asked, looking at her. "Riley's lucky he's got people to look out for him."

Ash looked at him sadly but didn't say anything. He looked away and watched Alex wander over to where Gates and Riley were on the other side of the barricade.

Abel caught Chris's eye while Zeke continued with whatever he was practicing, the light from his flames appearing and disappearing every few seconds.

"You want to work on anything?" Abel asked. "It's been a while since we've been down here."

Chris nodded, but Zeke spoke before Chris could say anything.

"I never asked," Zeke said to Abel. "What did you guys find at Matt's place?"

"We found the other three journals from Marion's doctor," Abel said. He looked at Chris. "Do you still have yours? We were worried Marion would have gotten her hands on it before we could get it from you."

"I've still got it," Chris said. "She didn't search me, so she didn't know I had it. What do you want me to do with it?"

"Best we give them all to Nixx," Abel said. "He might be able to find something in there that can help us win against Marion's Iron Army. You never know, we might find something more powerful in there. The other three are up in my room so, when we get back, I'll get the last one from you and give them to Nixx."

"Sounds like a plan. Alright, let's get some stuff done."

"Think I could join in?" Ash asked Abel. "It's been a while since I've tried new things with this ice ability."

Abel nodded. "Sure, feel free. Just let us know what you want to work on."

# CHAPTER TWENTY-EIGHT

# Medicinal Plants

"We've reached a solution on what to do about Matt," Vincent said, looking from person to person as most of them sat around the table in the group room.

Chris sat between Abel and Alex, opposite Ash and Gates. Riley sat happily on Gates's lap, keeping himself occupied with a book he'd been given, though he couldn't read it. Zeke sat on Gates's left, and Nixx sat next to him. As usual, Jacob was on one of the lone chairs near the middle of the room away from the table.

"Nixx says he'll be able to get what we need to stop the poisoning and help Matt heal," Vincent continued.

Riley looked up at Gates and pointed to a word on the page, making Vincent pause. "What's this one?"

Gates looked down at the book, before looking back up at Vincent again. "Constant."

"I want a few of you to go with him because, safety in numbers, you know," Vincent said. "I want at least three of you to accompany Nixx.

Jacob, I want you to be one of the people to go so everyone can get around quicker and you won't be gone as long."

Jacob nodded and Vincent looked around the table. "Any volunteers? We need at least two more people."

"I'll go," Gates spoke up. Riley tapped his arm and Gates looked down at the word Riley was pointing to. "Basic."

"The only place you're going is your bed," Zeke said, his stern gaze on Gates. "You're in no condition to be going outside of these walls. I'll go."

Gates rolled his eyes, shifting uncomfortably. It was clear he was still hurting but he wasn't going to admit it.

"OK, we've got Zeke and Jacob going with Nixx," Vincent said, looking at Chris, Abel, and Alex. "One of you want to go with them? Complete the group of four?"

Alex shook his head furiously, not liking the idea of leaving the security of the City walls. Abel and Chris looked at each other, neither of them sure if the other wanted to go. Since Gates was out due to his injuries, they needed someone else who knew what they were doing.

"I'd like to go but I kind of need to stay here with Jamie," Abel said. "So, Chris, if you could go, that would be great…"

"Yeah, alright," Chris sighed. "I'll go with them."

Vincent nodded, a satisfied look on his face. "That works well, since you know the plants we need. Alright, I'd like you four to head out early tomorrow morning. Unfortunately, it's too late now; there's no point wandering around in the dark, especially since it's not always friendly outside the City once the sun goes down. Two of you know what you're after, so try to be as quick as you can and make sure you get everything. There probably won't be any second chances."

"We don't actually know how to mix all these plants together," Nixx spoke up, everyone looking at him as Riley pointed out another word to Gates who answered him quietly. "We may need Heather once we've got everything. We don't really want to risk mixing it wrong and having it do something worse."

"The worst it can do is kill him," Ash said matter-of-factly.

Gates and Zeke both glared at her.

"That's what we're trying to avoid, if you hadn't noticed," Zeke said.

Ash rolled her eyes and leaned back in her chair, crossing her arms. "Not like it'd be a mass loss," she muttered to herself.

"You're extremely heartless, you know that?" Zeke snapped at her, while Ash avoided his gaze. "So, what? You'd rather he dies? You'd be happy if that happened, right? Well, sorry to break it to you, but some of us actually give a fuck about him. Your opinion is invalid here."

Ash rolled her eyes again but didn't say anything more.

"We're not arguing about this," Vincent sighed. He looked tired and obviously didn't want to play enforcer right now. "We've got our plan and we're sticking to it. Chris, Nixx, Jacob, and Zeke, you all head out early in the morning and be back as soon as you can. And, with that all said and done, have a good night, everyone."

With that, Vincent stood up and left the room.

Zeke shook his head, also standing up. "Whatever. I'm out for the night. I'll see a couple of you tomorrow."

He left the room, and no one else spoke.

"Alright, I'm out too," Gates sighed after a few seconds. He looked exhausted. He looked at Riley who was still trying to read the book. "Alright, kiddo, let's get you back to your mom. You should be in bed, too."

Riley seemed displeased with the decision but nodded anyway. Gates took the book and placed it on the table. It looked like a huge effort for him to stand while keeping hold of Riley.

"Bye, Chris!" Riley said cheerfully, waving at Chris as Gates headed for the door.

Chris waved back and they were gone.

Ash stood and followed Gates and Riley without saying a word.

Jacob looked at the four that were still in the room with him. "Well, that went well. I assume Ash doesn't particularly like Matt?"

Chris shook his head, and Alex shifted his position to face Jacob.

"You assume correct," Abel said. "I think their personalities clash a bit too much. Matt can tolerate it better than she can, though."

"Shows he's the more mature one, then," Nixx input.

Jacob sighed and got up out of his chair, stretching as he stood. "Well, I'll see two of you early tomorrow morning. Don't be late. We'll meet out at the front gates and go from there. I'll drop in and let Zeke know before I head out for the night. Try get there as early as you can."

Nixx and Chris nodded, and Jacob left the room.

"Sorry about throwing you under the bus with this," Abel suddenly said, looking at Chris. "It's just that Jamie hasn't been feeling too great today, so I figured it'd be better to hang around here tomorrow in case she needs me."

"It's fine, I'm happy to go. It's to help Matt," Chris said, seeing that Abel still felt bad about it. "Hopefully, this will get him back to good health."

Abel gave him a nod and a slight smile as he stood up. "Agreed."

Abel left, leaving only Chris and Alex. It was getting late, and Chris was thinking that he should get to bed as well, seeing as he had a very early morning coming up.

"Everyone has the right idea," Alex said, as he and Chris both reluctantly stood up. "I think it's about time I finish up and get some sleep, too. Good luck tomorrow, Chris. I'll see you when you get back. Just make sure you get everything to help Matt."

"Morning," Jacob greeted Chris and Zeke. He and Nixx were waiting for them near the front gate.

There weren't many people around this early in the morning, but there was a guard on duty checking anyone going in or out.

"Why are we out so early? The sun's hardly even up yet," Zeke complained, rubbing his eyes. "I'm pretty sure this time of morning doesn't actually exist."

"Well, it does today," Jacob replied. "Alright, let's head out. Nixx knows where to go. The first location is within walking distance of here so, once we've been there, we'll be moving around at a quicker pace. We don't have all day, and we need to get this done as soon as we can. Let's go."

He walked the few paces to the gate and pushed it open just enough so that he could leave. The other three followed. The on-duty guard just watched them leave without saying a word.

Once outside, Chris saw the line of workers quite a way down the wall. He assumed they were working on the defenses that Gates had been overseeing.

Nixx headed off down the Yellow Brick Road that led up to the gate, heading away from the City. Jacob followed him, leaving Chris and Zeke to bring up the rear.

"You think this will definitely help Matt?" Zeke asked as he walked with Chris.

"Heather assured me that it would, and we don't really have any other option but to trust her on this. She knows what she's talking about and she's the only one who can tell us how to help him," Chris said as they followed Nixx, who'd turned off left off the Road, out onto the grass. "We have to take the chance that she's telling the truth or it's a guarantee that Matt won't get better."

Zeke nodded and fell silent as they followed Nixx and Jacob into the woods. They weren't too far from the City outskirts. Chris could tell that Zeke didn't particularly wish to be out here today. He'd only stepped in to stop Gates from coming, and now he was stuck out in the woods with these three.

"So, what are we looking for exactly?" Zeke asked, watching where he was walking as they wandered deeper into the woods, Nixx still out in front. "Like, do we know what this stuff looks like?"

"I know what we're looking for and what it looks like, that's all that matters," Nixx said.

"Wonderful, so we'll be walking in circles."

Nixx chose to ignore Zeke's comment, taking a sudden left turn and coming to a stop. He crouched and looked at a plant while Zeke looked around and kicked the ground underneath his feet, the disinterest clear on his face.

Jacob didn't seem to care either way. He just looked around, making sure there were no threats nearby.

"You find something we need?" Chris asked, watching Nixx grab a few handfuls of what he'd found and hastily shove them into his bag.

"Peppermint. Did Heather say how much of everything we need?" Nixx asked, standing up straight and looking at him.

Chris shook his head. "She just told me what we needed and then said she could mix it together for us. She didn't tell me quantities."

"In that case, we'll just get as much as we can carry," Nixx said, leaning down and grabbing a few more handfuls. He put them in his bag and looked at Jacob. "Alright, we need to head back into Wonderland. Think you can get us into one of the forests over there?"

Jacob nodded. "Sure, that's why I'm here. Which forest do we need?"

"The one closest to the Room of Doors."

Jacob gave a nod, apparently knowing where that was. A few seconds later, his bright white light appeared. Chris and Zeke both shielded their eyes, but Nixx didn't even flinch.

The light died down, and Chris blinked rapidly and rubbed his eyes, trying to get his vision back from the brief moment he'd been blinded.

Nixx headed off into the dark forest and Chris realized he knew where they were. This had once been Nixx's domain. No wonder he knew where things were if they were within his area. Chris noted that this area had changed since he'd last been here and was now much eerier.

"The hardest one to find is going to be the Belladonna," Nixx said as they followed him. "We may have a bit of trouble with that and the Snapdragon. Belladonna is hard to find on a good day, but due to the state that Wonderland is currently in, it might take us longer. I don't know of anywhere to get it within Oz."

"What about the Snapdragon?" Zeke asked, looking around with an uneasy look on his face. "Also, I don't like the look of this place anymore. This isn't right. It doesn't feel right."

"Snapdragon is also going to be incredibly hard to find," Nixx said. Chris noticed that he'd lowered his voice. "It's very rare. Also yes, this place isn't right at all. We have to be very careful and try not to alert anything that lives in here now."

"What exactly are we trying to keep away?" Chris asked warily, his voice down as well.

Nixx turned to his right and Chris saw the clearing up ahead. Now, he knew exactly where they were.

"Depends on what's moved in since I've been gone," Nixx said. "Could be anything. Just make sure we don't get split up or else there may be a problem."

"What happens if we, for some reason or other, do get split up?" Zeke asked seriously, following Nixx and Jacob down the almost non-existent three stone steps.

This place was even more of a wreck than the last time Chris had stepped foot in it, which felt like another lifetime ago now.

The once beautiful wooden table was in multiple pieces, scattered around the open area in amongst broken and shattered pieces from whatever had been on the table.

The trees that had been on the left upon entering the clearing were either completely stripped of their leaves or just not there anymore. Chris could see a lot further into the forest than he'd been able to see last time, and he didn't like it much.

"If we get split up, try to get to the lake," Nixx said as he picked a book up off the ground and put it in his bag. "If you get to the lake, wait there and we'll all meet up. At least if you're in the open, you'll be able to see anything that comes running towards you before it tries to kill you and eat you."

"Well, what a wonderful thought," Zeke said, looking at Chris who shrugged in return.

Nixx gave a brief nod before continuing on his way, heading off to his left towards the stripped trees.

Zeke just shook his head, not saying anything as he trailed along behind.

# CHAPTER TWENTY-NINE

# *In the Woods*

"I swear it's getting darker the further in we get," Zeke commented as he dragged his feet, walking just behind Chris. "We shouldn't be in here."

"We need to go a little further and then we'll be able to move to a different place," Nixx called over his shoulder. "Stop complaining. You volunteered to come. You know what to do if we get split up in here."

Nixx finally came to a stop near a large tree. It looked like he'd found what he was after.

"Let's hope it doesn't come down to that," Chris said. "Is this the only thing we need from here?"

Nixx shook his head as he tore off pieces from the plant he'd found.

"No. This is the Carnation," he said. "There should be some Adder's Tongue not far from here."

"What exactly might have moved into this forest while you've been gone?" Zeke suddenly asked, really on edge now. "Because I don't know if it's just me, but I'm pretty sure I can hear something coming this way, fast."

Everyone stopped what they were doing and listened, no one saying anything.

"You're right, something is heading this way," Nixx said, tilting his head to the side. The urgency built in his voice as the ground started shaking. "We need to start moving before it gets here. We don't have long by the sounds of it."

"How long is not long?" Chris asked, the worry in his voice now. "Like a minute, or five, or...?"

"Thirty seconds, give or take," Nixx said. "Well, ten now."

Suddenly, a loud roar sounded out, very close by. The ground was still shaking and, before anyone could move, something huge burst through the trees, knocking some down, the roar now deafening. The giant figure stopped moving and just stood there, blinking rapidly as it towered over everyone.

"What the fuck is that?" Zeke asked, taking a few steps back as the creature roared again.

"Everyone stay completely still. No one move and don't say a word," Nixx warned, keeping his voice down. "Trolls don't have very good vision and can't usually see immobile targets."

"I assume it can hear us, though," Chris stated, his gaze never leaving the troll.

Nixx didn't say anything else, and all four of them stayed still, not daring to move a muscle. The troll looked around, still blinking as it surveyed the area.

Chris had never seen anything this big in his life. It was just below tree height, but it had still managed to knock over a lot of them, creating a path of flattened trees in its wake.

The troll looked down and made a grunting noise, sounding irritated and confused. It slowly looked around the area below it, knowing it had sensed something but unable to see what it was. Chris saw a movement off to his right. He wanted to know what it was, but didn't dare move because that would let the troll know they were there.

Whatever creature had moved attracted the attention of the troll. It roared again, the sound once again deafening before it started moving forward.

Nixx didn't even have time to shout for anyone to move; they were all in the troll's path. Everyone moved anyway. Zeke and Chris managed to dive to their right, out of the troll's way, while Jacob and Nixx went the opposite way.

Their movements made the troll realize they were there, and it forgot whatever had gotten its attention previously. It roared again, having set its sights now on the four of them.

"Everyone move, NOW!" Nixx shouted as the troll turned its attention to Chris and Zeke who were now luckily back on their feet. "Get out of its line of sight and get to the lake. We'll meet you there. Keep it off us and we'll get the Adder's Tongue!"

Nixx and Jacob were behind the troll, and it didn't see them move as they took off without waiting for an acknowledgement. The troll was too focused on Zeke and Chris.

"Which way's the lake from here?" Zeke asked urgently.

Both he and Chris backed up, keeping their gazes on the troll at all times.

"It's behind us, but I don't how far it is," Chris said. "We need to get this thing off us first."

The troll roared and suddenly moved, catching them both off guard. Zeke pushed Chris out of the way and stepped to the side. The troll blundered past them before turning to face them again, roaring in annoyance.

Chris got to his feet as Zeke joined him again.

"We've got to get around it," Chris said. "It already knows we're here. We have to get to the lake and this troll is in our way."

"I think we just have to run for it," Zeke said.

He took off to his right at a fast pace with Chris right behind him. The troll wasn't far behind, and they felt the ground shake as it chased them. They could hear it snapping the trees into little pieces as it passed.

Zeke risked a glance over his shoulder and saw Chris only just miss running into a tree. The troll was close on their heels, leaving a clear path showing where it had come from.

"We've got nowhere to get it off our trail," Chris called urgently, Zeke narrowly missing a tree this time. "We have to do something to lose it."

"Like what?" Zeke shouted back as the troll roared and picked up its pace behind them. "We're in a damn forest! We've got nowhere to go!"

The two of them kept running, and Chris tried to figure out quickly where they might be able to go to lose the troll.

"Up there!" Chris suddenly shouted, pointing ahead. "The ditch!"

Zeke didn't bother arguing. Both men picked up their speed, heading for a ditch in a clearing just ahead. Chris glanced behind and saw the troll gaining on them.

With no hesitation or any further thought, they jumped down into the narrow dirt ditch. It was deep enough that they could both reach the top of it, but they were shielded from view for the most part by a ledge of dirt.

Neither of them moved or spoke. They felt the ground still shaking around them as the troll ran right over the top of the ditch, causing some dirt to rain down onto them. It seemed the troll hadn't seen them jump into the ditch.

They stayed where they were, hearing the troll roar and the ground stopped shaking. The troll had stopped when it realized they were gone, and it was now looking around, trying to find them.

"How long do we stay here?" Zeke hissed, as the troll made an irritated snort as it searched for its prey.

"We can't let it know we're here. We have to make sure it leaves," Chris whispered back.

The ground began to shake again as the troll stomped around slowly, purposefully. It felt and sounded like it was coming back towards them.

"This is complete bullshit. This isn't what I had in mind for today!" Zeke snapped quietly. "We have to get back to the other two."

Chris nodded but didn't say anything. They both stood very still as the troll walked back over the top of the ditch they were in, heading back the way it had come. It looked like it had given up now that it had lost what it was after.

Chris moved a bit, pulling himself up over the ledge slightly in an attempt to see. The troll had its back to them as it made its way back through the path of destroyed trees and undergrowth it had created. Once it was far enough away, Chris hauled himself up and out of the narrow ditch. He helped Zeke out and they were both glad to be back on solid ground.

"Which way do we go?" Zeke asked. He brushed himself down then leaned over and tried to get some of the dirt out of his hair. He didn't like it. "We can't go back the way we've come because that's the way that thing went."

"I guess we keep going the way we're headed," Chris said, brushing dirt off himself as well. "Or we go to our left and try to make it to the lake, because that's more or less the way we needed to go before."

"Think it was a good idea to leave them like that?" Jacob asked as he watched Nixx inspect a plant.

The noise and ground shaking had died down a few minutes ago, and Jacob took that as a good sign. There was the occasional shake of the ground now, but nowhere near as drastic as it had been before.

"They'll be fine," Nixx said. "Chris knows where the lake is, and I doubt Zeke would let anything kill them. Hopefully he doesn't set the forest on fire. They'll be fine."

Jacob didn't say anything more as Nixx grabbed what he needed, putting the plants in his bag with the others before he stood up. He looked at Jacob before heading back the way they'd originally come.

"I'm sure they'll be fine," he repeated, sensing that Jacob wasn't convinced by his previous statement. "Don't worry, we won't be leaving without them. That's a guarantee."

"Well, I doubt anyone would be happy if only two of us returned," Jacob commented, walking beside him, assuming Nixx knew where he was going. "I don't think I'd like to have to explain why they didn't return with us."

Nixx shrugged as they walked, and Jacob saw the clearing up ahead with its ruined table. There was no sign of the troll, and the ground wasn't even slightly shaking anymore, so that was a rather good sign.

The two walked in silence, reaching the clearing. Nixx looked around sadly as they passed through it, noting the destruction caused by the troll.

"Such a shame," Nixx said, stopping by the ruined table and resting his hand on part of it as he surveyed the damage. "This used to be such a nice place but now it's all infected with evil creatures and it's just a generally miserable place."

Jacob stayed quiet, not knowing the right thing to say in this situation.

Nixx sighed. "Makes me wonder what everything would be like if I'd never left. If anything bad would have still moved in. What would the world be like if Marion was never in charge?"

"Unfortunately, there's no way to know," Jacob input as Nixx bent down and picked up a fragment of a teacup. "Life isn't that simple."

Nixx gave a nod and tossed the broken piece of teacup back onto the ground.

"We should keep moving," he said, readjusting the bag he had on his shoulder. "We've got to get to the lake and see if Zeke and Chris are there. If not, we'll wait until they show up."

He went to walk off, but something stopped him. A frown crossed Jacob's face.

"Well, that's unexpected," Nixx said, watching the little white rabbit stop in his path and look around. "Didn't think he was still around."

"The rabbit?"

Nixx nodded. "He's been around for a long time. I didn't think he'd be here anymore since Jamie isn't here."

"What's the importance of the rabbit exactly?" Jacob asked, feeling confused as they watched the rabbit move slowly around the clearing, not worried about them at all.

"Well, that's the question, isn't it?" Nixx said mysteriously.

Jacob sighed. He just wanted a straightforward answer.

"Everyone seems to have gotten the whole concept backwards, even Abel," Nixx continued.

"Right..."

"The original story was that it was Jamie's calling card after she was corrupted by Marion," Nixx said. The rabbit stopped and stared at them when it realized they were still there. "That it was her way of getting people down to Wonderland: send the rabbit up top and people would follow it for some unknown reason, ending up down here and then Marion could have more subjects."

"So, what's the real story?"

"From what I understand, it was actually Jamie's way of trying to get Abel's help, calling him to help her," Nixx said, watching the rabbit curiously move towards them, twitching its nose as it got closer. "Even if it was a part of her subconscious, she knew she needed someone's help, and Abel was the one she knew she could fall back on if something happened. He never got his hands on this guy, though."

"What would have happened if he did?" Jacob asked.

Nixx shrugged. "Who knows?"

# CHAPTER THIRTY

## Marking Time

Chris looked around as he and Zeke took a break. There had been no more sign of the troll, and they were currently in the clear.

"I didn't think it was this far," he noted. "Maybe we aren't going in the right direction."

"Well, you were pretty sure we were," Zeke commented, hands on hips as he watched Chris survey the area around them. "We're just going to have to keep walking until we find it."

Everything looked the same around this area of the forest. There was nothing to differentiate it from any other part.

Chris started walking again, Zeke trailing along just behind him. Neither of them said a word and the only sound they heard as they walked was dead leaves crunching under their feet.

"That's it," Chris suddenly said, pointing up ahead. "See, we were going the right way the whole time. I knew it."

Zeke rolled his eyes and followed Chris onto the lake shore. The lake wasn't as full as it had been the last time Chris was here. Chris just hoped he wouldn't have to swim across it again.

Nixx looked over as he saw the two men emerge from the forest. "About time you two showed up. We've got a few more places we need to be, so let's get moving."

He looked at Jacob and the bright light appeared. Nixx had already told him where to go next. A minute later the light faded, leaving the four of them in a new place that Chris didn't recognize.

"Damn, one day I'm gonna remember to shut my eyes so I don't get blinded by that," Zeke said, blinking to try and clear his vision. "Can we go home yet?"

Nixx chose to ignore the comment, instead walking away with Jacob and Chris following. Zeke took a moment to try and get his sight back before even attempting to follow them.

"We still have a few more stops before we go back," Nixx said once Zeke finally caught up. "Once we're back, we have to decide what we're going to do about mixing this all up."

"We don't really have any choice but to give it all to Heather and get her to do it," Chris said.

They walked across the barren landscape. The only thing that was really out and about were rocks, and none of them had moved. Yet.

"Unfortunately, I think you're most likely right," Nixx said, stopping at one of the large rocks. He looked around the base of it but couldn't see what he was after. "I don't know how it needs to be done, and she does. We really don't have any other choice."

"What happens to her once we've got all we need from her?" Zeke asked as they moved onto the next large cluster of rocks. "I mean we can't exactly … keep her."

"We shouldn't be killing her outright, either," Chris said.

Zeke sighed as Nixx stopped at the rocks and looked for something.

"We also can't let her go," Jacob said with a shake of his head as Nixx searched for the plants he needed. "I don't think we should kill her, but we can't let her out."

"What happens if she does get out?" Zeke asked, crossing his arms as Chris just looked at him. "She hasn't really left us with much choice on what to do. She'll tell Marion what we've been doing, and we can't risk that. She's going to die in the war, anyway."

"We'll figure it out once we know Matt's going to stay stable," Jacob said, Chris nodding in agreement this time. "Until then she's not our worry or our problem. Vincent's the one who decides, so it's up to him."

⊷⊷❖⊶⊶

"This is the last one," Nixx said, standing up straight and stretching out his lower back. "We have everything that we need, so we can get back to the City and decide what to do next."

"Should we report to Vincent first?" Chris asked. "Or do we go straight to Heather and hope that she knows what she's doing?"

"We should probably tell Vincent before we do anything," Nixx mused. Everyone else nodded. "Once we've done that, then we can go about the next step. Heather's the only one who can help Matt right now. We have literally no idea how we're meant to put all of this together; she's our only option."

"Probably good we didn't kill her, then," Chris said, looking at Zeke who rolled his eyes.

"Once we don't need her anymore, she's as good as dead," Zeke said, crossing his arms. "It would be better if she wasn't around to cause havoc. She's part of the reason that Matt's sick. If that's not reason enough for her to be killed once we've gotten what we need, then I dunno what is."

Chris didn't say anything, deciding that staying quiet was his best option right now. He didn't particularly wish to argue with Zeke right now, as Zeke could get very opinionated when he wanted to.

"Let's get back, talk to Vincent, and get Heather to mix this all together for us," Nixx said, looking at Jacob. "Once that's done, I'll get it down to the infirmary and hopefully it will cure Matt fairly quickly."

"She said it'll take a couple of days for the poison to clear from his system," Chris input, shielding his eyes as the bright white light appeared.

The light disappeared moments later, and they were standing in the group room in the castle. Zeke had once again forgotten to shut his eyes, but Chris didn't even feel bad for him right now since he'd been difficult all day.

"Alright, I'll head over to see Vincent," Nixx said, already walking away. "I'll find you guys when I have a clear picture on what to do. Chris, we might need you to help us with Heather and getting this made."

Chris nodded, although Nixx didn't see it as he was already gone from the room.

"What time is it?" Zeke asked Jacob. "We're a couple of hours behind Wonderland, aren't we?"

Jacob took his phone out of his pocket and looked at it. "About eleven. We weren't out for very long."

Zeke nodded. "Thanks. It definitely felt like a lot longer. I'll go check in with Blaine, see if he's awake."

"I'll go and check in with Vivian, see if she needs someone to keep an eye on Riley," Chris said. "I guess I'll see you guys sometime later on once we all know what's happening."

He headed off, walking quickly through the castle corridors and down to the infirmary, knowing that Vivian would most likely still be there. She would be there for as long as Matt was.

Sure enough, Vivian looked over when she saw him. "You're back."

Chris nodded and stopped next to the chair she was sitting in. She looked tired, like she hadn't had much sleep. It was all taking its toll on her.

"How's Matt doing?" he asked.

Vivian sighed. "Not good, Chris, not good."

"Well, we should be able to help him soon," he said. "Nixx has gone to talk to Vincent, and we should have everything we need to help him within the next few hours. Where's Riley? I came down to see if you needed someone to entertain him for a few hours."

"He spent the night in Blaine's room," she said. "I'm sure Blaine could use a break from him, let him rest a bit, if you wouldn't mind."

"Not at all, I'm always happy to help with him."

She gave him a grateful smile, and Chris left the infirmary, heading to where the bedrooms were located. He just had to remember which one Gates was in. He knew which one he was in, and he knew which one Ash was in, but it was a guess as to which room Gates currently resided in.

Taking a guess, he went to the door in the middle of two others and knocked on it, hoping this was the right room. A few seconds later, the door opened, and Zeke stood there looking at him. Chris assumed he must have guessed the right room since he'd said he was going to see how Gates was doing.

"You after Riley?" Zeke asked, knowing exactly why Chris was here.

Chris gave a nod and Zeke moved aside, letting him into the room. Gates looked over from where he was sitting on the bed. Riley sat opposite him and was playing around on Gates's phone.

"Hey, Chris," Gates greeted him.

Riley looked up when he realized Chris was there and abandoned what he'd been doing on the phone. He gave Chris a cheerful smile and a wave. After Chris waved and smiled back, he picked up the phone again, going back to whatever he'd been doing.

"How are you doing?" Chris asked Gates who shifted his position, still clearly feeling it.

Gates looked like he was faring a bit better compared to yesterday, but Chris could see straight off that he still wasn't completely well.

"You know, can't complain," Gates replied. "Wouldn't mind going home but, you know, kind of stuck here at the moment."

"You're not really, you're allowed to leave any time you want," Chris said. "You don't have to stay down here. No one's keeping you here."

Gates shrugged, watching Riley as he spoke. "Yeah, well, once all of this is done, then I'll be allowed to leave. I'm not about to go anywhere while there's the immediate threat from Marion. I'd rather know it's all been dealt with rather than wonder forever what happened."

Chris nodded in understanding and crossed his arms as he looked at Riley.

"How about we go do something for a bit? Give your uncle a bit of a break for a while?" he suggested. Riley shrugged but didn't look up from the phone. "Come on, let's find something to do. We should go and find Alex."

Riley's face lit up with a smile when he heard Alex's name. He handed the phone back to Gates, got off the bed, went over to Chris, and took his hand.

"Before we leave, can I ask you something?" Chris asked, looking at Gates.

Riley waited impatiently, pulling on Chris's hand, wanting to go and find the little blue cat.

"Guess so. Depends on what you want to know."

"You said you were engaged to Vivian's sister?" Chris asked, noting the frown that appeared on Gates's face.

"Yeah. But that was like ... seven, nearly eight, years ago. She wouldn't have waited that long for me to come back."

Chris nodded and Gates sighed.

"I just can't really imagine what she went through when it all happened," Gates continued. "I proposed to her and a week later I disappeared. Just really can't imagine what she went through because of that. We'd been together for a while and then I finally propose and then disappear seven days later. I don't think she'll be too happy to see me."

"I wouldn't say that." Chris tried to reassure him, but Gates shrugged. "She doesn't know what happened to you."

"I know, but I don't what I'm going to tell her," Gates said, looking down briefly. "I mean, I've been gone for almost eight years. I can't exactly tell her the truth about where I've been."

"I'm sure you'll figure something out." Chris looked down at Riley. "Alright, let's go find that cat."

Riley smiled and pulled Chris to the door. Once they were out, Riley let go of Chris's hand and headed off down the hallway, trusting that Chris would follow.

"Keep an eye on him," Zeke said just before he closed the door. "He's been in here all day so you might have a hard time keeping up with him."

"Note taken."

# CHAPTER THIRTY-ONE

# Curing the Sick

"Chris, Chris, I found him!" Riley called.

Chris entered the group room and saw Riley grinning at him as he pointed at the little blue cat curled up on a chair watching them.

"So, you did," Chris said. "You win. You found him before I could."

Chris had known the entire time that Alex was here; he'd seen him when they'd come back from the plant hunting expedition. He'd just needed to keep Riley occupied for a while because he was running out of ideas on how to keep him from wandering off by himself. He'd made sure the group room was one of the last rooms they checked in their search for Alex.

Riley began to play with Alex, who obviously didn't mind.

"Chris," Nixx said, appearing in the doorway. "We need you to come down and help us out. Heather won't say anything."

"You tried using Alice?" Chris asked, glancing over at Alex and Riley, seeing them both still occupied.

"Alice won't cooperate without you or Matt," Nixx said, making Chris sigh. "So, we could use a bit of help."

"Alright, I'll be down there in a second."

Nixx nodded and walked away, while Chris looked at Riley and Alex.

"Alex," he said, making the little cat perk up and look at him. "Can you please keep an eye on him for a bit? I have to go and help out downstairs."

The cat meowed at him, and Chris took that as a yes. He didn't have any other choice at the moment.

He looked at Riley who was patting the cat. "You stay here with Alex for a bit, OK? I don't want you wandering off, so just stay here and I'll be back as soon as I can. Promise me that you won't go disappearing on me or Alex?"

Riley nodded. "Promise."

Chris left the room, picking up his pace once he was out and heading down to the dungeon. He wanted this done as quickly as possible.

He went down the steps to find Vincent and Nixx waiting for him. "Can we make this quick?"

Vincent nodded. "That's the plan. She won't talk to us or do anything. We're hoping she'll be more receptive to you."

Chris sighed, moved past them, and stopped at the bars at the front of Heather's cell.

She glanced over at him. "Chris, how strange to see you down here," she said, before going back to pretending to look at the chipped paint on her nails.

"Stop playing games, Heather," Chris warned, making her roll her eyes and look at him with no amusement. "We got everything you said we needed. Now, we need you to mix it together for us because we don't know how to do it safely."

A sly smile appeared on her face. She knew she had all the power right now. Without her they could do nothing to help Matt without risking his life.

"Well, looks like you've got a bit of a problem, don't you?" she said. "I mean, I do know how to help, and I would, if I wasn't locked away behind these bars..."

"We're not letting you out," Chris said sternly.

Heather turned her back on him. "Well, then, I guess your little friend's going to die. Shame, really."

Chris looked over his shoulder at Vincent and Nixx. He shrugged, not sure what he could do to make Heather help. It was obvious she wasn't going to do anything for them unless they let her out, and Chris knew that wasn't a smart idea.

He turned back to look at Heather who was still standing with her back to them all.

"What do you want in return for doing this for us?" he asked, planning on trying to negotiate with her. He didn't know if he'd follow through on any promises, though. It crossed his mind that they were lucky Heather wasn't overly bright.

Heather turned back to face him, walking forward and stopping just in front of the bars. Chris moved back to keep his distance.

"Well, it all depends. Are you going to follow through on what you promise, or are you going to backstab me and throw me back in here once the deed is done? Because I don't trust you or your little friends up the back there."

Vincent and Nixx stood back, knowing that Chris would handle this a lot better than they could, and they didn't want to get in the way.

"That's strange, seeing how I don't trust you or your friends, either," Chris responded, crossing his arms and making Heather smile.

"Then, we're on the same page," she said, looking him over. "What I want in return for doing this, is to be let out of here and allowed to go home. You let me out and you don't try to get me again."

"I can't do that. I can't let you run back to Marion," Chris said with a shake of his head.

Heather moved back a bit, crossing her arms to mirror his stance. "Well, then, I guess he dies."

Chris sighed as Heather turned her back on him again and wandered back into the middle of the cell.

"I also guess you won't be able to find out how the Iron Army works, either," Heather suddenly said. She looked over her shoulder at Chris. "Shame."

"You know how they work?" Nixx asked, taking a step forward.

Heather turned to look at him. "They were partially my idea so, yeah, I have a bit of an idea. But you've got to let me out first."

Chris sighed. "If we let you out, you mix this stuff together and tell us how the soldiers work, otherwise you're straight back in here. If Matt dies or doesn't seem to be getting better, you're back in here. You do anything wrong, and you'll be down here for a very long time."

"Deal," Heather said with a smile.

She moved forward and reached out through the bars. Chris reluctantly shook her hand, agreeing on the deal.

Heather looked at Vincent, raised an eyebrow, and pointed at the cell door. Vincent didn't seem too pleased, but he walked forward, nonetheless, took out his keys and unlocked the door.

"Thank you," she said as the door swung open. "Now, where can I mix all of this together? Do you have, like, a magic lab around here anywhere?"

"You get a workstation and security," Vincent said. "Nixx and I will go with you, Heather, so you'd better not mess us around."

Heather gave him a smile. "Wouldn't dream of it."

"Alright, that should just about do it."

Chris stood with his arms crossed, watching Heather put one last thing into the mixture. The smoke rising from it made Chris uncomfortable, but he wasn't going to back away even though there were several guards with him.

Nixx had headed down to the workshop after watching enough of what Heather was doing to be sure it was safe. Vincent was bored and had left shortly after she started.

Heather looked at Chris and gestured to the concoction she'd created. "There you are. I assume you want this to go?"

Chris didn't respond, so Heather rolled her eyes and carefully poured the liquid into a bottle. She put the lid on and held it out. "Better take it before I drop it."

Chris reluctantly moved forward and took the bottle from her.

Heather sat down on the chair and put her feet up on the desk she'd been using.

"Nice place Vincent's got here," she said, looking around. She looked at Chris again with a sly smile on her face. "Whereabouts do you sleep?"

"You still have another part of the deal to fulfill," Chris said, not in the mood for her games. "This is only one half of it."

"Well, as far as I was aware, I only had to do this to be let out," Heather began. Chris knew there'd be a catch with her. "I only get one thing while you get two. I'd like something else and then I'll help you out with your army."

"What else do you want?" Chris asked, knowing there wasn't really any other way they could learn how the soldiers worked.

Heather pretended to think. "I want to be able to leave here by myself, no guards and no escorts as I leave the City. I get free rein when I leave."

"How do I know you'll just leave without doing anything?" Chris asked.

"You don't, but you have no other choice if you want to know how the soldiers work."

Heather smirked at him, knowing she had the upper hand when it came down to it. She knew what she was talking about, and she knew what they wanted to know. Chris didn't really have any other option.

"Fine," Chris said, and Heather nodded in satisfaction. "But I'm taking you down to the workshop myself. These guards will stay with you the whole time while you work down there with Nixx. And you don't go anywhere until Matt is better."

Heather nodded. "Guess that works. Lead the way."

She stood up and followed Chris out of the room, the guards not far behind. He led her down to the workshop.

"Got everything you needed?" Nixx asked as Heather went over to the soldier they'd half dismantled.

"I'm heading to the infirmary now," Chris said, holding up the bottle as Heather looked over what they'd done. "She's going to help you with these. The guards will be here the whole time in case something happens."

"I'm sure I can teach her a lesson if she tries anything," Nixx said, making Heather shoot him a glare.

Chris smiled in amusement, heading back out and up the stairs. He walked quickly to the infirmary, knowing they needed to get what Heather had mixed to Matt as soon as possible.

Vivian looked up he entered the room.

"We've got it," Chris said, holding up the bottle. "Anyone here that can do this?"

Vivian nodded and went deeper into the infirmary. A minute or so later, she came back with one of the doctors.

"She said you have what's needed?" the doctor asked.

Chris nodded and handed over the bottle.

"We've been told it has to go directly into the bloodstream. I assume you use all of it. We weren't told quantities, and we don't have time to waste," he said as the doctor nodded in understanding. "We've been told it'll take a couple of days to clear everything out of his system, so we have to wait and hope it works."

"I'll get right onto it," the doctor said. "I'll send someone to find Vincent if there's any improvement or further deterioration."

Chris nodded and watched the doctor head back into the infirmary, presumably to get everything he needed.

Vivian took his hand and smiled at him. "Thank you for this, Chris. You've no idea how much this means to me and Riley."

"Matt's a friend to me, as well," he said. "I wasn't about to sit back and do nothing. I couldn't help him when I was in the witches' castle, but I can help him now. It's not just me, though. Nixx and everyone else are also responsible for helping. None of us are about to let him die while there are still things we can try."

"Thank you," Vivian reiterated. "Seriously, thank you."

# CHAPTER THIRTY-TWO

## Healing

"Any news?" Zeke asked, sitting down opposite Chris.

"It's only been twenty-four hours," Chris said. "We'll have to wait a bit longer."

Ash and Riley were sitting in the middle of the room playing a board game Ash had managed to find overnight.

Gates also came into the room, clearly having nothing to do today, and joined Ash and Riley on the floor. He was moving a lot better, showing that he was healing, even if he was still tired and having a bit of trouble with some movement.

Alex was sitting on the chair next to Chris and he looked up at him. "How do we know if it worked?"

"He won't be sick anymore," Chris said.

"What did you do with Heather?" Zeke asked. "Vincent said you had to get her to do some stuff, so where is she now?"

"Hopefully still down in the workshop helping Nixx with the soldiers," Chris said.

Everyone stopped what they were doing as Vincent appeared in the doorway. He looked around at everyone in the room. The only ones missing were Abel and Jamie, and Chris hadn't seen Abel since he'd come back.

"Matt's awake," Vincent said. "But I'm going to say this now to make it clear: he's still very sick, so I don't want people in there crowding him. If you want to see him, there's to be no more than two of you at a time. Don't overwhelm him."

Everyone nodded.

"I thought it was meant to take a few days to clear out of his system. It's only been twenty-four hours," Chris said. "I didn't think he'd be awake for a few more days."

"Well, he's awake now, and he's been throwing up for the past fifteen minutes. That's why I'm warning you all that he's still very sick," Vincent said. "The plants are obviously doing something, but it looks like it'll take a few more days for things to calm down. So, as I said, no more than two at a time. Be respectful since he's so sick but I don't want to stop you from seeing him."

With that, Vincent left the room. No one said anything for a few seconds.

"Well, I don't know about you lot, but I'm going to see him," Zeke said, getting up from where he'd been sitting. "Anyone else?"

"I'll come," Chris spoke up before anyone else could. Gates looked at him and narrowed his eyes but didn't say a word. "I'll come back in a bit and someone else can take my place."

"That would be me," Gates said. "So, don't take forever or I'll come down there anyway. Fuck what Vincent says."

Riley looked away from the board game and frowned at Gates, not seeming too happy at hearing him swear. Gates looked at him apologetically but didn't say anything.

Zeke and Chris left the room. Zeke didn't say a word as he made sure to keep a few paces in front of Chris, clearly not in the mood to talk to him today. Chris didn't know what he'd done to make Zeke not like him very much.

When they entered the infirmary, Vivian looked over from where she was standing next to a closed bathroom door.

"Hey," she greeted them as they stopped in front of her. "Just give him a couple of minutes. He's still really sick."

"Vincent said he wasn't faring too well but he's awake?" Chris said as Zeke took a seat on the closest chair he could find. "Apart from being sick still, how's he doing?"

Vivian shrugged. "Better by the looks of it. A bit pissed off, but that's to be expected."

Chris nodded, hoping Matt would be OK in a couple of days. With any sort of luck, he'd be able to help when Marion finally decided to attack them. They still had no idea when that was likely to happen, so they were just preparing as well as they could in the time that they had.

Jacob and the other trainers were in the arena every day for hours working with people to get their abilities up to scratch so they'd be able to do what they could to take down the Iron Army.

Even though there were some abilities that hadn't worked against the metal soldier, Chris felt like they still had a decent chance of eliminating Marion.

Despite what Matt had said when they were stuck in the parallel world together, Chris was sure Matt would want to be the one to finally kill her. She'd wronged him enough that he'd want to eventually get his vengeance on her.

The three of them looked over as the bathroom door opened. Matt stopped in the doorway, holding onto the doorframe, and looked at Zeke and Chris.

He looked very tired and didn't say a word as Vivian helped him over to the closest bed. He sat on the edge of the bed, looking like he needed a few hours of sleep.

"Hey, man," Zeke said, getting to his feet. Matt nodded slightly. "Vincent said you were awake, so we thought we'd stop in and see how you're doing."

Matt looked up at him, meeting his gaze. "I'm doing just great."

Matt's attitude certainly hadn't changed over the past four months, Chris thought. Knowing him, it was probably worse since he'd been locked away for that entire time with barely anyone to talk to.

"You'll get better, just got to give it a bit of time," Chris tried. Matt looked at him, not saying anything. He looked a bit mad. "You'll be OK."

"Chris, I've been sitting in the dark for four months," Matt said, looking like he was trying to keep his words civil. "You, of all people, should know that right now, I don't have a lot of patience for time. I've lost four months of my life that I can't get back, so I don't really have any more time to waste."

Chris didn't say anything, deciding the best course of action was to stay silent. Vivian had been right when she'd said Matt was angry, but he had every right to be. He'd lost a lot of time.

"As long as you get better, no matter how long it takes," Zeke said. Matt switched his gaze to him and Chris figured he was less likely to get mad at Zeke if he said anything. "Do you remember much of what happened?"

"What do you mean?" Matt asked, sounding a bit calmer.

"Do you remember what happened before you got here?"

Matt looked at him for a few seconds before he spoke. "I can't tell you how I got back here. But I know more or less what happened over the past four months."

Zeke nodded and stood up. "Alright, well, we should probably leave you to get better. Blaine was going to stop in a bit later if you want to see him."

"Let him know to come by in a couple of hours. I think I need to sleep a bit before I talk to anyone else."

Zeke nodded. "OK, we'll leave you to get some rest then."

Matt gave a tired nod and Zeke indicated for Chris to follow him out.

"Chris," Matt called, making Chris stop and look back at him. "Thank you. Vivian tells me I pretty well owe you my life."

"It was a team effort," Chris said, but he could tell Matt didn't believe him. "I'll leave you to get some sleep. You know where we are if you need us."

Matt nodded and Chris smiled briefly at him before following Zeke out of the room.

# CHAPTER THIRTY-THREE

# Heather's Information

"Chris, hey."

Chris was sitting in a chair in the group room and looked up to see Abel walking towards him.

"Hey," he said in return.

"How's Matt doing?" Abel asked, crossing his arms.

The small blue cat wandered into the room and jumped up onto the arm of the chair, settling down as he listened to them talk.

"He'll get better," Chris said. "Going to take a couple of days, but he'll get there."

Abel nodded and looked around as Nixx stopped in the doorway. He didn't say a word, just indicated for the two of them to follow him as he turned and walked away.

"What's that about?" Abel asked.

Chris shook his head. "Guess we're about to find out."

Chris, Alex, and Abel quickly headed out of the room and caught up to Nixx, walking a few paces behind him.

The little cat meowed, making both of them look down at him as he trudged along with them. He seemed tired.

Chris shrugged at Abel, and they kept walking along the hallway and down the stairs that led to the workshop. The top door was open, but the lower one was still missing.

Chris frowned as they entered the workshop. "Where's Heather?"

Alex wandered over to the table, jumping up on it to inspect what was on there.

"That's the problem," Nixx said as Abel and Chris exchanged looks. "She's insisting on leaving, but Vincent's thrown her back in the dungeon. He doesn't trust her not to do anything, and she's rather mad that she's been denied that part of the deal."

"Is she going to try something?" Abel asked.

Nixx shrugged. "Honestly, Abel, we don't know. She's been down there all night now and she hasn't stopped muttering to herself. We think she's managed to contact Carmen or Marion."

"Great. The last thing we need is for them to launch their attack on us now," Chris said with a sigh. "What are we going to do?"

Nixx shook his head. "I don't know. Vincent was talking about killing her to try and prevent this war starting too soon."

"We can't do that," Abel said, making Chris nod. Abel had clearly changed sides, seeing how he'd voted for her to die earlier. "We don't know what she's told Marion, if that's who she's contacting. We need her to tell us."

"How? None of us are going to be able to force her to tell us anything now that she thinks we've reneged on the deal," Chris said. "None of us are intimidating enough for her to take us seriously."

Abel thought for a second, then looked at him. "What about Matt?"

"You really think I want to be up and moving around right now? Going anywhere near Heather isn't something I feel like doing," Matt said, looking at Chris and Abel. "In case you two hadn't noticed, I'm not exactly feeling the best."

"We know, but we don't really have any other ideas or anyone else that might get through to her," Chris said, desperation coming through his tone and making Matt sigh. "We've got to do something, or we may be in serious trouble sooner than we would have liked."

Matt looked at Abel for a few seconds before he looked back at Chris.

"I'm not guaranteeing anything," he said, shaking his head. "Also, I hope you know that I don't really have much patience left with that bitch. I hope you know she's going to be dead before the end of the day."

"I don't think you should be killing her," Abel spoke up.

Matt looked at him and crossed his arms. "Why not? All she's done is fuck us around. She's the one responsible for locking me away for four months, so you'll have to understand why I don't particularly like her."

"We know you don't like her, but you shouldn't be killing her. She might still have information or something we can use against Marion," Chris said.

"Well, too bad, this is the warning. You ask me to get her to talk about what she's been doing or who she's been contacting, and I'm killing her. I'm not about to let her live down there in the dungeon where she could keep doing it. She'll kill anyone as soon as she gets the chance."

Chris sighed and moved closer to Abel.

"We don't really have any other choice, Abel," he said, keeping his voice down. Abel glanced at Matt before looking back at Chris. "We have to do it. She doesn't seem to have much of use left that we need. Nixx knows how the soldiers work now, and she cured Matt, so what's she got left that she could tell us?"

Abel still looked unconvinced but shrugged in resignation. "I guess, if there's nothing else we can do…"

Chris looked back at Matt who was just watching the two of them. "Alright. You go and talk to her, get as much out of her about anything as you can, and then you can do whatever you need to do."

"Glad we came to an understanding," Matt said, a hint of sarcasm in his tone. "Now leave me alone. You'll have your information by the end of the day."

"Heather."

Heather turned around, startled by the sudden interruption. She narrowed her eyes, not sure where the voice had come from or who had called her name.

She turned around again, seeing someone standing in the back corner of the cell with their arms crossed.

"Still lurking in the shadows, I see," Heather commented, crossing her arms as well. She knew who it was now. There was only one man she knew who lurked in the dark. "I would have thought that four months alone in the dark was enough to put you off being unseen. Didn't think the darkness was your friend anymore."

"I just came by to say thanks for what you did," Matt said, pushing off the wall and walking forward a few paces. Heather moved back a bit as she watched him cautiously. "Because, you know, I could have been dead and out of the way if you hadn't given them the solution to what was wrong with me. You could have had one less person to worry about, one less danger."

Heather gave a shrug, but she stayed where she was and watched Matt move around the cell.

"Just doing what was right and helping out society, all that bullshit."

Matt gave a slight smile and stopped in front of her. "Because you really want to do the right thing. I find that very hard to believe. I've also been told that you've been down here talking to yourself over the past few hours. Why might that be?"

A small smile crossed Heather's face as she stepped forward one step, closing the distance between the two of them.

She leaned in as if she was going to tell him a secret. "Wouldn't you like to know?"

"Well, I wouldn't ask if I didn't want to know."

Heather smiled and stepped back again. "You're smart, figure it out yourself."

Matt laughed softly before all the amusement on his face faded. Without warning, he grabbed her and pushed her hard back against the cold stone wall.

She glared at him and tried to push him off, but she wasn't strong enough.

"You have two choices: answer my questions or die," Matt growled, leaning in closer to show just how serious he was. "It's your choice. Choose wisely."

The glare remained on Heather's face as she stared him down. Over his shoulder, she saw a guard pass the cell and not even notice the uninvited guest she had.

"You kill me and that's the start of this war," she hissed. "If I were you, I'd think twice before ending my life."

"Right now, I couldn't really care less about this fucking war," Matt snapped back, making Heather flinch. "You certainly don't want to push me right now. I'm far from in the mood to be messed with, so get talking."

Heather looked at him for a few seconds as she thought about what to do.

"Marion's aware of what's going on," she said, having decided to tell him the truth. She didn't feel like dying right now. "I was talking with Carmen last night using my wonderful witchy powers that connect us, so she's aware of everything you lot have been doing. You have less than a week before they come knocking on those gates, and that's if you're lucky."

"What exactly did you tell her?" Matt asked, not relaxing his grip on her. Heather stayed quiet, so he pushed her harder against the wall. "Talk."

Heather glared at him again before speaking. "I told her that you're here with the stupid housemaid and the boy." She noticed the look on his face. "Oh, what? Did I hit a nerve or something?"

"That's my family you're talking about, so watch your damn mouth," Matt warned. "Now keep talking and tell me what I came down here for."

"Your family?" Heather asked, raising her eyebrows. "You mean, that little brat is your kid? Man, no wonder I couldn't stand him."

Matt leaned in even closer, making Heather even more uncomfortable.

"You listen here," he said, his voice low but threatening. "I have a rather sharp dagger on me somewhere, so you'd better shut it with your bullshit and answer my questions, because I'm running out of time right now. I haven't got patience for people like you. I don't like having my time wasted."

A sly smile crossed Heather's face as she looked him up and down. "Can I take a guess as to where you've hidden that dagger?"

"You guess correctly, and I'll kill you. Answer the fucking question."

"What was the question again?" Heather asked.

Her innocent act was starting to really piss Matt off.

"What did you tell Carmen?" Matt snapped. His tone and the look on his face instantly wiped the amusement off Heather's face. "I'm gonna count down from five. When I reach zero, I'm gonna kill you, whether I have my answers or not. Five."

Heather hesitated, not sure if Matt was telling the truth. It wasn't often he lied and when it came down to it, she doubted that he'd lie about killing her.

"Four."

Heather looked over towards the front of the cell, hoping that a guard would come past before Matt could kill her, but there was no one around.

"Three."

She switched her gaze back to Matt whose facial expression was still the same.

"Two."

Heather knew that if she didn't speak up, he'd kill her without any hesitation. She wasn't about to die over something as small as information she'd told Carmen.

"One."

"Alright, fine," she said. "I told her that I'm locked up and that you're not dead. I told her that Vincent negated on his deal of letting me out once I'd fulfilled my part of the deal, which was helping you and then showing them how the Iron Army soldiers work. I didn't tell her anything else, I swear."

Matt looked her over, summing her up as he thought. He looked back at her face, no longer thinking.

"Zero."

Matt was quick. Less than a second after he'd said zero, Heather felt a sharp pain in her stomach.

Matt moved back slightly, and Heather looked down to see the hilt of a dagger showing where the rest of it was buried deep in her midsection.

"Good talk," Matt said, pushing the dagger in a bit harder.

She grabbed him to stop herself from falling. She'd never felt this kind of pain in her life.

"You said you'd spare me!" she managed to say as dark blood ran down and pooled on the floor.

"I never said that at all," Matt said. He pulled her closer, keeping hold of both her and the dagger. "I'll see you in Hell, Heather."

# CHAPTER THIRTY-FOUR

## War Triggers

Carmen suddenly doubled over in pain, holding her stomach.

"What is it?" Marion asked.

"Something's wrong," Carmen said. She kept one hand against the table as she straightened up a bit, still feeling the pain, just not as strongly as moments before. "My connection to Heather is broken. I think she's dead. Either that or she's severely hurt."

"Well, what do we do?" Marion asked, watching Carmen shut her eyes.

"Give me one second and I'll find out what's really going on."

Marion shifted position in her chair and watched Carmen who stayed completely still with her eyes closed.

Carmen opened her eyes again and hit the table in frustration. "They killed her! That's it, I'm completely done with those bastards. We're leaving tomorrow morning with the army. They are not getting away with this. I won't let them off that easy."

"Are you sure the army's ready to go out?"

Carmen looked at Marion and began pacing up and down the length of the room. "Oh, I'm sure. They've been ready for a while now. The Emerald City won't be completely ready for the attack yet. Heather said that their first line of defense isn't one hundred percent finished, which gives us the advantage."

"So, what's the plan?"

"We take the Iron Army out early tomorrow morning. We get close to the City but wait until the next day to attack. I want them to see us coming. Let them know we're going to raze their city to the ground."

Marion nodded, liking the idea of it. "Sounds like a good plan to me."

Matt crossed his arms as Chris, Ash, and Abel stared down at Heather's unmoving body.

"What do we do with her?" Ash asked, keeping her voice down. "We can't just ... leave her here."

"We have to get rid of the body," Chris said. "Ash's right, we can't leave her dead here in the cell."

"Does Vincent know this has happened?" Abel asked, shifting uncomfortably.

Matt shook his head. "No, and I don't think he'll be overly happy when someone tells him."

Ash looked at him. "You're the one who killed her, so you're the one who gets to tell Vincent the bad news."

Matt looked over his shoulder at her. Ash shrugged at him and placed her hands on her hips as her gaze went back to Heather's dead body.

Matt followed her gaze, thinking the entire time about what they needed to do. A guard walked past and paid no attention to what was going on. Vincent's guards were useless and slack, Matt thought.

"We have to burn the body," Matt suddenly said.

Ash was appalled. "You're joking. Jesus, Matt, she's already dead! Just dig a shallow grave and dump her in."

"That's not really any better, Ash," Abel said. "Even Heather doesn't deserve to be left in a ditch."

"Well, if she wasn't meant to be thrown into a ditch, why does the word 'witch' rhyme with it?" Ash asked back sarcastically as Abel rolled his eyes. "She's destined for the unending coldness of the earth. She'll be going to Hell anyway."

"What makes you say that?" Chris asked with a frown.

Matt crouched down, thinking as he looked the body over, the blood slowly soaking into the stone floor.

"It's an old folklore legend, an old wives' tale," Ash said, crossing her arms. "Witches, or anyone or anything that practices any kind of magic, goes straight to Hell with no way out."

"That's not true," Matt spoke up, everyone looking to him. "There's always a way out, which is why we have to burn the body. No body, no way of getting back."

"You said that anyone who practices any kind of magic goes to Hell," Chris said. Ash looked at him and nodded. "Does that mean that everyone who learns their ability will go to Hell? Isn't that technically a form of magic?"

Ash frowned, clearly having never thought of that. "That's a really good point," she said, looking at Matt. "What do you think?"

"I think we need to get this body outside the City walls and burn the witch," Matt said, standing up. He looked at Abel. "I can't shadow-step her out. I can only move fairly short distances at the moment. Help me get her out of here."

"Well, this is going well," Chris commented as they watched Heather's body go up in flames. "I don't know how we got past so many people with a dead body, but I think we've done alright."

Matt glanced at him before going back to watching the spectacle in front of them.

"We're so screwed," Ash said with a sigh, crossing her arms as she watched the smoke begin to rise. "This is not a good sign. We won't have long left if they know she's dead."

"Heather and Carmen were linked, so she'll know we killed her," Matt said, hands in pockets as he stared at the flames, the daylight around them slowly fading. "We have two days maximum. If it's not tomorrow, it'll be the day after."

"How are we even going to make it through all of this?" Abel asked, feeling the heat from the fire. "Gates is our first line of defense, and he's nowhere near ready to be fighting them off. Once they get through him, we're all as good as dead."

Matt looked at him as he thought about what Abel was saying.

"He'll be fine. He won't go down that easily, even if he's hurt," he said. "We have to let Vincent know what's going on because we have to be ready. Heather said we have less than a week and I don't think she was lying."

"Well, she's dead now, so we can't really ask her anything else, can we?" Ash said harshly. "I can't believe you killed her."

"She had it coming," Matt snapped back, not in the mood for Ash's attitude now. "She told Carmen and Marion everything she found out since she's been locked away here. She gave all our information to the enemy, so I didn't really have much choice. I did what I had to do."

Ash didn't say anything, deciding to stay quiet this time. She just stood and watched the flames.

"Someone stay here to make sure the whole thing burns," Matt said, walking off and heading towards the back gate where they'd come out. "I'm going to talk to Vincent."

"What do we do once the whole thing has burned?" Chris called.

"I don't know! Be creative!" Matt called back before he disappeared back into the City.

Chris looked at Abel. "Any ideas?"

Abel shrugged. Ash didn't contribute to the conversation at all.

"I guess we somehow bury what's left?" Abel suggested, the hesitation clear in his voice. He had no idea what to do. "We can't leave her out here in the open, so we kind of need to get rid of what we've burned."

Chris nodded, looking at Ash this time. "What do you think?" he asked, not even getting a glance; she didn't look away from the flames.

"I honestly don't care," she said. "As long as we don't get the blame for this, then I truly don't care what happens to the remainder of Heather's corpse. You two can deal with it, I don't have time for this. I'll be down in the arena if you want to talk to me about something that's not about this murder."

Ash tore her gaze away from the burning body and left, stalking through the partially-opened back gate and disappearing from view.

"She's a bit unhappy about this," Abel commented, looking at Chris.

Chris nodded, crossing his arms as the sun finally disappeared. The City lights illuminated the sky above it and a small area around its walls. The flames seemed a lot brighter now that the darkness had taken over.

"She and Matt still don't see eye to eye, and I think she's just mad that he killed Heather without any thought or discussion with anyone else."

Abel shrugged and put his hands in his pockets. "In all honesty, I think he did the right thing. Heather was dangerous, and she told Marion and Carmen everything that we know. If she didn't die today, she would have during the attack. Either way, she'd be dead."

# CHAPTER THIRTY-FIVE

# Last Minute Decisions

"So, what do we do?" Chris asked, the flames having died out less than ten minutes ago.

Abel shook his head slowly as they both stared at what was now mostly ash in front of them. Heather's body was no longer a problem. It was getting late, and they'd been standing outside in the cold for a few hours. Now they had to make the decision.

Everyone was probably asleep by now; Chris was sure it was nearing midnight. He wondered how well it had gone down with Vincent when Matt told him what had happened. If he had to guess, Vincent wasn't impressed and there was now going to be a big problem.

"I think we're going to have to walk a fair way out and bury what's left," Chris said reluctantly. "Somewhere it won't be found. Somewhere that no one will know of."

Abel was thinking about what they could do as he continued to stare at the few bone fragments and ashes. He was hesitant about Chris's suggestion but knew there weren't many options right now.

Where would they even go? Chris and Abel both knew very little about what was around the Oz area, except that it was dangerous outside the City after dark. And it would take too long to get over into Wonderland.

Unless they had someone who could get them around quicker.

"I'm going to find Jacob," Chris said. "Wait here and I'll be back."

Before Abel could protest, Chris headed back into the City. There was no one around as he walked quickly towards the arena, hoping Jacob was still there training someone. He'd been doing late nights lately, so there was a good chance that he was.

The arena came into view and Chris could see the lights were still on. Good, hopefully that meant someone was still there.

He didn't know if the lights were always on during the night or not. He'd never been to the arena this late at night. By this time of the night, he was usually sleeping, but right now he had other things to worry about. He could sleep in tomorrow if the Iron Army didn't attack too early.

Chris walked into the arena and saw a couple of people, but not Jacob. He felt his heart sink a bit. That was that plan down the drain.

Ben saw him and waved him over. "Hey Chris, don't usually see you down here so late. Anything I can help you with?"

"I was actually after Jacob," Chris said. "Is he here?"

"He was," Ben replied. "You just missed him. He had to go and take care of something about ten minutes ago. I'm sure if you hang around, though, he'll be back soon."

"It's kind of important and urgent," Chris said, wanting to keep this to himself but knowing he was probably going to have to tell Ben sooner or later about what was going on.

Ben frowned. "Anything I can do?"

"Unless you can get Abel and me into Wonderland with a click of your fingers, I don't think so, sorry," Chris said.

"Should I be wondering why you want to get back into Wonderland so urgently?"

Chris shook his head. "Probably better that you don't know."

Ben gave a nod of understanding. "Alright, then, I won't question it. But really, if you ever need any help, just let me know and I'm more than happy to do what I can. If I see Jacob, I'll let him know you're looking for him."

"Tell him it's urgent and to meet us outside the back gate."

"Will do," Ben said with a nod as Chris turned and headed back the way he'd come.

"What have you guys done now?"

Abel and Chris looked up to see Jacob walking their way. It had been roughly half an hour since Chris had gone in search of him and Jacob didn't look overly impressed. When he saw what they were standing in front of, he looked between the two of them.

"What the hell is going on?" he asked, pointing to the remains. "Do I even want to know what this is?"

Chris and Abel exchanged looks before they looked back at Jacob.

"Heather's dead," Chris said, figuring there was no point in lying to him. "Matt killed her and then left us here to make sure her entire body burned so she couldn't somehow come back. We were hoping you'd be able to help us out with burying what's left."

Jacob looked at him in shock.

"You want me to help you cover up a murder?" he asked, looking briefly at Abel before looking back at Chris. "You're kidding, right? What the hell is wrong with you?"

"Look, we know this is bad," Abel spoke up. "But all we need you to do is take us over to Wonderland so we can bury the remains far away from where anyone would think of looking and then bring us back. That's all we need you to do. We're not asking you to cover up anything."

Jacob seemed incredibly hesitant, looking between the two of them as he thought about what was the right thing to do.

"Does Vincent know?" he asked.

"Matt went to tell him, but we never heard anything after he left," Chris said. "As far as we know he does know, but we're not a hundred percent sure. We just really need to get this away from prying eyes."

Jacob looked at the remains, the bones and ashes hard to see in the dark as the City's lights didn't quite reach to where they were standing.

"Alright, fine," Jacob said, throwing his hands up. "But I don't want word getting around that I helped you with this."

"It's come to my attention that Heather is dead."

Vincent looked around the room disapprovingly with his arms crossed, completely ignoring the fact that Matt was with everyone today. He was far from in the mood to deal with Matt ever since he'd told him what had transpired overnight.

"I've got to say, I'm not very happy about this," he continued. "This has pretty well screwed us completely. We're vulnerable right now and they know it! They'll be able to get past our defenses when they attack. We're nowhere near ready to defend ourselves!"

No one said a word as Vincent looked around at everyone.

"You're all incredibly lucky that I don't kick some of you out of here right this minute," he said angrily. "I know who's been talking to who, so I know who I should be getting rid of, but unfortunately there are some of you I need to make sure this city remains standing."

"So, you're basically saying that you just need everyone so you don't lose your control," Matt stated, a bitter look on his face as Vincent looked at him. "You're unbelievable, you know that? What are *you* even going to do when they attack? You're always telling *us* what to do but you've never once mentioned how you're going to contribute towards this fight."

"I've been coordinating everything so, when the time comes, we're not caught off guard!" Vincent snapped, not liking Matt's challenge. "You shut your damn mouth and don't say another word or you're out of here. I don't need you on this, Matt, so stay quiet. You have no power here."

"If you really want me to leave, I'll leave," Matt said, standing up. "None of us came here to help you protect your city. We came here to get help for Jamie, and we got it, thank you. We didn't have to hang around and help you with anything and you're treating us all like your soldiers. None of us have to stick around and I'm certainly not going to wait around to die for you. I'm going home."

He walked out and Gates sighed, pushing himself up out of his chair. He didn't say anything as he followed Matt out of the room.

"If he wants to go, let him," Vincent said as Zeke quickly followed Gates. "If anyone wants to leave, be my guest. You don't have to help but just know that if you walk out of those gates, you're not allowed back in."

No one moved or said a word as Vincent made eye contact with each of them.

"That's what I thought," he said. He sighed. "Look, if what Matt said to me last night is true, today is the last day we have to prepare ourselves for the attack. I need all hands on deck right now, because if we don't get everything ready then the Emerald City will be razed to the ground and everyone in it will most likely die."

"You're not seriously going home, are you?" Gates asked as he watched Matt move around the room, grabbing anything that was his. "You can't just ... leave!"

"Why the fuck not?" Matt snapped back, stopping what he was doing and looking at Gates and Zeke. "Vincent doesn't want me here and, in turn, I don't want to be here. I want to go home and live my fucking life. I have a damn family now, Blaine."

"You think we don't want to go home?" Gates asked, indicating himself and Zeke. "Because, believe me, Matt, we do. But we can't, not yet. You can't just up and leave in the middle of this. You've waited nearly eight years to get your hands on Marion and finish her for good, and now you're just gonna walk away?"

Matt stayed silent, clearly having nothing to say as he looked at the floor. He sighed and looked at Gates again.

"Everything is still going to be there when you get back, Matt," Gates said. "They can wait for you for one more day. They've waited this long, so what's one more day gonna do?"

"I just want my life back," Matt said sadly. "Just want my damn life back, Blaine. I've lived the past five years without Viv and now she's back and we have a kid. They've both been locked in that witch castle for the past five years. Riley hadn't seen anything outside those walls until now. I just can't stay here."

He turned his back and looked around the room, making sure he had everything.

"Fine," Gates said. "Then, guess I'm going home too."

Matt frowned, looking over at him. Gates was serious.

"You're their first line of defense," Matt stated, getting a shrug from Gates. "If there's anyone who can't leave, it's you."

"I don't care," Gates said seriously. "I'm not letting you leave us down here. You've been gone for the past four months and now you're going to up and leave again? This time for good? How is that fair on us? We all came down here together, so we all go home together."

Matt looked between Gates and Zeke, not sure what to say.

"We stick together, Matt," Gates continued. "You don't get to leave without us. We either all go home together, or we stay down here and finish Marion off together."

Matt looked between the two of them again. Zeke didn't say a word. He'd do whatever they needed him to do.

"You sure?" Matt asked, both of them nodding. "Well, alright, guess it's settled then."

# CHAPTER THIRTY-SIX

# Enemy at the Gates

Both Chris and Abel looked when they heard sirens begin to blare. They exchanged looks, abandoning what they'd been doing. They sprinted out of the arena, closely followed by Jacob.

Nixx, Ash, and Alex were already at the City's front gate when they got there, the sirens still sounding. Chris noticed that the guard who normally checked people before letting them into the City was gone and the service area was all boarded up.

"Where's Gates?" Abel asked, looking around at everyone. "Zeke? Matt? Where are they?"

Ash shook her head as Alex clung onto her, fear in his eyes and evident on his face.

"We don't know," Ash said. "They were all gone. No one knows where they are. We think all three of them left either last night or early this morning."

"What? Why would they do that?" Abel asked. "We knew Matt was probably going to leave, but why the other two?"

Everyone shrugged, no one able to answer him.

"We're all so dead," Alex commented, shaking his head furiously as he continued to cling onto Ash's arm, not wanting to lose her. "Without Gates as our first line of defense, we're all dead."

"Look, we can handle this, OK?" Jacob tried to reassure everyone. "We've got enough people to help, and we can do this. We're not going to die, that's a promise."

"We've only got the civilians and ourselves for this," Nixx spoke up. "Trying to create our own Iron Army was taking too long and I wasn't anywhere near finished. We only have ourselves against them."

"We still don't know what abilities can and can't affect them," Alex noted.

"We've got a rough idea," Nixx said. "It seems physical ones, such as yourself, or Gates and Ash, are able to hit and affect them but they seem to have a magical resistance to non-physical ones, such as myself or Chris. Abel should be OK since his is a bit of both."

Abel nodded but didn't say anything. The sirens still sounded, and Vincent was still nowhere to be seen.

Nixx looked at Jacob. "Think you and Alex can go and round everyone up?" he asked. Alex shook his head again. He wasn't about to let Ash go. "Anyone who's signed up and ready, we need down here as soon as possible. We don't have long."

Jacob nodded but Alex continued shaking his head.

"Alex, please," Ash said, putting her hand on his. "I'll still be here when you get back, you'll be fine. Jacob will keep you safe."

Alex looked like he was on the verge of tears as Ash pried him off her and pushed him towards Jacob who grabbed him and headed off at a fast pace.

"We're just going to have to make do with who we have," Nixx said. "Chris, you and Ash head up into the watch tower; the one Gates was going to use to his advantage. Marion and Carmen should be outside the gates, seeing as the sirens are still sounding. Stall her as long as you can."

Chris nodded and indicated to Ash to follow as he headed over to the watch tower. They both ran up the steps and, when they reached the top, they looked out of the pane-less window to see what was happening outside the gates below.

"Oh God," Ash commented. What she saw was enough to make her regret staying. "We are so dead."

"So, what's the plan exactly?" Gates asked as he, Matt, and Zeke stood back and watched what was happening at the City gates.

The three of them were quite a distance away, unable to be seen from the City but able to see what was happening.

"We need to get Marion and avoid everyone else as much as we can," Matt said. "The warding barrier that protected the City is gone. The Army managed to dissipate it when they came through. Part of what they can do, apparently. So that makes it easier on us."

"OK, so we get Marion, but how do we avoid the remainder of the Army?" Zeke asked, looking at Matt who was focused on what was happening.

"We attack from behind before the others can make their move, make us the focus of the Army," Matt explained. "If we can keep the focus on us long enough for the others to get their shit together and help, we can pull this off. Marion and Carmen will most likely stay out of the way because they won't want to die, so that's when we take the chance and we grab Marion."

"What do we do with her once we've got her?" Gates asked. "You going to kill her?"

Matt shook his head. "No, that's an easy way out for her. She has to suffer first. I'm going to lock her up and see how she likes being trapped in the dark forever."

Gates nodded, not really caring what happened to Marion. As long as she was out of his way and he could go home, that's all he cared about. The quicker this was over, the quicker he could leave.

"The Army should attack us if we hit them first," Zeke said. "From what Nixx was saying when he was pulling them apart, whoever or whatever attacks them first will get their attention before someone else hits them. If we keep them focused on us, the others can launch their attack as well and maybe even split the Army."

Matt gave a nod. "Sounds like a plan. We'll give them a couple minutes before we hit."

"Send Vincent out to talk," Marion demanded, calling up to Chris and Ash. "All I want to do is chat and we can put aside our differences and come to some sort of agreement."

"We're not sending anyone out," Chris called back. "We're not stupid, Marion. No one's coming out those gates until you leave."

"Where is Vincent?" Marion asked, arms crossed as she looked around before looking up at him again. "I haven't seen or heard anything from him since this all started. Now we're here and he still hasn't shown his face. I'm beginning to wonder if he even exists."

Ash appeared next to Chris, getting his attention. She'd disappeared for a few minutes to see what was happening with Vincent.

"He's gone," she said to Chris, keeping her voice down so Marion wouldn't hear her. "He's completely gone. No one's seen or heard from him since yesterday when he was talking to us. Dorothy said he's not within the City walls, so he's left. He's abandoned us all and left us here to die."

Chris looked at her for a few seconds as what she said sunk in.

"Come on, I don't have all day," Marion called again. Ash and Chris both looked down at her. She gave them a bit of a smile. "Don't tell me Vincent's gone and left you all?"

Chris's expression fell. "You already knew that, didn't you?"

Marion shrugged. "Maybe I did. Is it really worth fighting over a lost cause, Chris? The Emerald City is as good as dead. If you all leave now, you'll survive, otherwise you're all as dead as Heather."

"Maybe she's right, Chris. We should go," Ash said. "What's the point if Vincent's gone? He clearly didn't want anything to do with this, and he just left us all to die. This city is gone."

"Ash, people live here," Chris said. "We going to just abandon all of them? Leave them all to die?"

"They're not our people, Chris!" Ash exclaimed as Chris shook his head. "We need to leave."

"Just because they're not 'our people', doesn't give us the right to abandon them and write their death sentences," Chris insisted. "If you want to leave, then leave, but I'm not going."

Ash shook her head. "I'm not leaving you here. We need to go."

"Then go!" Chris snapped. "I'm not stopping you. Leave. I'm not going anywhere."

Ash went to say something, but looked out the window instead, something having caught her eye. She frowned and Chris followed her gaze. Carmen and Marion also turned to see what was going on.

A wall of flames had appeared behind the Iron Army. The grass was completely on fire, the smoke rising high into the sky as Zeke and Gates both stayed a fair distance away.

Most of the soldiers turned to face the culprits.

"I thought they'd left," Ash said. "They've come back!"

"Maybe they never left," Chris said, watching some of the soldiers move towards the wall of flames, clearly not bothered by it.

Gates had his barrier up, shielding both himself and Zeke. Matt was nowhere to be seen.

"We have to take the chance and attack now while they're distracted," Ash said, clearly having changed her mind now that the others had shown up.

"You're leaving," they both heard, making the two of them jump and look around.

Matt was leaning against the wall at the top of the stairs.

"We can't just leave. What about all the people that live here?" Chris asked.

"Take as many people as you can and leave," Matt replied. "We can't afford much time here and the longer you wait around, the more likely it is that you'll die within these walls. The Army will tear the walls down once they're done with Gates and Zeke. They'll kill anyone who's left. If you value your life, you leave now."

With that, he was gone. Chris and Ash looked at each other.

"Let's go," Ash said, once again jumping ship and deciding that her life was worth it again. "Leave Matt to it, he clearly has a plan."

"You sure?" Chris asked.

If it was anyone's advice he'd take, it was Matt's. He wasn't often wrong and usually knew what he was talking about.

Ash nodded.

"We'll go let everyone know what's happening and we'll leave," Chris said. "No one's going to die here today."

# CHAPTER THIRTY-SEVEN

# Attempted Plans

"What's going on? Why's there smoke?" Abel asked as Ash and Chris joined everyone else on the stone street.

"We're leaving," Chris said.

Everyone frowned, even the citizens who had been rounded up to help with the defense of the City.

"Matt, Gates, and Zeke have it all under control," he continued. "We're not needed, and Matt said everyone needs to leave right now."

"We can't leave," Jacob said with a shake of his head. "I know it doesn't matter to any of you Wonderlandians, but this is our home. This city is our home."

"Neither Oz nor Wonderland is my home," Chris said, the statement coming out a bit harsher than he'd intended. "I'm sorry, Jacob, but you've got to leave. Everyone has to get out of here if they don't want to die."

Jacob shook his head. "Looks like I'm going to die here, then. I'm not leaving. We can't let this city burn."

Chris looked at Abel, Nixx, and Alex, his companions from the very beginning.

"Anyone else staying?" he asked. "Matt's buying us as much time as he can but it's not long. Either we leave now, or we go down like those walls will."

"I'll go get Jamie and meet you at the back gate," Abel said, not waiting for a response before he ran off.

That's one person on our side, Chris thought, looking around at everyone else.

The civilians were still standing around in their groups. There was no way they would be able to take down the entire Iron Army by themselves. Death was inevitable for them all.

Alex moved over to Ash and grabbed onto her arm. Nixx moved over to them as well. That was everyone who had originally come over from Wonderland into Oz.

Chris looked at Jacob again and got a sad look in return.

"I'm sorry, Chris, but I'm not leaving," Jacob said. "I can't leave this city to be destroyed, not without putting up some semblance of a fight. I hope you all make it back to your respective homes and good luck."

"I understand," Chris said, nodding. "This your home and you'll do anything to defend it. Good luck to everyone here. Hopefully, we'll see each other again one day."

He held his hand out to Jacob, who reached out and shook it firmly.

"It's been a hell of a run," Jacob said with a grim smile. "Good luck, guys. Keep safe."

⊰✦⊱

"This is going really badly," Zeke noted as he and Gates continued to move backwards.

Gates was just in front of him, keeping the barrier in place between them and the Iron Army soldiers. The soldiers kept coming, seemingly not worried about the barrier or the flames.

"I just hope Matt knows what he's doing," Gates said, taking another step back. "If I take even one hit, I'm pretty well gone. I'm not up to full strength. We can't risk it or we're both dead."

"Well, what do you suggest we do?"

Gates shook his head. "I truly don't know. We need someone else to hit them from the other side but nothing's happening. I think everyone's left."

"Wonderful."

Gates looked back at Zeke and stopped moving. He lowered his hands, and the barrier disappeared. The soldiers continued to advance towards them but were still a little way from reaching them.

"What are you doing?" Zeke asked, stopping where he was, a few paces behind Gates.

"What the fuck are we doing, Zeke?" Gates asked seriously, turning to face him. "Why are we doing this? Why didn't we just leave? We might not even make it back home at all because, let's be real here, those soldiers can't be defeated."

"You took one down by yourself," Zeke reminded him.

"That's different. This is an entire army of them," Gates said with a sigh. "Everyone in that city is as good as dead. We need to get out of here because I want to go home. I don't want to die down here! I never wanted this!"

Zeke looked at him sadly, understanding where he was coming from. "What do you suggest we do, then?"

Gates looked over his shoulder to see where the soldiers were. They were a bit too close for his liking, so he turned and put his barrier up again.

"We have to lead them into the City," he said with a shake of his head. "As much as that's not a good idea, I don't see any other choice. This is an open field and Matt's not going to be able to grab Marion unless there's some way he can get in and out quickly. If she's inside the walls, we can work as a team, grab her, and disappear for good."

Zeke gave a nod, fully on board with this plan. "Let's go then."

"We need you all to move out of the way," Matt said as Jacob just stared at him. "We're bringing the soldiers through the gates."

Jacob was now in charge of Oz's small army of civilians. Everyone respected him and listened to him and, now that Vincent was gone, everyone looked to him as their leader.

"You're not doing anything of the sort," Jacob said, staring an unimpressed Matt down. "Once they're inside these walls, we're all doomed. You can't let them in here. They'll destroy the City."

"You had your chance to leave," Matt snapped, but Jacob stood his ground. "So, get the fuck out of my way. Once Zeke and Blaine reach this gate, I'm opening it for them. They'll come in, very closely followed by those soldiers. You all stand no chance against them, so move or die. It's your choice."

"We're not going anywhere," Jacob said bitterly. "We're not about to turn our backs on our city. You open those gates and we're going to stand in their way. They'll have to go through us to destroy this place."

Matt glared at him, hearing the commotion outside. "Fine, have it your way. You've made your choice."

Jacob returned Matt's glare, and Matt turned his attention back to the gate. He knew Gates couldn't risk taking any hits, so the moment the two of them made it to the front gate, it had to be opened, otherwise there would be two casualties before the army even stepped inside the Emerald City.

"Someone get to the top of the guard tower and call down when they get to the gate," Jacob instructed his group of civilians.

One man rushed over to the guard tower, doing as asked, and ran up the stone steps to see what was happening outside.

Jacob looked around at the remainder of his small group. "I need everyone to move back so there's a good distance between us and the gate. Once they're through, we have to push back and defend ourselves and this city. I need two people on the gate with Matt, to help him with it. We don't need anyone dying for no reason."

Two people moved and joined Matt at the gate. Matt gave Jacob a nod of respect, acknowledging his change of heart, and Jacob nodded grimly back.

"Stay together, keep in the group, but move back," Jacob instructed. Everyone did as they were told with no hesitation. He looked at Doug, Ben, and Ruby who were in the first line of defense. "Everyone in the front line, you're the first line of defense we have. It's down to everyone here, but most of us probably won't make it out of here alive, so I respect you and thank you for what you're all doing here today. We're not going down without a good fight."

"They're nearly at the gate!" the man in the guard tower above shouted down.

"Alright, get ready to open the gate," Matt said to the other two that were with him. "You two, what are your names?"

They both looked at Matt.

"Gordon," the man said.

"Delilah," the woman said.

Matt nodded. "Well, Gordon and Delilah, I appreciate your help. Thank you."

"Matt, open the fucking gate!" Zeke yelled from the other side of the gate. "Like, open it RIGHT NOW!"

Matt, Gordon, and Delilah tried to get the gate open, but it was heavy and slow going. Suddenly, a steel sword broke through the center of the wooden gate, narrowly missing Matt and Gordon. It disappeared back through the wood, only to break through again in another spot, closer to the bottom.

"Move back," Matt instructed, roughly pushing Gordon and Delilah and backing up with them. "Go join your group, we don't need to open the gate. They'll get through on their own."

Matt left them on the street and ran up into the guard tower, taking the steps two at a time. He reached the top and, looking out the window, saw what was going on outside the front gate.

Gates and Zeke were backed up against the gate. Five soldiers pressed in, continuously attacking them. Gates and Zeke ducked and dodged, the soldiers narrowly missing them each time. Each time the soldiers missed, their swords sliced easily through the wooden gate.

Behind them, the remainder of the army was also beginning to move towards the City.

Marion looked up and saw Matt in the guard tower above.

"Sacrificing your friends, Shade?" she called up with amusement. "How noble of you. Open the gates or they're dead."

Matt glared at her for a few seconds before looking down at Gates and Zeke again. Both were nearly impaled but, somehow, they still managed to just get out of the way.

Marion sighed and said something to Carmen who was standing next to her. Carmen nodded, clicked her fingers, and the soldiers stopped moving.

Gates and Zeke exchanged looks but didn't say anything. Marion walked over to the two of them, stopping just in front of Gates.

"I'm honestly surprised that you're up and about," she said. Gates stared her down as Carmen looked up at Matt, who didn't acknowledge her. He was too busy watching Marion. "Last time I heard, you were seriously hurt. I'm surprised you're even on your feet, right now."

"Guess I heal quickly," Gates retorted.

"You're clearly still hurt enough to not defend yourself or this city properly," she said with a smile. "You keep avoiding letting your stupid little barrier get hit. Are you too hurt to use it?"

Marion looked at Carmen and nodded at her. Carmen clicked her fingers again. Two of the soldiers closest to Marion reanimated, moving forwards to stand beside her. Before either Zeke or Gates could move, the two soldiers grabbed them and held their swords to their throats.

Marion looked up at Matt. "Come down here and talk to me face-to-face. Or Carmen will give the order and they'll both be dead."

"Matt, don't do it," Gates called, feeling the soldier that had him move the blade against his throat a bit more.

Matt looked down at them, knowing he didn't have any choice but to go down there and face her. He disappeared from the window.

Marion looked at Gates and Zeke and smiled. "Guess you two mean enough to him after all."

Neither of them said a word as the gate opened just enough for Matt to step out. The gate swung shut behind him, and he stayed where he was, a few paces away from Marion.

"Let them go and we'll talk," Matt said.

"If I let them go, you'll just leave and we won't get to talk," Marion said. "Open those gates and let us in. You give us control of the City, and you can leave with your friends. Everyone else in there will be publicly executed, one by one, for daring to stand against us."

"That's not happening," Matt said. "You're not executing anyone. You can have the City but let them all go."

Marion gave a bit of a laugh, moving over and stopping in front of him, leaving a slight gap between the two of them.

"You do what I say, nothing else," she said. "You're my bitch, Shade. It's that simple. You were locked away for four months and I was in control. I'm still in control, so, do as I say, and open those gates."

"Not gonna happen."

Marion sighed. She went to say something, but there was a sudden clash of thunder, loud enough that it shook the ground. They all looked up and saw lightning flash across the sky.

Matt looked back at Marion as more thunder shook the ground. The sky darkened, and rain suddenly poured down, soaking everything and everyone in just seconds.

"Guess things aren't going your way right now, Marion. Maybe you're not as in control as you think," Matt said, realizing they were getting help after all. He knew what Abel could do, and it looked like he'd learnt a few new things with all his recent training.

There was another flash of lightning as the daylight disappeared entirely, sending everyone into darkness. Without thinking, Matt grabbed Marion and, by the time the next flash of lightning lit up the sky, they were both gone.

Gates quickly moved, putting his barrier up and pushing back against the soldier that was holding him. The soldier was unable to keep a hold on him and let him go. Gates felt someone suddenly grab him. The lightning flashed again, showing Matt briefly as the rain continued to pour down.

Next thing he knew, Gates was inside what looked like the Wonderland castle, water running off him and pooling on the floor. Matt appeared moments later with Zeke and disappeared again seconds later.

Marion was nowhere to be seen, and Gates wondered where she was. Gates and Zeke exchanged looks, then Matt appeared again with the remainder of their group. Everyone was soaking wet, Alex hating every minute of it.

"Thank you," Matt said, looking at Abel who was squeezing the water out of his hair. "We appreciate the help. You've really learnt some useful things."

"Jacob helped unlock it all," Abel said. His expression saddened. "What are we doing about him and his people? Where's Marion?"

"She's in the dungeons," Matt said, everyone looking to him as the water continued to collect on the floor beneath everyone's feet. "It'll all get upgraded to hold her and there's a warrant out for Hunter. There'll be people eager to hunt him down."

"We have to let everyone else fight it out and defend their city against Carmen and her army. There's nothing more we can do," Gates said. "This isn't our fight anymore, it's theirs."

# CHAPTER THIRTY-EIGHT

## Future Plans

Ash looked up as Chris walked over to her and she put down the book she'd been reading. The small blue cat sleeping on the floor next to her twitched a bit, and Chris wondered what he was dreaming of.

No one else was around. The castle was quiet, which was a nice change from everything that had been going on over the past few months. This was the first time in a long while that Chris actually felt like he was able to relax even slightly and not have to worry about anything happening.

"You think Marion can be kept in the dungeons forever?" Chris asked.

"I really don't know, Chris," Ash said with a sigh and a shrug. "Matt has people working on reinforcing the dungeons as we speak, but it could take a while. Someone has to stay here to make sure she doesn't get out."

Chris looked at her sadly as Ash avoided his gaze.

"That mean you're staying?" he asked.

"This is my home, Chris. Where else am I going to go?" she asked. "I have nowhere else and, as I said, someone needs to be here in case something happens. I assume you'll be leaving?"

"I have to, Ash. I'm really sorry," Chris said as Ash shrugged and continued to avoid looking at him. "This is your home, not mine. I have family back up top. They're probably wondering where I've been for the past however long it's been. I don't even know how long I've been down here, but I can't stay. I have to go home."

Ash gave a nod of understanding. "I assume Abel and Jamie are going too, seeing as he knows the way out?"

"You'll have to ask him."

"Well, just know that everyone's welcome to stop in any time they want," Ash said, finally looking at his face. "I want to hear from at least one of you in the not-too-distant future."

Chris gave a bit of a smile and Ash smiled back briefly.

"I'll see what I can do," he said. "If I have to, I'll send you a letter or something once in a while."

Ash laughed, which woke the cat who was suddenly alert. Ash looked at him and picked him up off the floor, putting him on her lap. Alex meowed at her, then closed his eyes and relaxed again.

"Feel free to stay a few more days before you go home. I assume you'll be going with Abel seeing as you don't really know the way out," Ash said. "You should probably go and check in with everyone before you decide what to do. And don't you leave without saying goodbye to us first."

Chris smiled again, Ash smiling back longer this time.

"I'll see what everyone else is doing and we'll see where it goes from there."

"You can't keep me in here forever, Shade," Marion said bitterly.

Matt stayed where he was, leaning against the wall opposite her cell, arms crossed as the single candle above him continued to flicker. A few citizens of Wonderland were working on increasing the security of this part of the dungeons. The last thing Matt, or any of them, wanted was for Marion to get out.

They were in the lowest part of the dungeons, where Alice had been kept when she'd been locked away here within the Wonderland castle.

Matt wondered briefly what had happened to Alice. Had she managed to escape from Vincent's castle or was she still there? Would she ever see daylight again?

"I can keep you in here for as long as I want," Matt said in reply to Marion's previous statement. "Not nice being locked behind bars, is it? You're lucky because you're not shackled to the wall. You should thank me for being nice."

Marion glared at him from where she was sitting near the bars at the front of the cell. "I don't see how this is being nice."

Matt pushed off the wall and strolled over to the front of the cell. He crouched in front of Marion, the bars the only thing separating them.

"You're going to rot down here for the remainder of your life, no matter how long that'll be," Matt said, noting that the glare never left Marion's face. "You can't do anything about it. I'm in control and you're the prisoner this time. You're powerless."

The smirk appeared on Matt's face as Marion stayed silent, clearly having nothing to say in her defense.

"We're going to get Wonderland back on track," Matt said. He leaned forwards a bit more. "And there's nothing you can do about it. Your reign here is over."

He stood up, moving back to his original position against the wall.

"So, you're going to leave me in here forever," Marion stated. She still sat in the same place on the floor at the front of the cell. "What are you going to do? How will you even know if I get out? I somehow doubt you'll be staying down here in Wonderland just to keep an eye on me. Don't you have a family now?"

Matt's expression didn't change. He knew what she was doing. She was trying to get a reaction from him to get that feeling of power back, even if it was just for a few seconds.

"You're right, I won't be staying down here," Matt said, smirking again at the annoyed look that crossed Marion's face as she realized he wasn't about to fall for her manipulation attempt. "Yes, I do have a family now and they deserve to live a proper life, a life far away from here. I also believe that I'll be told if you ever disappear. I have my connections."

"Let me guess, someone I don't like will be staying behind to keep an eye on me?" she said.

"Well, considering you don't like anyone, yes, you're correct."

Marion crossed her arms, mirroring Matt's stance, even though he was standing, and she was sitting.

"Is it Ash?" she asked, already knowing the answer. "Because I don't like her at all."

"You're kind of smart, you know that?" Matt said with amusement. "But yes, Ash is staying here. This is her home and she's staying here in the castle. She's in charge now."

Marion narrowed her eyes at him, not liking the idea of Ash being in charge. This wasn't Ash's castle, this was hers.

"You're all dead when I get out of here, that's a promise," Marion growled.

Matt laughed. "Well, then, I look forward to opening my front door and seeing you standing there ready to murder me and my family one day. You'd best make sure you get to me before I hear you're gone or else I hope you can run faster than me."

"Hey guys."

Abel and Nixx looked up as Chris stopped next to them.

"Hey, Chris," Abel said with a smile. "What's up?"

Nixx also smiled, then went back to looking through one of the doctor's journals.

"Just thought I'd come by and see what you guys are up to," Chris said with a shrug. "Any plans on what you're going to do now that this is all over?"

"Same as everyone else I guess," Abel said. "Gonna go home. You planning on leaving as well?"

Chris nodded. "Yeah, I can't stay down here. Everyone back home is probably wondering what's happened to me seeing as I haven't been able to contact them since I've been down here. They've probably reported me as missing by now."

"Yeah, that's one reason I returned back up top every so often. I didn't stay away for too long if I could help it," Abel said. "Didn't really want to turn up one day and find that I was a missing person."

"Speak for yourself," Gates said, wandering in and stopping next to Chris. "I have to go home and pretend I don't know where I've been or what's happened over the past nearly eight years."

"You looking forward to going home, though?" Abel asked.

"I don't know, I guess," Gates said, grabbing the closest chair and sitting down. "In all honesty, I'm kind of terrified."

"Why's that?" Chris asked.

"Ah well, where do I begin?" Gates said. "For one, I haven't been up top for nearly eight years. Two, I'm probably going to have to completely restart my life because I somehow doubt my fiancée would've waited all this time for me to come home. Three, I have to lie to my entire family about where I've been by pretending that I don't know. Four, a lot has most likely changed since I disappeared. And five, I don't know what I'm going to do when I actually get back up there."

"I'm sure everything will work out. You've just got to do it before you know what's really going to happen," Chris said. "If you overthink it, you'll talk yourself out of it."

Abel nodded in agreement.

"Yeah, I know, but that doesn't mean it's any easier for me," Gates said, looking at the floor as he linked his fingers together, thought on his face.

"The three of you going home at the same time?" Abel asked, snapping Gates out of his thoughts.

Gates shook his head. "Didn't think it wise for all of us to show up at the same time. We decide that I'll go home first. A couple of days later Zeke will go, and then a few days after that Matt will go back with Viv and Riley. Thought it might be easier that way. We all have our stories straight and know what each of us will say, so we can back up each other's stories. We've got the whole thing planned out, and now we've just got to do it."

"You're more than welcome to leave with me and Jamie in a couple of days," Abel said. "We thought we'd give it a day or two before we went for good, just to make sure everything's going to be OK down here."

"You mind if I tag along?" Chris asked Abel. "I don't actually know my way out of here, whereas you know your way around."

Abel nodded. "Sure. Anyone who wants to tag along can. I don't mind showing everyone the way home."

Chris looked at Nixx. "Any ideas on what you're going to do now?"

Nixx shrugged, still focused on the journal, although he'd been listening to their conversation.

"Not too sure at the moment," he said. "I'm sure Ash won't mind if I hang around here for a bit until I figure out the best thing for me to do. I can't really go back to my domain, seeing as it's been overrun, and I don't think I wish to get eaten by a troll any time soon."

"Fair enough," Chris said. "Hopefully, you find somewhere equally as good to stay."

# CHAPTER THIRTY-NINE

## Leaving Wonderland

"Well, I guess this is it, then," Abel said with a sigh as everyone stood around in the throne room. "Guess we're all going home today."

Matt was currently talking to Gates and Zeke, while Ash was discussing something with Nixx.

Chris glanced at Abel before looking at Alex and crossing his arms. Alex lounged on the throne, clearly not feeling like joining in any of the conversations.

"Alex doesn't seem too happy about everyone leaving," Chris said.

"I think he'll miss everyone," Abel said, following Chris's gaze. "He seems to have taken a liking to everyone and now we're leaving him."

"Time goes by at the same rate down here and up top, doesn't it?" Chris asked Abel.

"Yeah, so Matt and the others have been gone for nearly eight years, both here and there. You've been gone for about six months, give or take."

Chris sighed and looked at Alex again who was still sulking.

"I don't know how I'm going to explain to people why they haven't heard from me in nearly six months and why I haven't been home at all," he said.

Abel shrugged. "Honestly, Chris, I don't know. You're going to have to figure that out for yourself, I'm afraid."

Chris nodded. He'd been wracking his brain, trying to think of a decent explanation for a while now. Hopefully, he'd get an idea before he got back home or before someone dropped in to see if he was home. He probably had millions of missed calls and messages that had gone unanswered that he was going to have to deal with when he got back to the surface.

"I should go and say goodbye to everyone who's not going with us," Chris said. "Ash won't let me leave unless I say goodbye to her, and I should also go talk to Matt before I leave."

"Yeah, I should probably do the same," Abel sighed. "Just can't wait to be able to go home for a good while. I know Jamie can't wait to get home. It's been a while since she left Wonderland."

Chris nodded and headed over to Nixx and Ash, halting next to her.

"Hey, Chris," Ash said with a smile. "I assume you haven't come over here to say you're staying, have you?"

Chris smiled. "Afraid not. I actually came over to say goodbye to you guys."

Ash nodded. She'd known this was going to happen sooner or later. There wasn't anything she could say that would stop Chris from leaving.

"Well, it's been fun," Ash said, pulling him into a hug. "Not gonna be the same without all of you here."

She let him go, and Chris looked at her sadly. She returned his gaze with a sad one of her own.

"I'm sure everything will be fine down here," Chris said. "You'll keep everything under control. You and Alex."

"I appreciate the confidence you have in me," she said with a sad smile. She reached out and took his hand. "If anything happens and I need help, I'll probably come knocking on your door."

Chris gave a bit of a laugh. "Alright. Anyway, I'm going to go say goodbye to a few more people and then I'll probably be heading off. You take care of yourself and Alex, OK?"

"You too, Chris," she said, reluctantly letting go of his hand as he turned away.

Chris headed over to Alex, who was still sprawled out on the throne just watching the groups of people in the room.

"You're leaving, aren't you?" Alex asked, looking up at Chris with sadness on his face and in his voice.

Chris nodded. "Afraid so."

"I don't want you guys to go," Alex said, pouting and crossing his arms. He stayed on the throne, clearly unhappy with everything that was going on.

"I know, but you'll be fine down here without us," Chris reassured him, but Alex shook his head stubbornly. "You've got Ash here with you. She's not going anywhere, and I know you like having her around."

Alex gave a bit of a shrug, making Chris sigh.

"Just make sure you stop in once in a while?" Alex asked softly. "Please?"

"We'll see what happens," Chris said truthfully. He didn't want to make a promise he might not be able to keep, and Alex gave an understanding nod. "You look after Ash for me, OK?"

Alex gave another nod, seeming a bit happier. Chris gave him a bit of a smile before heading over to where Matt was still talking to Gates and Zeke.

Matt looked away from his conversation as Chris stopped next to the three of them.

"Chris," Matt said. "Come to join the conversation?"

"Came over to say goodbye," Chris said, and Matt nodded. "Didn't think I should leave without saying goodbye to you first."

"I appreciate it," Matt said. He indicated to Gates. "Apparently he's leaving today with you and Abel, so we were just talking a bit before he goes and leaves us for a few days."

"Probably be more than a few days," Gates said. "Depending on how everything goes for us, really. I don't know when I'll see you guys again."

Matt gave a shrug, arms crossed. "You never know. However it goes, I'll see you sometime soon."

Gates nodded and Chris looked at Matt again.

"Any plans on what you're going to do for a few more days down here before you head home?" he asked.

Matt shrugged. "Going to head back over to the domain we used to reside in. Probably board it all up and close it up for good so no one else can find it or get inside while I'm not here. Last thing I want is someone destroying the place, all the hard work we put into it. Me, Viv, Riley, and Zeke will stay there for a few days. Close it all up and then go home when the time comes."

"Sounds like you have it all planned out," Chris said. "I really hope everything works out for you, Matt. For all of you."

"I appreciate it," Matt said, his tone grateful. He put his hand out in a friendly manner. "You take care of yourself, Chris. Maybe we'll run into each other down the road again one day."

Chris shook his hand, and they smiled at each other.

"You too, Matt. Look after yourself and your family."

Matt gave him a nod and let his hand go.

Gates sighed and looked at Chris. "Just let me know when you, Abel, and Jamie are ready to head out. I'm ready to go whenever you're ready."

"We shouldn't be staying much longer," Chris said. "Once we've said our goodbyes to everyone, we should be ready to head out."

"Sounds good, just come find me when you're about to go.," Gates said. "I'll be here."

# CHAPTER FORTY

## Going Home

"Feels like forever since I've been back in this part of Wonderland," Gates commented as they entered the Room of Doors.

Everything was how it normally was within the round room, the floor intact and doors shut. It was a lot different to when Chris had been here the first time, when he'd first stepped foot inside Wonderland.

"We still need to go further than here," Abel commented as the door shut and locked behind him.

Gates shook his head. "You guys have to go further, but this is where we part ways."

Chris and Abel frowned at him, while Jamie stayed silent.

"What do you mean?" Abel asked. "We're not at the correct set of doors."

"Your door is different to the one I have to go through," Gates said. "I know which door will take me home and it's one of the ones in here.

It'll take me straight to where I need to go. You guys have your doors, I have mine."

"You sure about this?" Chris asked.

"Yeah, I'm sure," Gates said, smiling slightly. "I know where to go. It might have been nearly eight years, but I still know how to get home. You guys take care, OK?"

Jamie smiled at him and Abel and Chris nodded.

"Look after yourself, Blaine," Chris said, holding out his hand. "I hope everything works out for you when you get home."

Gates gave a slight nod and shook Chris's hand. "I hope so too, Chris. Anyway, I should let you all get on your way. Take it easy and remember you can always stop by if you want to."

"Same goes for you, too," Abel said. "Don't be a stranger."

"Hopefully, we'll see you again someday," Chris said. "If you're ever in Pennsylvania, you stop in, OK?"

"Will do," Gates said. "Now get going. We all have homes to get to."

Abel, Jamie, and Chris continued on their way. Chris glanced over his shoulder once and saw Gates just standing there, watching them. He waved and Gates turned away.

"Do you ever wonder what happened to Jacob and the Emerald City? Do you think they could have beaten the Iron Army?" Chris asked as they walked.

"I doubt it," Abel said. "Carmen probably razed that city to the ground because Matt killed her sister. We could barely touch those soldiers, so I can't see how the Emerald City citizens could have made any difference at all."

"I hope Jacob at least got his family out," Chris mused. "Maybe we'll find out one day."

"Yep, but not today," Abel said with a nod.

They continued to walk in silence until Abel finally came to a halt.

He gestured to the four doors in front of them before looking at Chris. "Well, this is it. This is how we get home. You ready to step through one of these doors?"

Chris nodded. "Are *you* ready to step through one of these doors for what will hopefully be for good?"

Abel gave him a smile. "I have my doubts about it being for good. But I can hope that it's for a good while."

Chris smiled back in amusement before contemplating the four colored doors in front of them.

"Are we taking different ones?" Chris asked as he crossed his arms.

"Afraid so," Abel said. "Jamie and I take the blue door, but I unfortunately don't know which door you need to take. The green door goes to Miami, so I don't think that's the one you want. So, for you it comes down to the black door or the red door."

Chris looked between the red and the black door, trying to decide which one to take.

"Well, I guess since it's narrowed down to two doors, it's a fifty-fifty chance," he said. "Either way, I'll be able to get home eventually, back to the real world anyway."

"It's your choice which door to take," Abel said. "But either way, we should really get going. You don't need my guidance anymore. Hopefully, we'll run into each other again sometime down the track, Chris. It's been a good run, man, and thanks for all the help over the past few months."

Abel extended his hand. Chris accepted it and shook it with a smile, before turning and giving Jamie a quick hug.

"See you both around, and good luck," he said, stepping back from her.

Abel smiled at Jamie, then gave Chris one last look, before opening the blue door.

Chris waved as Abel and Jamie stepped through the doorway. The door clicked shut and they were gone.

Chris sighed, going back to looking between the two doors. Which should he take? The red or the black?

He needed to make a decision, but who was he kidding? He already knew which one he'd take. It wasn't going to be the red one.

Without any more thought, Chris went over to the black door. He hesitated slightly then pulled it open and stepped through.

The bright light and cool air hit him, making him shiver as he heard the door shut and lock behind him. He looked around as his eyes adjusted. He was standing near a large tree, where the sun had broken through the leaves at the top.

Chris looked around a bit more and realized where he was. He was back home.

He looked behind himself and at the tree. The door was gone, no trace of it whatsoever. He frowned, wondering where it had gone and if that was normal. Whatever, he thought. He was home and that was good enough for him.

He walked around the tree and something at the base of it caught his eye. He stopped and stood for a few seconds, looking at the rabbit hole he'd followed Abel down all those months ago.

He was back in the same place as he'd left.

He smiled to himself. It had all come full circle and now it was almost as though nothing had happened. He'd been gone for months and all that was left now were the memories of what had happened.

He sighed, figuring that he should probably head back to his house as he felt the tiredness suddenly catch up with him after such a long few months.

Something else caught his attention in the grass. He walked over to what had caught his eye and picked up the book he'd left on the riverbank. It wasn't in the best shape anymore. It had spent months out in the weather, so of course it wasn't going to be in the same condition as when he'd left it there.

He couldn't help but smile. It hadn't been moved at all and had been in the same place for months. It was a bit amusing, to say the least. It seemed so normal, unlike the adventures he'd experienced since he'd last seen this book.

The smile remained on his face as he tucked the book under his arm and began his walk home.

It was nice to be back.

Gates looked up as the door to the police station opened, and two people entered. He looked down at his hands again, linked in his lap. He wasn't sure how he felt about this right now, mostly because they'd called Skye and not his parents, which had been the complete opposite of what he'd hoped would happen.

But there was no backing out now that he was here.

"Oh my God, Blaine! It *is* you," he heard Skye say. He hadn't thought he'd ever hear her voice again and he blinked away some tears.

Skye and some guy he didn't know came over to him. She pulled him into a very tight embrace, Gates hugging her back automatically.

"They said they'd found you, but I didn't really believe it at first, but, oh my God, you're really here!" she said, keeping hold of Gates who didn't want to let her go either. He chose to ignore the man standing next to Skye, though he had a decent idea of who he was.

"I can't believe you're really here, where have you been?" Skye said.

Gates held her a bit tighter as he answered. "You wouldn't believe me even if I told you."

———❖———

"You know you're not going to be able to hold us forever, don't you."

Alex jumped and grabbed onto Ash's arm. Ash stopped and stared into the darkness of the only other occupied cell in the dungeons.

Hunter stepped forward so they could see his face in the flickering candlelight. "I hope you've got a way of contacting the rest of your little friends in a hurry."

Ash glared at him, but refused to engage, turning and pulling Alex along with her.

"I want every door checked twice a day, in here and down where Marion is," she said to the guard who stood by the main dungeon door. The guard nodded. "And, under no circumstances, is *anybody* to interact with either of them, except to give them food."

Neither Ash nor Alex spoke as they walked up the stone steps leading out of the dungeons, both finding it hard to not think about Hunter's words.

*By Daryl Walker*

The Other Side of Andy

***Motionless series***

Motionless in Wonderland

Something Motionless This Way Comes

The Iron Army

www.ingramcontent.com/pod-product-compliance
Lightning Source LLC
Chambersburg PA
CBHW030647020726
47493CB00006B/1917